'While filled with touches of magic woven into its worldbuilding from the very start, the warmth and intimacy of this book's focus on its two principal families felt more like social drama or historical fiction at times.

The stakes rise over time, and certain expected tropes do appear - individual heroism, a looming sense of threat and mysterious antagonists, and of course a quest - but these all felt grounded by the richly drawn family of characters at its heart. This means that although the danger has land-wide implications, it feels all the more personal. It also means that when combat and conflict happen, the matter-of-fact, unflinching manner with which Hemsley treats it hits all the harder.

A book of effective, contrasting tones; sweet, enduring characters, and in part a rumination on inequality and difference, I recommend this read to anyone looking to be surprised by something a bit different.'

Michael Jarvis : *review on Amazon*

'The Gifts is a fascinating book. Part fantasy, part adventure story, it's filled with magic, mystery and suspense. Set in a parallel world, where forces of good and evil are both subtly and obviously drawn, the story is a quest on the part of the main characters to find the hidden power behind the system which allows one race – the Hued – to live with wealth, comfort and power and another – the Talthen – to put up with oppression and disdain at every turn.

I would recommend The Gifts as a clever, engaging and highly unusual read.'

Deborah Jenkins – *author of 'The Evenness of Things'*

'It's a fantasy type story in that it takes place in a world other than our own and that it has characters with magical aspects but I still found it very rooted in the themes and concerns of our own world.

Fantasy is not a genre I would normally pick up. But even though the dominant race in the story are people who are literally very brightly coloured and gifted in highly unusual ways, the whole concept didn't seem too alien. I think this is because it was a very interesting exploration of themes such as justice, equality, race which all feel very close to home. These themes made it much more than a trivial story.

It's quite a saga of a story set over a long period of time, but I think the ending is all the better because the story has built up to it slowly. This is not a simple crisis that is resolved, there has been deep pain and a huge price to pay for those characters seeking to transform their world.'

Sheila Bridge – *author of the 'Live Life Loved' Blog*

The City

The sequel to The Gifts

Cathy Hemsley

ISBN: 9798778940055

DEDICATION

This book is dedicated, with many thanks, to my late friend and fellow novelist, Edwina Goodwin. You are much missed.

ACKNOWLEDGMENTS

Acknowledgements and thanks go to my wonderful family: husband Phil, children Lizzy and Beck. Especial thanks to Beck who first thought of the Hued, their gifts and the original plot, and designed the covers for this and for The Gifts.

Thanks also to my many friends and fellow writers who have encouraged, supported and commented on these two stories: to Hilary, Izzy, Sarah, Sheila, Steve and Trevor.

CHAPTER 1
SARE

Ezera Mertrice hated these sorts of jobs.

Escort duty - now that would be fine! She appreciated getting out of the city for a few days on a trip to Gathen, Peveque, or the northern hills. Such jobs meant good pay, usually. Good company too, and the chance of tangling with a few would-be robbers. She liked a straight-forward fight.

Tax collection was not as fine, although she could deal with it on most days. It was only on rare occasions that there was trouble. Some dullard farmer, scratching a living, whose harvest had failed and who would have to be hauled away, kicking and struggling. Usually with a wife or family clutching at him, screaming and begging. It wasn't just the ragged, half-starved children, earth-floored hovels and empty barns that had started to trouble Ezera over the past few months. It was the amount of tax involved. A few coins, just pennies sometimes. Powers above knew the City didn't need the handful of coins that they dragged from the dullards. But Jarial said, whenever she ranted about it, that it had to be done.

"We have to enforce the law, Zera," he'd say. "They may complain about it, but you know it has to be like that. It's always been like that. To keep the city safe."

Despite what he said, as far as Ezera was concerned, tax collection was not fine. But today's job - well, her heart had thudded in her chest when the captain, Levin Bluestone, had slapped his hand against his thigh, grinned and said, "Right! Some sewer-rat of a dullard has tried to burn down the manor at Saroche. They've got a prisoner, so it's straight-forward. Couple of day's riding, collect the rat. Public punishment, his village to witness it. It's only a scabby little place called Sare, apparently, so just ten of us should be enough."

And now, two days later, they stood in pale spring sunshine and stared down at a thin dullard man who knelt in front of Levin. His swollen face drooped over his bare chest. Dried blood stained his cheeks and bruises marked dark lines over his back and shoulders. Heavy chains hung from the manacles on his wrists. He muttered, through torn lips, "It wasn't me. I didn't do it." A woman crouched by him, wailing and crying, as two bare-footed children clung to her skirts. The other villagers stood in a trembling circle around the man and the guards. The village chief, a grovelling, pale-faced man, took the woman's arm and pulled her away. "I apologise," he said in a fearful, humble voice to the captain. "His wife, his children ... You must understand."

Levin turned to Ezera.

"Your turn, I think," he said, passing her the whip. "You know the drill. Flog to death."

Ezera picked up the whip and ran her fingers along the edges of the flint and bone shards knotted into the leather. This wasn't what she'd joined the City Guard for. She liked the camaraderie, the training, using her gifts. She knew she was good at protecting Hueds when they travelled. But judicial torture and execution weren't on her list of favourite assignments.

She shook her head.

"No." Her voice sounded surprisingly loud. "No, I won't. Prison - yes. But not this. Not with his family standing here."

One of the villagers lifted up his head and stared at her. He was tall, with thin cheeks and a narrow nose. His skin was light brown and his eyes were pale blue. He stood with his bare arms folded defiantly. Ezera could see the strength in their knotty, wiry sinews. She caught his eye, then glanced away.

"What? Coward or bloody dullard sympathiser are you

all of a sudden? Are you sure you want to say no, Sergeant Mertrice? To disobey a direct order?" Levin snapped.

Ezera hesitated. But only for a second. She'd fight like a wildcat to protect the city. But this? No. These sort of sadistic, public punishments only made for more resentment. Just kill the poor sod, and do it quickly. Sword through the heart - she'd do that, yes. But not this.

"With all due respect, Captain," she said. "A clean kill, yes. But a public flogging is excessive, in this case."

Levin came up close to her. "Weakling," he hissed in her face. "It'll be a week mucking out the stables and cleaning the privies for you when we get back. Shame we don't flog our own ... I'd enjoy that."

He snatched the whip from Ezera and advanced on the prisoner. The dullard flinched backwards and gasped, "It wasn't me! Please ... I beg you ... "

Levin slapped his hand across the dullard's face, knocking him into the dust.

"Right, you, get the scum up," he said to the other guards. "Pull his arms out. Hold him steady. Let me show you how this should be done."

He brought the whip down hard across the man's shoulders. The dullard flinched and moaned as the blood came. A woman in the watching crowd screamed, then clutched her hand over her mouth.

"Now, remember, you're not aiming for a quick, easy death," Levin said. "You're aiming for pain. Drawn-out punishment. Deterrence ..."

With each word he slashed the whip down. As he did so, Ezera saw the tall dullard watching stand straighter, clenching his fists by his side as he stared at the rivulets of blood. His pale eyes were wide as if he needed to suck in all the horror and never forget it.

When it was over, the man dead, the whip frayed and the ground spattered with gore, Levin dropped the bloody whip into the dust by the body. He wiped his hands on his jacket and turned to the village chief.

"Now, I reckon you've had a lesson here," he said. "Don't forget it. I don't want to have to come back to this pathetic bunch of hovels to remind you. You, you, and you ..." He pointed to ten of the dullards then turned to the guards. "Shackle them up. A year or so in prison should help you all remember, I reckon."

Ezera gasped. Levin turned to her.

"They should be grateful it's not decimation. This is for arson. Had you forgotten that? The council said punitive measures," he said. "And they said they'd leave it to my discretion. If you don't like it, complain to them, not me, and don't snivel. Now, help get these brutes shackled up!"

He strode away. "By the walls, but my arm aches like the blazes! Tough little git, wasn't he? " he said to the guard holding his horse.

As Ezera pulled the manacles and chains from the packhorse, she glanced at the torn, blood-stained body crumpled on the ground. The tall dullard went to it, gently turned the body over and closed its eyes. He covered his face with his hand and knelt, head bowed. A woman crouched by him, sobbing, then she wiped the blood from the battered, pale face with the corner of her skirt.

Ezera handed the chains to a guard. "You do it," she said.

"No stomach for it?" he sneered.

Ezera shook her head. "Not for this, no!" she snapped.

"Don't blame you. Not when we've go to do this all again the day after tomorrow, after we've sent this rabble to the prison."

"What! Do this again?"

The guard seized one of the ten dullards, a young and terrified woman. "Turns out it wasn't him that started the fire," he said, as he clamped the manacles on her shaking wrists then gestured to the body. "That one was caught in the barns the next night, spying out the manor in order to try again, they said. Probably nicking food judging by his scrawniness, I reckon. Anyway he swore it wasn't him. Then two days later some turncoat informer gave the captain the name of the real culprit. In another beggarly power-forsaken hole seven miles away." He spat into the dust. "They're all scum, damn them. Selling their own folk for a piece of Hued gold? They're not worth the scrapings of muck off my boots."

"What? You mean ... We did that to an innocent man?" Ezera exclaimed.

The guard shrugged. Levin turned around, stepped towards her and grabbed her arm.

"Innocent? He's dullard trash. He'll be guilty of something," he hissed, his face close to hers. "They're all as bad as each other and don't you forget it. We had orders, remember! The council ordered a deterrent!"

"Orders?" Ezera wenched her arm free. "You and the council and their orders can go to hell!"

She strode towards her horse. As she passed the group of villagers kneeling by the body, the tall dullard stood up and looked directly at her with narrowed blue eyes and a stern frown on his face. Ezera glanced at him and their eyes met again. She stared back for an instant, feeling a strange urge to put her hand on his shoulder and to say that she was sorry. But she walked on, her back straight and her head proud, then mounted her horse and rode away, ignoring Levin's shouts and curses and threats.

As the City Guards rode away from Sare, Durston Halthe watched the shackled villagers trailing behind in the dust clouds rising from the horses' hooves. His father, at the end of the chain, turned his head and looked back at him. Durston could only lift his fist in defiant farewell. There was no point in going after them, not yet. Not with his cousin Alric dead, his wife and children sobbing and hysterical, Durston's mother distraught, his brother trembling, trying to be brave, and his young sister curled-up in a terrified ball of misery. He was needed here for a while. He'd guessed what would happen when he'd received the message from his father about his cousin's arrest. He'd known how much it would cost the village. Durston would have to try to help here, for a couple of weeks at least, before returning home. But one day, he swore to himself, he'd go after them and try to rescue his father.

He clenched his fists and frowned as he stared after the column of prisoners, with the green-skinned snake of a captain riding at the front. The captain had known that Alric was innocent, but still went ahead with his execution, and still took ten villagers! And now he was going on to another village to do the same again!

"By the Powers above and the Virtues below, one day I'll find that vicious bastard, that foul Hued captain, and I'll tear him slowly limb from limb. I swear it!" Durston muttered.

And the other soldiers? Them too, except for the one who'd met his eyes and who'd refused to flog his cousin and then had ridden away. Durston had noticed her earlier when they'd ridden into the village. She had sat upright and balanced in the saddle with a sword loose by her side and a bow and quiver slung across her back. The black jacket of the City Guard uniform had fitted tightly around her waist and breasts. The colour of her skin, a warm chestnut brown, was unusual in the midst of the green, orange, blue and other brightly-coloured Hueds. Her eyes and her short, wavy hair had matched her skin. She had almost looked like a dark-skinned Talthen; as if, like many, she had been tanned from working in the fields all summer. But she definitely wasn't Talthen. She wore her symbol, a lightning-bolt, on her collar and he'd seen the matching mark on her left hand. Even so, when he'd first noticed her, he'd felt a treacherous desire fill him. And later, when she'd refused the captain's order and their eyes had met, there had been something else. Something deeper. A shared feeling. She'd been outraged too. And now, despite the turmoil of grief and fury and desperation, her defiant face rose unbidden into his mind.

CHAPTER 2
THE FIREMAKER

One good thing at least, Ezera thought as she slammed the door of the guardhouse and strode up the street, Jarial would have finished work by now. She glanced up at the sky. Almost sunset. Yes, he'd be at his house. She'd go straight there, she'd not bother going home to wash or change, she'd go straight to him.

She remembered when she'd first seen him, six months ago, at a bar in the lower city. He'd been on stage, playing a guitar, with two other musicians. His accompanists were clearly musically gifted. They languidly raised their fingers and music flowed with ease from their empty hands and from the marks on their palms. But Jarial had strummed manually and with passion, stamping his feet to the rhythm, as if he and he alone cared and could carry the melody. Then he had looked up, seen Ezera staring, winked and started to sing. It was a wild, strange song about mountains and a man hunting for deer in dark forests. The words and melody caught Ezera. His confident hands summoned haunting, moving chords from the strings. The song finished and the other two merely bowed casually, but he bent his head down in silence for a moment, looked up, saw Ezera and lifted his left hand. She saw the flame-shaped mark on his palm. He snapped his fingers and sparks flickered for a moment on the ends of his fingers, shining orange light on his scarlet face and beard, and reflected in his blazing red eyes. He's a firemaker, not a musician, she had realised, as he had put his guitar on its stand, sauntered over and offered to buy her a beer.

Two days later, he'd turned up at the guardhouse and asked her for archery lessons. The lessons had lasted about a week before it had become obvious that he was more interested in her than in hitting the target. At the remembrance of how their hands had touched when he'd taken an arrow from her, and how he'd put the arrow and the bow deliberately down on the grass, moved towards her and kissed her firmly and determinedly, without question or ceremony, she walked faster up the street and around the corner to his house.

Before she knocked, Jarial opened the door.

"Ezera!" he smiled. "By the walls, it's been weeks. It's good to see you. You are as beautiful as ever."

"And filthy," she said. "I came straight here."

"You couldn't keep away, could you?"

"No, but don't boast about it."

He leaned forward, stroked his finger along her cheek and chin and down to her breasts, then kissed her forehead, her cheeks, her mouth. She stood on tiptoe to kiss him back and fling her arms around his neck.

"Jarry, Jarry," she whispered. "Powers above, I've missed you!"

"Me too. Come in, come upstairs. Bed, then food?"

"Yes. Bed, then food. You know me. Maybe a bath afterwards?"

It was deep evening when they came downstairs and through the house to the enclosed, herb-filled garden, tucked under the shadow of the eastern city walls. Scents of lavender and thyme drifted up as Ezera brushed past the plants on either side of the path. On the flagstones Jarial's bronze firebowl stood empty on its tripod. Next to it was a stone bench facing a table laden with glasses and bottles of wine.

"Oh, it's good to be here again, to be clean at last," Ezera said, as she sat on the tasselled rugs and cushions spread on the bench. "And wine too! Did you expect me?"

"You said you'd probably be back yesterday or today. I've been watching out for you," he said as he poured out two glasses. "Here."

"Thanks! By the walls, I need this after that assignment!"

"No, don't gulp it back! This is good wine, not cheap vinegar. It needs to be savoured, like this," he said, swirling his wine round in his glass, then sipping it.

"You'd better pour me another then, so I can appreciate it."

He sat down beside her, ran fingertips across her lips and put his arms around her. As she rested her head on his shoulder he tilted her chin up and looked into her eyes.

"How was it?" he said.

"Foul. It was about as bad as it could be, Jarry."

"You thought it would be tough, didn't you? Well, it's done now. You're back."

"Yes, back at last. It was ..."

Ezera remembered the tears of the woman who wiped the blood away from the face of the dead man, and she leapt up and paced around the firebowl.

"Jarry, it was awful! Those villagers, they were half-starved, terrified, and then ..." Ripping some leaves from a sage bush, she tore them into shreds and dropped them onto the dead cinders in the firebowl. "We had to flog someone to death and take ten prisoners. And then Levin ... He is - there are no words for him! It might have been attempted arson, they may be only dullards, Talthen, but even so they didn't deserve that."

"Talthen?"

"That's what they call themselves. We might call them dullards, but they hate that name, Jarry. They're Talthen."

"Are they? Does it matter? Dullards, Talthen, they're still not Hued. They are only peasants, Ezera. They are not important. Forget them."

She shook her head.

"Zera, stop pacing around. Forget it. It's done with," Jarial said, standing up, taking her hands and pulling her close. "Come here."

She tipped her head up so he could kiss her, and she closed her eyes to feel the warmth of his lips on hers.

Suddenly, she remembered the pale eyes of the Talthen man who had stared so intensely at her. She opened her eyes and stepped away.

"What is it?" he said.

"Nothing. No, it's nothing. I'll try to forget it."

"More wine?"

She nodded and relaxed against the cushions as he tipped the rest of the bottle into her glass.

"Good. I assume you're hungry?"

"Yes. Incredibly hungry!"

"I can do something about that at least, my lady. Your desires are my commands," he said with an exaggerated bow, before going into the house. He returned with plates and wide terracotta platters that he placed on the table.

"Buttered roast chicken with tarragon and garlic; fresh white bread, baked today; and the best peaches I could find," he said, passing her a loaded plate.

"Oh, yes." She tore hungrily into a leg of chicken. "I've missed your cooking too. Perfect. Just what I needed!"

"Wonderful! Food, drink and bed ..." He winked. "I'm glad to have been of use."

"One more thing, though," she said, licking her fingers.

"Is the woman never satisfied?" he exclaimed, spreading his arms wide in mock appeal.

"No. How about some fire? It may be spring but it's cold. It almost feels like there could be a frost tonight. See?" She gestured upwards, where tiny glints of stars were appearing in the darkening sky.

"Fire? Immediately, my lady."

He stood by the firebowl and held his hands out, palms upwards. Ezera leaned forward to watch. She thought she'd never tire of watching him do this. As he lifted his hands, ghostly outlines of coals and logs appeared in the bowl. They hardened into reality. Sparks hissed from Jarial's fingers, and fell, spitting and crackling, onto the wood. Little tongues of pale green flames glimmered among the logs, danced, seemed to hesitate then grew. Smoke rose as the flames waved and curled round the red-glowing coals. Slowly the fire took hold. Jarial breathed in deeply, shut his eyes and raised his hands higher as if lifting a great weight. His sinews and veins stood out sharply in the growing light. More coal and wood appeared and kindled. The firelight and warmth blazed out and filled the garden with golden light. Jarial dropped his arms.

"Jarial? Are you all right?"

"Yes," he said, raising his head and staring at her. "Of course. Why shouldn't I be?"

"Oh. Right."

Ezera shook her head. She knew, almost certainly, that Jarial was finding it harder to use his gift. But he, along with many others, refused to admit it or discuss it. No one would. But she suspected that she wasn't the only Hued to find that their gift was weakening. She knew that her responses were marginally slower, her instincts less tuned, her sword arm weaker, her arrows less accurate. But, for Jarial and others, the subject was taboo. As she finished the chicken and bread, she decided to say nothing. She had a more serious subject to discuss. For a while he sat next to her, eating peaches and pouring out more wine. They listened to the fire crackling and the faint sounds of talking and laughter from in a nearby tavern. Jarial's guitar leaned against the bench. He took it up and strummed a few chords, then started a quiet song about two lovers meeting on the city walls. Ezera listened until he'd finished, then put her hand on his arm.

"No, wait a while, Jarry. We need to talk. I've got something to tell you. Jarial, I'm going to leave the City Guard."

"What! Why? Zera, by the Powers, why?"

"That bastard Levin. I can't take him and his sadistic bullying a moment longer."

"Levin? I know he's a swine, but I thought you could handle him. He doesn't dare bully you, does he?"

"No, not more than anyone else. Only what military

discipline allows. I don't let him push me too far. But it's the Talthen, Jarry. I just can't stand by and watch such pointless cruelty anymore. He killed an innocent man, Jarry! If I'd had known - I could have stopped him, but I didn't!"

Jarial stared at her. "Innocent? That's beyond bearing. No Hued should do that."

"And we took away ten prisoners! Shackled, dragged off. One was a young girl, she only looked about sixteen. Powers alone know what will happen to her there. And two were old men who could hardly walk. The prisons are about full anyway. I know the council authorised a deterrent, but it's wrong. We are Hued! We are not bullies and sadists and murderers!"

Jarial nodded.

"You're right. I know we have to tax the dullards: to maintain our position, to keep ourselves safe, but we shouldn't resort to tactics like that. Do you want to make a formal complaint to the council about it? You know my mother. She's on the council."

"Madame Latisse? I know of her, I know she's your mother, but you haven't introduced me to her yet."

"Well, I will, all in good time. But you could talk to the council."

"No. I've tried that before, several times. I'm not going to waste my effort on them. They don't listen. They insist on punitive measures. But it only makes it all worse. The resentment it creates! Powers above, Jarial, there are thousands more of them than us! If they rise up against us ..."

"They won't. They're nothing. We've no need to be afraid of them. They're not that organised or powerful, and they're too frightened."

"And too hungry! They're half-starved, Jarial."

"Well then. And that's not our fault, is it? We can't help the bad weather, or their harvests failing. Anyway, don't worry, they won't attack us. They're too scared and too weak."

Jarial was sitting by her, his arm around her, but she moved away, turning to face him.

"How do you know? You've never been more than a few miles from the city. You've no idea what things are like out there."

"Yes, I have. You tell me often enough."

"So what if I do? It matters! Jarial, I can see terrible things happening if we carry on letting bastards like Levin torture and kill as much as they like!"

"You're exaggerating. The council keeps him and the guard in order. They know what they are doing."

"No, they don't. We might be safe at the moment, with the walls and the guard, but what if our gifts fail? If we have to buy or trade food with the Talthen?"

Jarial slipped from the bench and knelt in front of her. He stroked the sides of her arms, then grasped them, looking intently at her.

"Zera, never mind that. Forget the dullards or Talthen or whatever they're called. You said you're going to leave the guards. What are you going to do?"

She was silent.

"Fighting is your gift, Zera. If you aren't in the guards, what then? Leave the city for some forsaken garrison town?"

"No - not that."

"Well, tell me. Some menial job here? Cleaning, skivvying, waitressing?"

Ezera drew in a deep breath, closed her eyes and shook her head. She finished her wine, stared at the fire then looked steadily at Jarial. The firelight glowed on his cheek and reflected scarlet in his eyes.

"I'm going to leave the city."

"What!"

"No, Jarial, listen! I've had three days to think about this, ever since we left Sare. You know my uncle, Cairson Watergiver?"

"Cairson Watergiver? The renegade dullard-lover who's

deserted the Hued? I didn't know he was your uncle. That traitor?"

"Don't you call him a traitor. He's not! I visited him in Marden for a day on the way back and talked to him. I'm going to join what he's doing there."

Jarial stared at her, his eyes narrowed.

"You're joking. Join those traitorous, cowardly fools in that ridiculous venture of his? You've been listening to that crazy half-breed, Berrena Rochale."

"They're not fools, Jarial. They know what they are doing."

Jarial stood up.

"Oh, yes. Giving up their gifts, deserting the city, hobnobbing with dullards, all for some mad rumour that the gifts will fail, started by Lord Sapphireborne years ago and spread by Watergiver and that black witch!"

He poked the burning wood of the fire with a stick, then turned back to her.

"Don't you give up your gift, Zera. We are Hued, remember. We have been given the gifts to be used, not thrown away."

"I'm not going to stop using my gift."

"Good! You can't - you shouldn't. Powers above, Zera, the gifts are not like some old knives that you just throw out when they are broken or rusty. The gifts - they are our heritage, our treasure, our responsibility. We should use them to keep ourselves and Hueron safe."

"Jarial, listen! Listen to me!" She stood and took his arm. "I want the city to be safe too. But if the gifts fail we need dullard, I mean, Talthen friends!"

"They are not going to fail. That's just scaremongering."

"My eldest cousin, Aven, I remember hearing that she believed the gifts were failing. Her, Cairson, Lord Sapphireborne, Lady Sarielle Rochale; they were not stupid. They had good reason to believe that the gifts were going to fail!"

"Really? But Lord Sapphireborne is dead and Sarielle

Rochale has gone into exile. They're hardly great or lasting examples. And Aven? She was your cousin, then? Anyway I know of her - one of the missing four, isn't she? I was barely twelve, but I remember it, of course. No one understood what that strange mission was really about, let alone why all of them disappeared. Anyway it was twenty years ago. Panicky nut-cases, that is all they were. Them, and that scaremongering Berrena Rochale. You shouldn't let them influence you."

"I don't! I think for myself, Jarry! But Cairson is right, I'm sure."

"So what if he is? Zera, are you serious about leaving - about joining them? Why?"

"I've spoken to him. I'm going to help them. I'll teach those in Marden to fight. And we'll learn how to make and use weapons, without using gifts. It's the only way we'll be safe, should the worst happen." She paused, and looked steadily at him. "Come with me, Jarial. I want you to come with me."

Jarial stepped back and folded his arms.

"Abandon the city? Our home? Run off and fraternise with our enemies and let Hueron decay and rot? No. Never."

"Jarial, you said you loved me. And you know how much I love you. So, please, think about it. I don't want to leave you!"

"Then stay! If you love me, stay! I'm not leaving. We should stay here, Ezera, stay and stand by our own. Hueds are not cowards. They don't run away. I never thought you'd be a coward."

She drew a deep breath and stood up, her fists clenched.

"Don't you dare call me a coward. You're the coward! Too frightened to face the truth, too frightened to admit that our powers are weakening. You're wrong, Jarial, and you know it."

"If you think I'm such a coward, maybe you had better leave. I'm surprised you're bothering with a coward like me."

Ezera picked up her jacket, sword and bag.

"No - wait. Wait, Zera! I didn't mean that!" Jarial exclaimed desperately, leaping up and grabbing her arm. "But - but if you go, if you walk out of here, that's it between us. Are you sure? Is that how little you love me?"

She shook off his hand and stepped back.

"I'm not going to be blackmailed like that!" She paused. "Jarry, you know I love you, but I'll do what I think is right. You could come with me! If you loved me, you would!"

"So ... You're going. Just like that."

"Yes." She held out her hand, but he ignored it. He turned to the firebowl, held his hand over the fire and the flames died. The garden plunged into gloom.

"Jarry ... please ..." she said, touching his arm.

"It's your choice. Your choice to go. Not mine," he said, his voice bitter and his face averted. "Go on then. Say goodbye and go."

"Powers be with you, Jarial, then. Goodbye it is! Come to Marden to find me if you change your mind," she said, then turned and left.

CHAPTER 3
CEODRINNE

Durston ran his hand over the planed wood. It felt smooth and splinter-free. He nodded with satisfaction, lifted the board and leant it against the back wall of his workshop, next to the others, before moving on to the next job, making the two trestles to lay the boards on. He laid a plank on his work bench and started to saw.

A figure darkened the doorway. Durston looked up. The sunlight shone behind the figure and he couldn't make out their face, only feathery brown hair in an auburn halo against the light.

"What do you want?" he asked, as he sawed.

"They said, in the market, to come here. I need to buy shields, wooden swords and arrows."

It was a woman, with a Hued accent. He put down the saw and looked up.

She stepped forward and looked around at the workshop, at the bed shoved in one corner with a darned blanket roughly thrown over it, at the wood shavings that littered the dirt floor, at the damp plaster coming away from the wall on one side. She raised her eyebrows.

"This is the place?" she asked. "Can you sell me shields, swords, arrows?"

Durston straighted up and stared at her. It was the brown-skinned Hued woman from the City Guard, the one who'd refused to flog Alric to death three months ago. What was she doing here in Ceodrinne?

When she saw his face, she hesitated, but then looked squarely back at him and shrugged.

"Well?" she said. "I need twelve training shields, twelve simple wooden swords and a hundred arrows. They said in the market place that you did fletching."

"Aye. I do."

"So, how much? And how quickly can you do them?"

"And how many whips would you like with them?"

He heard her sharp intake of breath. But she lifted her chin and frowned at him.

"Yes ... I thought I recognised you. You were that dullard, I mean, Talthen, from Sare."

"Aye. I was there." He stepped forward. "Do you really expect me to sell weapons to cursed Hueds like you? To kill more Talthen, no doubt?"

He grabbed a chisel from his workbench, strode forward, seized her arm and yanked her close. As he held the tip of the chisel to her throat he snarled, "By the Powers, no. Never! I saw what you black-hearted guards did to my cousin, to my father. I should kill you and all your breed."

"Just try it. I'm fast and I'm strong," she hissed, "This will be in your liver before you've even drawn blood."

Durston felt a sharpness stabbing into his side. He looked down and saw she had a dagger point pressed against him. He moved the chisel away slightly from her neck.

"Nay. I wouldn't anyway. Because you didn't. That's the only reason I'm not going to try to kill you. Why didn't you?"

"Why not? By the walls, not all Hueds are like that bastard Levin!"

"Who?"

"The captain. Levin Bluestone. The one who flogged your - cousin, was it?"

"Levin Bluestone ..." Durston repeated. He had a name now.

She lowered her dagger.

"Truce, right? Put your chisel down. What sort of weapon is that anyhow?"

He stepped back and put the chisel on the bench, within arm's reach, in case he needed it.

"I'm sorry about your cousin," she said. "But there was nothing I could have done to save him, nor the others."

Durston stared at her.

"Save him? You're a Hued, in the cursed City Guard. Why are scum like you talking about saving Talthen? And coming here to buy weapons for the guard? Powers above, tell me, or I will kill you, I swear!"

She narrowed her eyes and looked at him searchingly, up and down, then laid her dagger on the bench next to his chisel.

"I'm not in the City Guard. Haven't you noticed? I'm not wearing the black. I left a week after your cousin's death. It was ... well, it was one brutality too many. I left the city too. I'm with the Hueds at Marden, under Cairson Watergiver. My name is Ezera Mertrice."

She held up her left hand and Durston saw a pale lightning-bolt shape on her palm. Then she reached her hand out, palm upwards, towards him. He shook his head and ignored it. He'd heard of the Hueds, two hundred or more, in Marden estate. He thought they were foolish visionaries, most of them, fence-sitters and doubters mixed in with a few traitors and spies. He wouldn't trust them as far as he could throw his workbench. But this woman seemed different.

"I'm not your enemy," she insisted. "Tell me your name."

He gazed at her warm brown skin, wide eyes, white teeth almost smiling at him. The same physical desire that he'd first felt on seeing her returned, and with it that sense of a deeper, stronger desire. Not lust - a finer, stronger connection. He moved towards her and took her hand.

"Durston Halthe," he said. "From Sare, but I work here."

Their eyes met as their hands joined. Durston could see her dilated pupils, her breasts rising and falling with her breathing, her parted lips. She moved closer to him and lifted her head for an instant, then rapidly stepped back. He saw her brown skin, brown hair, brown eyes: Hued hair, Hued colouring. He saw her symbol, a lightning bolt, displayed on her jacket. He dropped her hand.

"Anyway, to business," she said brusquely. "I came to

Ceodrinne with Cairson and a couple of others. We're trying to buy seeds, food, grain. Your town chief, in the market, sent me here."

"To buy weapons?"

"Training weapons, that's all! I'm training the Marden Hueds in self-defence! Look, Durston," she continued, and gestured to the chisel and dagger on the bench. "I'm no fool. Cairson up in Marden, Lady Berrena Rochale in the city, they think we can build bridges, be friends. Hued and Talthen. But I'm not so naive. It's not going to end that easily. I don't want to be sitting in Marden House, with rampaging Talthen outside, trembling for my life with scores of untrained greenhorns and no weapons, no preparation, no shields, no arrows, nothing."

She paused.

"You're not persuaded easily, are you?" she said. "Listen, I don't know which side I'm on yet. I'd like to stop swine like that bastard Levin flogging, raping and torturing their way round dullard - Talthen villages. But I'm not going to let Hueds, or myself, be flogged or murdered either. Not without a fight. Do you understand?"

"Aye. But you leave Levin Bluestone to me. He's mine ... I'll not rest until I find him and cut his black heart out." Durston added in a quiet mutter.

"So, you can make the arrows blunts, if you want, for now. For training. But will you sell them to me, or do I have to go to the next town down the river?"

Durston nodded. "All right. Hued gold, though," he said. "And I charge Hueds double - them rich bastards can afford it, I reckon."

Ezera nodded. "Fine by me, it's not my money."

"Twelve shields, twelve swords, a hundred arrows. They'll be ready in three weeks. I have to go to Sare every few days, thanks to your City Guard, to help my brother work the land. So I can't do them any faster."

"Fair enough."

"And, I want you to come - no one else. Don't send

anyone else to collect them."

"Me? Why?"

He grabbed her hand. He wanted to pull her into his arms and kiss her. Something about her face made him think he could. But he held back. Instead, he put her dagger hilt into her palm.

"I don't sell weapons to Hueds. But for you ... I will."

CHAPTER 4
THE COUNCIL

Berrena Rochale bit her lip and looked around the council chamber, at the city councillors sitting arrogantly or carelessly on the curved benches, at the scattering of curious Hueds in the balconies. There were not so many as before. She was becoming less novel, less controversial. Some whispered to each other, many looked dismissively at her, a few stared with obvious distaste or even hatred. She knew what they called her. The exile, the freak, the witch, the traitor. But for the sake of the few that agreed with her, for her family, she had to persist. She remembered how her father had argued and persisted, and eventually died, in this very chamber. She drew in a deep breath.

"Please, for the Powers' sakes," she said, holding her hands out palms upwards. "You see my mark. I am one of you, I am Hued, I am on your side. I beg you, for your own sake, listen to me!"

"No. We have had enough, "said the president of the council, her lime-green eyes harsh. "You are simply wasting council time with your paranoia! This list of demands ..." She studied the notes in front of her, then steepled her fingers and leaned forward, staring fixedly at Berrena. "Repeal the taxes on dullard towns, an amnesty to all non-violent prisoners, end the dullard labour gangs ... Well, they are presumptuous enough. But your others! Ban the word 'dullard', greater trade with the - the so-called Talthen! Even to sell them food and goods at reduced rates, on the grounds that they are, according to you, in danger of starving! Are you trying to bankrupt the city?"

"No," said Berrena. "I am trying to save the Hued."

"Yes, yes, we know your logic. We have heard it a

28

thousand times. But now this new farrago of hints and warnings! This mad tale of travelling wizards plotting evil, of them telling you our powers will fail. It is nonsense! Arrant and time-wasting nonsense!"

Several other councillors nodded. One muttered to the leader, "We should move on. Just get rid of her. She's crazy."

Berrena stood as tall as she could and clenched her fists by her sides.

"It is a warning," she said. "A warning and a chance. You have to listen!"

"We have heard enough. We have already given you enough of a concession."

"To be allowed to stay three nights, not just one, in the city?" Berrena exclaimed. "Just three nights? That's hardly a great concession!"

"It is quite enough. You will have to be satisfied with it." The president banged her gavel. "Lady or not, Hued or not, Berrena Rochale, if you keep wasting our time with threats and fear-mongering, we will reconsider having you detained in the dullard prison for a month. Audience dismissed! We will take a recess and continue with our normal business in half-an-hour."

Berrena sat down on one of the chairs at the side of the chamber, as the councillors and audience got up, stretched and gathered their documents. Her legs and arms trembled. To be threatened with prison again? Cairson, her father's friend, had told her what the prison was like. Of the brutality, of the misery and starvation, of the forced labour and deaths from exhaustion and beatings. She had been past it once: a grey stone block five miles outside the city walls. Even from that distance she could sense the despair and agony inside its windowless facade.

Most of the councillors ignored her as they passed through the door next to her chair. But one, a younger man, came up to her and quietly said, "Lady Rochale? I want you to know that I, and some of my friends, believe you. But we are too few. And the council will never vote for measures like those - that would cost us so much and be so risky."

He bent closer to her and took her hand. "Langron ... is that where you and Lady Sarielle live? We may join you," he added in a whisper, then quickly walked away.

She watched him leave, feeling a tiny bit of encouragement. There was always hope, even if the Hued did lose their gifts in the near future, as her meeting with the Magi had revealed. She wondered how she would cope when she lost her insight into others' characters, along with her invulnerability. Then she shook her head. There was no point in speculating. What was coming, was coming. At least they had a time to prepare. If only the council would listen! She stood up, shoved her papers and pens back into her bag, pulled her jacket on and hoisted the bag onto her back. As she turned, an older woman took her arm. The woman had hungry eyes and grey streaks in her orange hair.

"You said 'travelling wizards'. Did you mean the Magi?"

Berrena nodded.

"Have you seen them? Spoken to them?" There was a desperate urgency in the woman's voice.

"I saw them, that is all. Mother spoke to one of them."

"She did? Sarielle? I must know - did they say anything about my son?"

"Your son ... Headon. Headon Alcastor?"

The woman nodded.

"No. No, there was nothing. No news, only lies and deceit. I am sorry. You must be Thera Redstone," Berrena said.

Thera turned away, releasing Berrena's arm.

"I knew it. Sarielle would have sent to me. She has lost her son too ..."

She turned and crept away, her head bowed.

Berrena walked towards the gate, thinking of Thera, the Magi, Headon. Her own son and her husband were missing too ... Riathe, Felde: where were they? It was weeks since Felde had ridden away in search of the Magi and their son. Her hand fluttered to the Binding. His heart was still beating within her blood. He was still alive, at least. But what was happening to them? She had to trust that if he was alive, there was still hope. And Riathe had inherited the same invulnerability that she had. Her son would not be hurt.

Yet again, Berrena debated riding out in search of them, but she knew it would be folly. She had no idea where they were, which road they'd taken or would return on. No, all she could do, like so many before her, was return home and wait. Like she had twenty years ago, when Felde, her brother, Headon and their companions had ridden south, sent by her father, on that futile and tragic mission. She had waited for months, and only Felde had returned. Perhaps this time he would find out the truth, rather than the lies from the Magi about what had happened to Headon, Aven and Iselle, and to her brother Vallan. She had to struggle even to remember what Vallan looked like now. The pain of losing him blended with the fear of losing Felde and Riathe too, so much so that she had to pause, resting on a bench on a quiet street, until the tears in her eyes cleared.

.

CHAPTER 5
TRAITOR

Jarial climbed the steps up to the city wall on the south-eastern side. At the top waist-high parapets, interspersed with stone benches, edged the wide pavement. A breeze fluttered the flags above the gates, hiding then revealing the coloured symbols embroidered on the thirty or so standards of the council leaders and richest Hued families. High above them, the bright silk of the seven flags of the founders of Hueron slowly bloomed and rippled as the strengthening wind filled them. The clouds shifted and the morning sun brightened the purple, red, blue and green of the cloth and reflected off the gold finials on the tops of the flagpoles.

As the wall curved south, the Saroche river curved around it. Many people sat on the benches, chatting or, shielding their eyes from the bright summer sun, idly watching the Hueds strolling along the winding paths bordering the river over a hundred and twenty feet below. Others leaned on the parapets, gazing down at the kingfishers and herons diving into the deep pools near the tree-lined bank, and the pleasure boats and yachts drifting downstream.

Jarial ignored the view of the river and wide plain spread below him. He walked north, past the east gate, stopped and gazed towards the far eastern horizon. Ezera was out there, somewhere, in one of the alien dullard villages and towns. He leant on the white stone of the parapet and watched the carters and riders on the main road going to and from the north-east gate. He hoped, despite it all, that she'd be among them, coming back to Hueron and to him. He had only seen her once in the last two months.

She'd come back to the city and knocked at his door.

When he opened it, she had briefly raised her hand in greeting. That was all. He had said nothing. He could not trust his voice. Instead he had stood and watched her, waiting for her to make some further gesture or word of reconciliation. But her words were curt. "I need my summer cloak," she'd said. He'd handed it to her and she'd strode away without looking back.

He shaded his eyes from the sunshine and just made out the outlines of the most distant hills. Ezera said that from the highest of those hills it was possible to see bracken and heather-covered moors, and from them Marden was visible, twenty-three miles from the moors, far into the unknown distance-shrouded country. Ezera was right. He'd never travelled more than fifteen miles from the city. And he did not want to. Why should he? Why leave the safe, familiar beauty of Hueron for the dirt and squalor of rough dullard towns? Even travelling to Hued estates would be unpleasant: riding through hostile settlements, stared at by resentful, hungry eyes.

He gripped the cold stones. He sounded like Ezera. Resentful, hostile dullards ...

He turned away from the view and sat on a bench. The sun had warmed the stones behind him. He leaned back and stared at his mark on his palm. Ezera and the others were wrong to leave. Those mistaken weaklings who had deliberately chosen to abandon their gifts and live outside the city were dangerous fools. The Hued gifts were given to be used! It was wrong - criminally, morally wrong - to throw them aside.

Jarial took his symbol from his pocket. He held his breath, gripped the symbol tightly and felt the comforting, tingling warmth as a flame appeared and trembled on his other palm. It was pallid in the bright sunlight. He breathed slowly out and held the flame then grew it until its dancing, golden blaze outshone the sunshine and filled his cupped hand. The breeze grew and the flame danced. He closed his hand over the flame to extinguish it.

"I swear, by the gifts and the walls, no! I won't! I won't leave the Hued. I won't turn my back on my heritage!" he muttered.

But Ezera was right. It was getting harder. If only he could earn enough money with the music: with his guitar, his songs, the dances and flute tunes that he wrote. Last night he'd played a small club in the northern quarter: songs he'd written about the founding of the city, ballads based on tales his mother had told him about the persecution of the Hued by the fierce and evil Sarochen, love songs about a young girl meeting her lover after dark; wild lonely flute tunes and fast, swirling dances. He'd been cheered and clapped, but had barely earned enough to cover a meal and a few drinks. He needed to earn more. Then he wouldn't have to spend his time going around restaurants and bakeries and inns to light fires, fuel ovens, set blazes going in numerous fireplaces. Today he'd already lit fires for sixteen restaurants in the city centre, eighteen bakers including one right over on the west side of the city, and there was more work to come. He rested his head on the back of the bench and closed his eyes for a moment. Below him he could hear people chattering and bargaining in a market in a nearby street, smell stews and grilled meat from food stalls. Above him, only a clear blue sky.

He stood and walked to the north-eastern gate, intending to descend and walk to Clementine Park for his next job: to create and light a bonfire for a summer party. As he reached the steps, he saw a dark-skinned woman threading through the market traders and the people coming into the city from the north-eastern road. She walked with a determined step towards the gate. Her long jet-black hair hung loose and Jarial could see the darkness of her skin. He knew who she was. He ran down the steps.

"Rochale?" he said. "Lady Rochale?"

She nodded.

He paused, staring at her.

"Traitor," he said, at last. "You and that double-traitor,

that renegade and dullard-lover, Cairson Watergiver!"

"Cairson?" she gasped. "Traitors?"

"Telling people to run away. To stop using their gifts, to leave the city. Deserting the city, their gifts, their home, their responsibilities! Lying, twisting, undermining ... The council should have you and him strung up."

He stepped towards her, his fist raised. Berrena lifted her hands and moved back, fear on her face.

"No, no," she stuttered. "No, that isn't true. I've never told anyone to stop using their gifts! I don't tell them that ... I just ..."

"Just what?"

She squared her shoulders, paused, then looked steadily at him.

"I have only told Hueds, giftless Hueds, those who have already lost their gifts or are losing them, that they are welcome in Langron or Marden. That is all."

"Liar! Lying half-breed freak! By the blood and the marks, then, why are so many leaving? Why did she go? She still had her gift! You and Cairson, between you, you twisted her, corrupted her ..."

"Who?"

"She was one of the best in the guard! And now she's mouldering, exiled, miles away, when she should be here! Protecting the city! How many more will you and that treacherous Watergiver take?"

"'Tis not my doing," she said, gently laying her hand on his arm. "I don't know who you have lost, but neither Cairson nor I are to blame. People make their own choices."

He wrenched his arm from her.

"It was your doing!" he said. "She wouldn't have chosen to leave the city otherwise! To leave me, to join our enemies!"

"Perhaps you should go after her," she said. "You are a fire-maker, are you not? You could help them."

"No!" he muttered, putting his hands to his forehead. "No, no, I can't ... We, the Hued, we have to stay here. It's the only way. We have to stay here and keep ourselves safe."

"I don't think you will be safe here. Please, please believe me. That is all I am trying to do. To save the Hued."

"No!" he snapped, straightening up. "No. You're wrong. She's wrong. Leaving the city, running away, that's wrong. It's cowardly! We are Hueds, not cowards. We should stay here and protect ourselves, our homes, our city, each other, not scurry off like frightened rabbits to hide in some power-forsaken dullard rat-hole. You're wrong!"

He spat at her feet, turned and stalked away.

CHAPTER 6
PLOTTING

Durston finished binding the feathers on to the last arrow, tied it up in a bundle with nineteen others and placed them in the almost-full barrel. He'd completed the swords and shields last week, now all he had to do was wait for Ezera to come. As he tidied up the workshop, he debated going to Marden to take the arrows to her, but he had other more pressing things to attend to. Tomorrow, Powers willing, he'd walk to Sare, see how his mother and brother were managing, and help with the farm work for a day or two.

It was late evening, and too dark to work anymore. He lay stretched out on his bed, with his hands behind his head, and gazed at the flickering shadows and lights the lantern cast on the roof beams. He thought of Ezera's vibrant face and wide brown eyes. Then he shook his head, blew out the light and tried to banish her image in sleep.

A quiet rap woke him. It was completely dark. He judged that he'd been asleep for about an hour. There was a faint glimmer outlining the door of his workshop.

"Aye, who is it?" he said.

"The smith sent me to you," a voice whispered. "Let me in. I need to talk to you - privately."

Durston picked his way past the piles of wood, benches and barrels to the door. His bare feet crunched on curls of wood shavings. As he opened the door, pale light from a lantern shone in his eyes. A man, wrapped in a dark cloak, held the lantern. Durston could only see a glimpse of the man's face.

"I don't know you," he said. "What do you want?"

"To talk. Here ..."

Durston heard the chink of coins and the man held a gold piece out towards him. He took it.

"Very well. You'd best come in," he said, opening the door wider.

The man slipped through, placed the lantern on a bench, brushed sawdust off a stool and sat down. He kept his cloak wrapped around himself, still hiding most of his face. Durston shut the door then watched him warily.

"What's this about?" he asked.

"Revenge."

Durston started. He clenched his fists.

"Against who? Against me? 'Tain't no one that I've injured, that I know of."

"Against the Hued, who else? The City Guard in particular."

"Revenge against the Hued? Dangerous talk. You'd best tell me who you are before you go any further."

"I will. But first, swear by the Powers above and the Virtues below that you will keep this meeting, my name and what we talk about, secret."

Durston thought for a moment. But he could see no harm in listening. He nodded.

"I swear," he said.

"Bind it, then."

Durston stared at him. Did he mean the blood binding?

"Spit!" The man spat into his left palm and held it out. Durston remembered his grandfather doing the same to seal a bargain. He spat into his hand too and grasped the other's. The man's hand felt small and bony.

"Tulketh Jobe," he said, unwinding his cloak. He was dressed in good-quality linen with a stout leather jacket, and a fine gold chain glinted inside the white cambric of his shirt. Rich, thought Durston. A rich Talthen? Unheard of. Even so, he was slightly built, shorter than Durston by a head. His face was pale with high cheekbones and a strong chin, and the lamplight shone onto his reddish hair.

"Well, Tulketh," Durston said. "I'm Durston Halthe. What's this about?"

Tulketh tightened his thin lips as his prominent grey eyes, shaded by sandy eyelashes, scanned the room, then he darted to the door, opened it, quickly looked up and down the street, and sat down again.

"I told you. Revenge. Revenge and justice - and liberation," he said, his mouth a tense line as he stared at Durston.

"Liberation?"

"From Hued rule."

Durston breathed out a long, slow breath. At last, he thought. Yes, liberation. From taxes, prisons, oppression, starvation. If only it were possible. He sat down near Tulketh.

"How?" he said, leaning forward.

Tulketh narrowed his eyes. "I ain't going to tell you all the plans," he said. "But things are moving. We reckon that within a year we can raise an army big enough to take the city. Ten thousand men."

Durston gasped.

"By the Powers!"

"Aye. A liberation army, we're calling it."

"Impossible!" Durston grabbed Tulketh's wrist. "Look at us," he said, gesturing towards himself. "When did you ever see a stout, let alone a fat, Talthen? Thin ... half-starved ... most of the Talthen be too weak, too hungry, to keep themselves alive, let alone take on the city. And even ten thousand is too few. The walls, the guards ..."

"Mayhap. But we'll have other help."

"What?"

"'Tis secret. But 'twill make the difference. Trust me. I've told you enough. Now, listen. This is why I'm here. We need help. People to make weapons, armour, arrows. We pay you in Hued gold, then you make for us, in secret, what we need. And when the time comes, you join us."

"How do you get Hued gold? Durston exclaimed.

"Nought to do you with." Tulketh stood up. "Agreed?"

Durston stood too. "Hued gold for arrows? I'd be stupid not to agree, wouldn't I?"

"Aye. Right then. We'll come, pay you, and arrange a cache - somewhere deep in the forests to the north. You'll make the weapons and hide them. There'll be caches all round the countryside, ready for the signal."

Durston spat on his left hand and held it out.

"Aye. Agreed," he said.

After his strange visitor had left, Durston strode to and fro, his hands clenched, his heart beating hard against his chest. Tulketh had said he'd return with money and orders. An army, a liberation army! To take the city! And, surely, the prison too. That would not be forgotten. There were hundreds of Talthen, like him, who had brothers, husbands, wives, family locked up, starved and enslaved in that foul place. His father was there and Durston had no way of knowing if he was even still alive. If he could rescue his father, bring him back to Sare, then find and kill that green-skinned Hued bastard ...

CHAPTER 7
DRIZZLE

It started to drizzle. Ezera dismounted and pulled her summer cloak out. As she did so, she looked around at the fields. The corn in one lay sodden and flattened. Even a city girl like herself could see that there wasn't much chance of a harvest from it. On the other side of the road some sort of vegetables - cabbages or beans, she didn't know which - stood rotting and brown between water-filled ruts in the muddy soil.

As the drizzle thickened, Ezera pulled the hood over her head and rode on, with the pack horse trudging alongside her. The horses' hooves splashed through rain-specked puddles and the wind blew rain over them until her trousers and boots were soaked. Her hands felt numb from the wet and cold. She shivered, but at least she had her cloak. Even though it was only thin wool, it kept the worst off her face and body.

She remembered how Jarial had glared at her when she'd collected it. Ezera, stubborn from birth, as her father had always said, had bit her lip as she knocked on his door. She wasn't going to be the first to apologise or beg or ask. She'd waited for him to greet her or to say something - anything - any hint of regret or of a changed mind, a desire to have her back. But there had been nothing in his face except stony blankness. She had shoved her hands into her jacket pockets and stepped back to stop herself running to him and flinging yearning arms around his comforting, strong warmth. And he - the cold-hearted swine! - he'd just stood there. It was clear he didn't want her back.

At Ceodrinne she tied up the horses outside Durston's workshop, knocked and strode in. Durston looked up from chiselling a piece of wood, and nodded.

"Ah, 'tis you. 'Tis ready, just let me finish this mortise," he said.

Ezera tossed her cloak onto a workbench and perched on a stool to watch him.

"You've got a leak in your roof," she said, glancing up to where water dripped onto the sawdust and wood shavings on the floor.

"I know. Shove that bucket under it, would you?"

He tapped on the chisel a few more times, then laid it next to the hammers, other chisels, clamps and set squares on the workbench.

"Done. Right. Your kit is there, in that corner. Under the blanket."

"I hope you've kept it dry."

Durston glared at her. "Dry? Oh, aye, 'tis dry enough. Perhaps your ladyship would like to check it? Count the arrows?"

Ezera slipped off the stool and pulled the blanket aside.

"Thirty gold, as we agreed," Durston said.

"Yes. The money's in my pack, there," she said as she knelt by the pile of arrows, wooden swords and shields. She picked up a bundle of arrows, then turned over a shield and inspected it. She stood up, holding one of the arrows.

"These are good. Neat, smooth fletching. Very high quality. But there's far more here than I asked for."

Durston nodded.

"Do you want paying more?"

"Nay."

"No? Why?"

"I have my reasons."

Ezera stared at him, but his face remained impassive.

"Sure?"

"Aye."

She put the arrow back and picked up a sword.

"Well, fine, it's your choice," she said. "We will need more, even so. Another lot, same amount?"

"Right. It will be another two weeks, though."

She swung the sword to and fro, then weighed it on her palm.

"Very good too. I like the feel, the balance. Smooth wood, perfect weight for training. You know what you are doing with weapons. Do you fight with swords as well as make them?"

Durston picked up another sword.

"Try me," he said.

Ezera glanced around. "It's a little crowded in here. Outside? You don't mind a little rain, do you?"

"Nay. Outside is fine. But I don't have so many spare shirts that I want to get this one soaked," he said, peeling it off.

Ezera pulled her jacket off and tossed it onto her cloak. "Good point. No point in that getting wet either, I guess."

In the lane rain poured from drenched thatch and trickled down ruts and between stones. A flurry of wind threw raindrops into their faces.

"On guard?" Ezera said. He nodded.

He was faster and better than she expected. She'd taken it slow at first; with her gift, she knew she had an unfair advantage. But after several blows, parries and counter-blows she realised that he had speed and strength that matched hers. Once or twice he had broken through her defence. Maybe she could risk going a little faster. Durston held up his hand.

"Don't you pull your blows or go easy on me," he said harshly. "Don't coddle me! I ain't a newbie. I want to see just how good you are. How good a gifted City Guard soldier really is!"

"Fine! If that's what you want ..."

She hammered blows onto him, not caring if he could defend himself or not. After a few minutes she had hit his arms, legs and body several times. Dark-red bruises bloomed on his side and over his ribs. He was panting and sweating.

"Enough?" she asked. "It's a good thing none of your villagers are around. They'd get the wrong idea, seeing us, despite the training swords."

"Aye. But carry on. I ain't done up yet."

"Tough *and* stubborn? Right, try this!"

Ezera attacked as fast as she could, with counter-thrusts and a subtle feint that she'd learnt in City Guard training. But Durston must have come across this. He whipped his sword up to block her. Instead, she resorted to a basic, quick flurry of side-swipes and upper cuts. She was too fast for him. She forced him back against the wall of a cottage. Water dripped from the thatch into his fair hair and clear blue eyes. Ezera stepped back and twisted, intending to swivel round for greater speed and knock his sword away. But her shifting foot slipped in the mud. She crashed down sideways and cursed loudly.

"Are you hurt?" Durston panted.

"No! Just stupid! Stupid, stupid mistake!"

He stepped forward and reached his hand down. She grasped it and he hauled her up. Suddenly she was close to him, close enough to see droplets beading on his shoulders and clinging to his hair, and to see his bare chest rising and falling. He put his other arm around her and pulled her closer still. She couldn't help herself. She slipped her arms around his waist, lifted her chin and stared steadily into his strange blue Talthen eyes. As they kissed, rain ran down from their hair and over their skin. Ezera's fingers glided over his smooth, wet back muscles. Then Durston released her and stepped back.

She gasped as if she'd been struck. What the hell was she doing? She ought to feel anger or revulsion, but all she felt was amazement.

"Powers above, Durston ..." she breathed, moving back from him. "Don't ... No, don't. We really shouldn't."

He looked at her steadily, took a step towards her, then

turned away.

"Nay. I guess not," he said, and strode back into his workshop.

She followed him. He grabbed a cloth, towelled himself dry and put his shirt back on. Ezera pulled on her jacket.

"You're a good fighter," she said.

"Mayhap. But you beat me easily," he growled.

"Of course," she said, holding out her palm. "See my mark? I wouldn't be in the City Guard if I couldn't take on and beat most people in a one-to-one fight. City Guards are expected to be able to easily handle five or six dullards. I mean Talthen."

Durston nodded sullenly, then turned away.

"I'll help you load up your horses," he said.

CHAPTER 8
A LIBERATION ARMY

The tap on the door came after midnight, a week later. Durston saw Tulketh Jobe outside.

"We need two hundred arrows for the army," he said, putting a lantern on the workbench.

"What about shields, pikes, armour, swords?"

"They're being made by others. I need to show you the cache. We'll need to arrange to meet at some point northwards of here."

"Aye. But first, sit down, Tulketh. I need to ask you. What about the prison?"

"The prison - aye. 'Tain't forgotten. We'll take that first, and the garrison towns, then the city. Liberation, and revenge."

"By the Powers, I want to do more than just fletch arrows for this. I'll join, I can fight, I've learnt sword drill since I was eight. I can recruit for you from Sare. I know of dozens there who might join. If you're planning to attack the prison and the city, then you need every man you can get."

"Aye, we do." Tulketh stroked his chin and eyed Durston reflectively. "You want revenge, like so many. How many in Sare?"

Durston thought. His uncle, his aunt, Alric's brothers and sisters, and all those who'd seen their family members or friends taken off to the prison.

"Fifty, I reckon."

"Good. You're in. You're one of us."

"And you reckon ten thousand men will be enough! 'Tain't. You'd need more, far more. 'Tis well nigh impossible, Tulketh. There's forty thousand people there. You can't starve them out: they have all the food, weapons and water they need. The walls are a hundred and twenty feet high. 'Twould take far more than even ten thousand."

"I told you, we've got help."

"What help? Tulketh, if I'm to join in, I want to know."

"Don't worry, Durston, we've got more people involved than you'd believe."

"How many?"

"Hundreds scouting and recruiting, like me. You can trust us."

"Aye, that's the point. Who's 'us'?"

"You're sworn to secrecy, remember. And we'd know if you blabbed. Not that 'twould make much difference, now. It's started and nought will be able to stop it."

"Well, then," Durston said, slamming his fist down on the table. "Then tell me!"

"'Tis me, Ulban Hirsche, and others."

"Ulban Hirsche - I've never heard of him."

"He's a landowner, a Talthen, from in the forests east of Langron. He has powerful friends." Tulketh paused. "I've got your word?"

"Aye!"

"The Magi."

Durston stood up. "The Magi? Powers above!"

"Like I said, powerful friends, more powerful than any Hued. Have you ever seen them?"

Durston nodded. "Two weeks since. They passed Ceodrinne travelling south."

"South, returning home from visiting Ulban. They've promised to help the Talthen against the city, when they return in spring next year. With them on our side ..."

"The Magi - aye. Wizards ..."

Durston remembered the six wizards, leading a procession of scores of servants, horses, carts laden with goods, and attended by their new apprentices. Their robes, their jewels, their staffs; their aura of power and confidence.

"They'll help us against the Hued? Truly? But why?"

"They be no friends to Hueds, you know that. And they'll have their reasons, no doubt. I heard that they've seen how we are treated, and decided 'tis not to be borne any longer. Anyhap, 'tis between them and Ulban. I ain't in their inner councils."

He paused, and looked up at Durston. "Satisfied?" he asked. Durston nodded.

"Spit and shake, then, to seal it," said Tulketh. "Good. Now, to business. First, let me trim this light. Dark as the inside of a black wolf in here ."

Tulketh reached over to the lantern on the workbench. His hand knocked it and the door swung open. The candle inside tipped over and rolled over the wood shavings on the bench. Durston leapt forward and seized it.

"Watch what you are doing, you fool!" he gasped.

Tulketh eyed him curiously. He took the candle from Durston and held a curl of shaving to the flame, until it started burning. Durston turned pale. Tulketh dropped the blazing wood onto the bench and Durston flinched, then grabbed a cloth and threw it over the flames.

"Scared?" Tulketh said.

"Don't you know how dangerous fire is in a place like this?" Durston said, pointing round at the scattered pieces of wood, jars of polishes and wax, varnishes, paint, dust coating everything. "For Powers' sakes, be careful!"

"Calm yourself down. I ain't going to set fire to your precious workshop."

"Fine! Just watch it!"

"Jumpy, ain't you?" he sneered, putting the candle back into the lantern.

"So'd you be if you'd seen someone burnt in a place like this," Durston growled, shutting the door of the lantern. "I ain't a coward, I just ain't too fond of fire getting loose around here. So we'll keep the lantern shut, right!"

"Have it your own way. Anyhap, as I said, to business. I need to fix where to meet you so as I can show you the hiding place for the stuff."

After Tulketh had left, Durston lit his own lantern, and dragged a blanket off his bed. In the corner of the workshop stood a pile of arrows and wooden shields. Tulketh had eyed the pile but said nothing. Durston realised he'd better hide them. They were for Ezera. He sat down on his bed with his head in his hands. What a fool he was! It was bad enough making her extra swords and arrows, simply because she seemed to care about Talthen. And, he had to admit, because he wanted her to survive. Now he had committed to making weapons for both the Hued and this 'Liberation Army'. As if that wasn't bad enough, he'd agreed to join the army. He could find himself fighting against Ezera.

As he lay back on the bed and he wondered: if such a massive army could be raised, what would happen to the Hueds at Marden, and to Ezera? No doubt they would be attacked and massacred. A sudden, unwelcome pang of fear hit him. Perhaps he should warn her as well as making additional weapons for her? But he was sworn to secrecy, and she already suspected that rebellion against the Hued was looming. Anyhap, she was a Hued City Guard and a gifted soldier. He'd heard of City Guards that could take on ten Talthen at once with ease. He'd heard of their reactions, their accuracy, their speed. Her mark indicated how gifted she was. And she, and the others at Marden, were not unarmed.

But if the Magi were going to help, perhaps even the invulnerable City Guard would be defeated. He could only hope to the powers above that, if they did, Ezera would survive. Durston imagined the Magi simply lifting their hands and the walls crumbling, the guard failing, the Liberation Army storming into the city. To have the Magi on their side! He remembered the sight of them riding past ... He had stopped, along with dozens of others, to gaze at the procession, the grey-clad well-fed servants, the thoroughbred horses, the stately Magi themselves, the pride on the faces of their apprentices. On five of them, anyway.

The sixth apprentice had been a thin, young lad who had ridden at the tail of the procession. He was abnormally pale. His skin and hair was almost white. He kept glancing back and around, with an intense apprehensive stare, as if searching for help. Durston had wondered why the Magi had picked someone so fragile and nervous to be an apprentice, and why the boy kept riding on when his reluctance was so apparent.

CHAPTER 9
GIFTLESS

Ezera bounced on her toes to ready herself, stepped forward and brought the wooden sword round and up. It clattered against the other woman's sword.

"Good!" Ezera said. "That's it! Hold your sword steady, tilted slightly, so that the cross-piece protects your hands. But you have to turn the blow with the flat, not the edge, otherwise you'll ruin your cutting edge."

The woman nodded. Ezera glanced around at the others fighting in pairs on the wide lawns at Marden House. She'd decided to start teaching them how to parry the middle, upper and lower cuts, after having spent a month teaching them the attacking cuts. Most of them were competent, if slow.

She clapped her hands.

"Right, everyone! We'll swap around - partner with someone else. Just keep going through the practise strokes until you're really smooth. Until it's almost automatic. Tiron, you partner me."

Tiron nodded and strode over. He was an ex-baker, a determined, wide-shouldered man used to hefting around sacks of flour and heavy trays of bread.

"You're shaping up well, Tiron," Ezera said. "We'll go a bit faster. I'll attack, you defend."

Before they started, she saw Cairson standing on the gravel terrace between the manor and the lawns. As they sparred, he walked over to them, leant on his stick and watched. Then he called to her. "Ezera, can you pause for a moment?"

Ezera dropped her sword. "Take a breather, Tiron," she said and jogged over to Cairson.

"Yes, uncle?"

"How is it going?"

"Well enough. Most of them are improving. I'll start teaching them counter-attacking and evasive footwork next day. Tiron is learning fast. He'll be good. And a couple of the women have become surprisingly competent at archery in just a few lessons. But they all need to practise more. At least an hour a day!"

Cairson nodded. "Yes, well, we won't have that discussion again. They do have other responsibilities, though I accept that this could be important too."

"Of course it is! But I know about their other jobs. That's why we started so early this morning."

"However, that is not what I wanted to ask about."

He took her over to the pile of training weapons.

"Zera, where did these come from?"

"The wooden swords? Durston Halthe, the Talthen in Ceodrinne. He supplied them. You know that!"

"So many?"

"Yes. Twenty-four." Ezera paused and shrugged. "Yes, er, he gave me a few extra." She still couldn't understand why he'd done that.

"A dozen extra, by the sound of it."

Ezera picked one up and swung it around.

"Does it matter? They're good. Well-made. Don't splinter too easily, good and sturdy. He did us a favour, uncle. Two dozen training swords, two dozen shields, two hundred arrows."

"And the cost?"

Ezera tossed the sword back on the pile. "Er, well, yes, uncle, it was expensive. But we need them!"

"Very well. I'll not press it. Just don't break too many, will you?"

"Right."

"But what about those?"

He walked over to a bundle of swords lying rolled up in a cloth.

"The sharps?"

"Yes. Real swords, not training ones, I notice. There's a dozen here, and you've got more in your armoury."

"We will need them, uncle. There's nearly a hundred people here. They all need to be armed. Just in case!"

"They're City Guard swords, aren't they?"

She put her hands on her hips and stared defiantly at him.

"Some of them were mine," she said.

"Some!" Cairson smiled. "Yes, but not even you, Ezera, own thirty-odd swords. How did you get them?"

"They're borrowed! That's all. The guard in charge of the armoury in Hueron agreed to lend them to me ..."

Ezera thought of the other thirty swords, the dozens of spears and fifty or so daggers, not to mention the quivers, scabbards, belts and leather greaves that she'd charmed and wheedled out of the friendly guard, swearing by the walls and Powers above that she was only borrowing them, before smuggling them out on the cart to Marden. She probably shouldn't tell Cairson about those.

Cairson shook his head and patted her shoulder.

"By the gifts, Ezera, you are incorrigible! Well, I will not enquire too closely ..."

"Good. I'll carry on then." She picked up one of the swords.

"One more moment, niece. I have another issue with you," Cairson said. He paused and looked grave. "You were fighting very impressively just then. So fast, so accurate, so instinctive - even when only training. Zera, you were using your gift."

"Yes, of course I was! What of it?"

"We agreed that here, in Marden, we would stop relying on the gifts. That we would live as Talthen; simply, by our own unaided manual efforts."

Ezera shifted her weight from foot to foot impatiently.

"Yes, yes, I know, but ... but it's not that simple for me! I can't ... It's not like a piece of armour that I can take off. It's part of me. Uncle, you should understand that!"

"Nevertheless, you shouldn't use it. You should learn, should try, to rely on your natural strength, not your powers."

Ezera rammed her sword point into the grass.

"How?" she exclaimed. "Tell me how and I'll do it!"

Cairson raised his eyebrows. "You never were very persuadable, even as a child. Zera, can't you simply slow down somewhat? Ignore your gifted instincts? Rely only on your normal senses?"

She shook her head. "No, I can't. It doesn't work that way! And how can I train these properly if I'm not the best that I can be? Uncle, I can see what you're getting at, but it's just not possible. It's just idealistic dreaming!"

She picked up the sword, grabbed another one, and strode back to Tiron.

"Right! We'll carry on! Uncle, you'd better keep out of the way!"

Tiron hesitated.

"With those?" he said.

"Sharps? Yes. We need to go to the next level."

She saw the worried look on his face.

"They can be safer. People get more bruises with training swords because they wave them around and are more careless," she said. "Besides, you need to get used to the different weight and balance. Trust me. You won't be able to hit me, and I'm not going to hurt you. Simple: slow attack and parry. We'll just go through the practise strokes."

Steel hit steel. Tiron was getting better: using his weight and strength to the full. Soon he'd be good enough to really challenge her. She grinned at the thought. Lack of proper training was making her rusty and sluggish. She needed a skilled and relentless opponent.

She parried his upper cut, whirled the sword around, down and then slowed to give him a chance to react. He fumbled his defence and she pulled her blow so that it just tapped his arm.

"Good, but raise your sword to head level to stop mine, then you respond quickly with a down cut, like this ..."

They parried. Tiron defended then attacked. She turned it easily. He speeded up, obviously keen to get through her defences.

Something changed.

Ezera didn't know what, but something felt different. Something was missing. She lowered her sword and glanced around. It was quiet. The other pairs had paused. Some looked at her, puzzled. Cairson stared at something yellow on the grass then knelt to pick it up.

"Are you all right?" Tiron asked.

"Yes ... Yes. Fine! Carry on!"

He hefted his sword, lifted it high, then rapidly slashed sideways. Ezera lifted hers to parry but the sword felt as heavy as lead, not steel, as she raised it. What was wrong with her? Why were her muscles so weak, her arm so slow? She panted with the sudden, strange effort. Tiron's sword came too fast. She was too slow. The blade slammed into her leg. She heard the crunch of steel cracking into the bone and felt her muscles ripping as she fell sideways.

Someone screamed. Tiron dropped his sword and knelt by her. His face was aghast.

"Powers above! I didn't mean ..."

Ezera tried to sit up. She grabbed her leg. Blood, warm brown blood, pooled onto the grass from the torn flesh. Searing pain tunnelled through her nerves. She bit her lip in an effort not to moan with pain. She'd never been injured this badly.

"Get help ..." she gasped, as she tried to staunch the pouring blood. "Wrap something round it ..."

The wound gaped open. She could see the white bone, split by the sword point. As the others stood round, open-mouthed and useless, Tiron yanked off his shirt and tried to bandage her leg. Suddenly Cairson was there, his face pale.

"You, and you, run to the house and get help, a healer, one of the recent arrivals was a healer - get him, get someone!" he shouted. "Here, Zera, lie back. Tiron, let me help."

As they wound the cloth tightly, Ezera felt her head reeling. Don't faint, she told herself. She collapsed onto her side. In the grass, by her face, spattered with her blood, she saw something. It was the thing that was missing. Her symbol. Her lightning bolt.

It was dead.

CHAPTER 10
PANIC

Another inadequate fee for an evening's music, thought Jarial sourly, jingling the few coins in his pocket. Hardly worth it. If he didn't love the performing so much he'd give up. As he walked to the first cafe on his list, he hummed a tune from one of the songs, then shifted it into a minor key, turned a phrase around and elaborated it. He thought of Ezera, and a melancholy yet seductive five-note phrase came to him. It was only mid-morning and the street was quiet. He started to softly sing the new tune, weaving bitter words and harsh poetry into the music.

At the cafe the owner was flicking cloths over tables and shuffling chairs around. Jarial stopped singing, nodded a greeting, and went through to the kitchen at the back.

"Just be quick, will you," the owner called. "I've got twenty pies that need baking."

In the kitchen, Jarial held his symbol and visualised firewood, kindling, flames. As he pictured them he felt the flow of the gift, pulling fire and heat into the oven before him. Logs, twigs and a few hesitant flames appeared. Jarial held them, and concentrated on increasing the heat and the fuel.

Something snapped. The flames died. Jarial heard a glass smash in the café followed by the gasp of the owner.

He stared at the oven. The logs and twigs were still there. He reached his hand towards them but they were cold. Then he realised something else. He could no longer feel or sense his symbol. He felt as if it had vanished. Opening his hand, he stared at it. It was still there: his warm red, flame-shaped symbol, looking unchanged. But he couldn't connect to it. It was as if his finger had been cut off and lay dead on his palm. He lifted his hand and peered closely at the shape, but as he did it slid from his palm and onto the floor. It shattered. Red-orange shards bounced on the tiles and scattered around his feet.

Jarial knelt down and picked one up. What was going on? How could this happen? Symbols were alive, indestructible, dying only when a Hued died. But his was ruined and broken. He grasped the fragment. The sharp edge cut into his hand, but he ignored the pain and crouched down, holding his fists to his head as he tried to suppress his panic.

He stood up and stared at the dead, cold logs in the oven. He tried to use his gift, frowning with unaccustomed effort and clenching his hand tightly around the shard, but nothing happened. No flow, no connection. He was giftless. Ezera had been right and now he had lost his gift.

No one must know, he thought. He picked up the remaining pieces and put them in his pocket, turned, and ran through the cafe. The owner sat at a table, staring nowhere and looking stunned. But Jarial ignored him and sped down the street towards his house. What should he do? Go to Marden, find Ezera, admit he was wrong, live with dullards? Run away?

In the street he saw others staring at symbols in their hands or picking slivers of coloured glass from between cobbles, looking confused or appalled. One woman laughed hysterically, another crouched and sobbed as she stared at her symbol in her palm. With relief, and then with fear, Jarial realised. He was not alone. The same loss had happened to them, perhaps to all the Hued. What Berrena Rochale had foretold had happened.

Jarial's mother had mocked Berrena's warnings, saying: "Her father, Lord Sapphireborne, had the same ridiculous idea; that the Hued gifts would weaken and might even fail. But he was a fool. Imagine sending your son off on some far-fetched mission to investigate your theories! Along with four other Hueds, and none of them returned, you know. And then his wife, Sarielle Rochale, suddenly announces, after his death, that she is going to go and live with dullards! It's no surprise that his daughter is infected with the same pernicious ideas. It's my belief that the stress of losing her father and her brother has turned her brain."

Now Jarial wondered if his mother was wrong and Berrena right. He could remember, even though it was almost twenty years ago, his parents discussing the scandal of Lord Sapphireborne's death and the missing Hueds; the rumours about him plotting to seize power, and the tales about his exiled black-skinned daughter and her dullard husband.

Jarial remembered something else his mother had said. She was on the City Council, and yesterday she had complained that Berrena Rochale had insisted on another meeting with the council.

"Claiming Hued status, calling herself Lady Rochale! Wasting council time with her scaremongering and her preposterous demands that we should treat dullards as equals," she'd snapped. "Trying, yet again, to frighten us into believing her outrageous prophecies!"

The meeting was this morning, which meant, Jarial realised, that Berrena would be in the city. He turned and ran towards the city centre.

CHAPTER 11
BERRENA'S LOSS

The street was quiet at this time in the morning, with few people using it, apart from a small group of Hueds walking ahead of Berrena. It was a longer route to the city hall from the north-eastern gate but she preferred it. It went past a college where, on a clear sunny morning like today, there would be groups of students sitting on tree-shaded benches discussing art or poetry or music, and clusters of earnest children gazing at their symbols. Faint ghosts of objects - fruit, paper, bread, cups, egg - appeared in the children's hands as they practised. Berrena liked to stand and watch. But this morning she did not linger. She walked on, rehearsing in her mind what she would say to the council to persuade them to take some action. She was not sanguine, but at least she had been granted another audience. She would have to be polite and persuasive, she would only ask for small changes such as a reduction in taxes, she would not be a fear-monger, but the thought that they might send her to the dullard prison made her stomach shrink.

Suddenly, silently, the world shifted and tilted around her. For an instant Berrena felt as if she was a taut rope that had been disconnected and flailed wildly. The group of Hueds in front of her stopped walking. Berrena saw their symbols fall then shatter as they hit the pavement. The sharp sounds of glass fragments skittering over the stones broke the quiet of the street. She looked around. Behind her, down a side street, in the park across the street, people stood motionless, staring at their symbols or kneeling to pick up coloured pieces. Some gasped in panicked alarm or gazed around in consternation. Others bent to scoop up the remnants of their symbols and ran rapidly down the street.

Berrena looked at her hands and arms. They appeared no different. She staggered to a bench on the pavement and sat down. Her legs trembled and a cold sickness gripped her stomach. She hunted through her pack until she found her small penknife. Holding her breath, she sliced the blade across her fingertip. It cut easily through her skin and the sharpness of the pain shocked a sob from her. The pain - the agony! Suddenly her head swam and blackness clouded her vision. Dizziness and pain filled her senses. She fell sideways, clutching her hand, gasping, until the blackness faded. Shuddering, she heaved herself slowly back up and looked at the stinging, bleeding cut. The welling blood taunted her.

As she gazed at it and tried to overcome the terrifying feeling of faintness and dread, a hand touched her shoulder. She looked up into the troubled, lined face of an older Hued woman, with sea-blue skin and incongruous white hair. The woman held out her hand. On her palm lay a perfect image of a fish. But it had broken in two.

"Lady Rochale?" the woman said with quiet fear. "It's dead. This is what you said would happen, isn't it?"

Berrena stared at her in horror. The woman's face was empty. There were no emotions, no desires, no truth or falsehood. Berrena shuddered and wrapped her arms around herself as she fought against an instinct to scream at the blank mask facing her.

The woman stepped back and stared at Berrena's expression, then at her broken symbol and the confused and frightened faces of the Hueds running past them. She scurried away.

The blood ran down Berrena's finger and dropped black specks onto the white pavement. The cut throbbed with unbearable significance. Her invulnerability was lost. "What has happened?" she whispered. "Felde, Riathe ... the Magi ... Have they got something to do with this? Oh, Powers above, what has happened?" Her hand fluttered to the shared heartbeat. If that had gone too, she would be utterly broken. But it beat on, as strong and reassuring as ever. Her husband was still alive. If only she could know if her son was too.

She reeled along a street leading towards the north-east gate. Suddenly, the red-skinned, fire-making Hued who had raged at her a week ago came around a corner, ran to her, seized her shoulder and pulled her around to face him.

"You said this would happen!" he shouted.

She stared at him in fear and confusion.

"I remember you," she said. "You - you spat at me."

"You deserved it. And now - look around you! Is it true? Have the gifts gone? You said this would happen, didn't you? How did you know?"

"Aye, they've gone. I didn't know it would happen like this ..." she whispered. "Not all at once. Not instantly, without any warning! Oh, what has happened? Is it the Magi? Riathe, Felde ... what have you done?"

"Who?"

"My son, my husband! Felde, Riathe!" She could not help it. The names burst from her in a cry. She clutched her breast and breathed in and out deeply, in great shuddering moans. He gripped her shoulders harder and shook her.

"What have they got to do with this? It's you. You witch! You had something to do with this!"

"Nay! Nay! Look!"

She held out her hand to him so show him where her blood trickled from the cut on her finger.

"See! I've lost mine too. My invulnerability, my insight ..." she said.

"What do you mean?"

"My skin. It was my symbol. No one could cut it or hurt me. And that's gone. I tried to cut my finger, with my knife, and ..."

"What? How can your skin be your symbol?"

"I don't know. And I could tell what people were like, if they were good or evil, what their gifts and desires where.

I've lost that too. How will I live without that? Believe me, please! I didn't want this to happen!"

She looked at his furious, twisted face.

"Please, let me go," she pleaded. "It's not my fault! I must go home! I can't - I can't help the city anymore ..."

He dropped his hands and she turned away and stumbled along the street. She walked quickly, using narrow circuitous streets and lanes, the gate. She had to get home, to Langron. To somewhere safe where she could learn how to deal with her loss. How to use knives with care, how to use cloths to handle oven-hot dishes, how to read the deceptive faces of other people. In the side streets people scurried round corners, looked from side to side, darted into doors and locked them. As she emerged onto a main street she came upon heaving, chaotic groups of fearful-looking Hueds and heard loud shouts of arguments and panic, and the ominous roar of raging voices coming from an intercepting thoroughfare. She threaded her way through the crowds, avoiding eye contact.

"That's her!" someone shouted. "That's the half-breed who said this would happen!"

"Traitor!" someone else yelled.

Another person hissed, "She must have known. She must have had something to do with this. Treacherous dullard witch!"

The hissings and shouts grew louder. Berrena started to run. The gate stood only a few hundred yards away.

A man, his face contorted with ugly fury, grabbed her arm.

"You! I bet you're enjoying this. Watching us fail. Watching us turn into no better than dullard peasants!"

"Nay!" she said, but he snatched a fistful of her hair and yanked it back. She screamed.

"Bitch!" he said.

Others came crowding round. Some muttered, many glared. Someone said, "Let her go. It's not her doing."

The man let go of her hair and rounded on the speaker,

shouting incoherently. As he did, Berrena pulled free, pushed through the throng and ran for the gate. But there were forty or fifty Hueds gathered near the gates and shouting at the guards. She could see the walls, the City Guard, but she couldn't get there. Someone pulled at her pack, another at her jacket. They seized her arms, their grips tight and painful. She struggled uselessly. The men and women around her swore, shouting curses at her.

"Powers above, leave me be!" she pleaded. "Help! Oh, for the Powers sake, help!"

Beyond the mass of heads she could see the firemaker, the red-skinned, red-bearded Hued. He must have followed her. He stood and watched, an appalled expression on his face.

"Help! Please - help me!" she cried.

He held his arm up, as if to ward off a blow and looked away. Berrena stared as he turned around and stumbled away.

The furious man suddenly smacked the side of her face with his open hand. The pain of the blow staggered her. She fell sideways and curled up on the ground in terror. Someone kicked her. She whimpered with the pain. She couldn't stop herself. Only now did she realise how overwhelming and disabling pain could be. Another kick came, another blow, and all she could do was roll up into a sobbing ball of agony. She couldn't think, couldn't speak, could barely breathe.

A voice shouted, "By the walls! What the hell is going on here?"

Berrena peered through the legs surrounding her. The guard captain strode towards them, his sword in his hand.

"Hell's curses! That's it!" exclaimed the captain. He turned to the guards behind him and yelled, "I don't care if you think you can't fight anymore. You've been trained, haven't you? Your weapons are sharp, aren't they? Use them, you idiots – clear this street! Now! Get these fools out of here!"

Berrena curled up tighter. She didn't dare to move. Around her came shouts and yells and the metallic hiss of swords being unsheathed. An arrow struck the cobbles beside her head. She waited for the blows and cuts that would probably kill her.

The tumult raged about her. Then it faded. The street fell quiet. Someone shook her shoulder. Tentatively she peered up at them. It was the guard captain. Most of the crowd had gone.

"Are you all right, my lady?" he asked. "Can you stand?"

She nodded. Warily, she sat up and rubbed the bruises on her side and shoulder. Her arm and cheek were bleeding profusely. She dabbed at the cuts with her skirt. A few guards stood round her and the captain. Some held the reins of horses standing nearby.

The captain turned to the guards. "That's it. I'm leaving. Those that want can join me and Lady Rochale as we go to Langron. Or stay here, and go to the council for orders."

No one moved.

"Right! It'll be you that regrets it, not me. Now, open the gate and shut it after us. Keep it shut. If you're going to stay here, you'd better keep it shut, locked and barred, believe me!"

He mounted, and turned to Berrena. "You'll have to ride with me. One of you, help Lady Rochale up in front of me."

Berrena scrutinised his face. But it was no use. She could no longer tell whether to trust him or not. Despite shaking with fear, she allowed one of the guards to help her mount in front of the captain. They rode through the gate with his arm tight around her and his other hand on the reins. The gates crashed shut behind them.

"Are you rescuing me?" Berrena whispered. "Why?"

"Returning a favour," he replied. "Two years ago you persuaded my brother to take his wife and children to Marden. Now it seems you were right, when you kept saying we were all doomed. I know they are safe - safer - at least."

Berrena nodded. "I see. Thank you."

"And now? Without our powers? I don't want to be trapped in the city! I've got more chance to survive in Langron, I reckon, than here in Hueron. We should have listened to you. Now that our gifts are gone, the city will follow. It will be destroyed, without doubt."

CHAPTER 12
TRAPPED

Jarial turned away and stumbled down an alley. He leant against the wall, closed his eyes, and slid down until he sat on the ground with his head rolled back against the rough bricks. Then he slumped forward, his hand over his mouth as he fought a sudden nausea. He could not believe he'd seen such appalling violence. Not in the city, not by Hueds, not so many against one unarmed woman. He should have gone to help her, but what could he have done? There were twenty, thirty furious Hueds attacking her. Still, he knew what a coward he had been. He crouched, his eyes closed, and listened to the shouts, the curses, the cries, and then he rolled sideways and vomited into the gutter.

He wiped his mouth, shuddering at the memory, then forced himself to stand up. He ought to do something. Ezera would. If only he had her courage. Despite the trembling in his legs he went back towards the main street, his mouth set in a determined line and his fists clenched, and he peered round the corner.

Most of the crowd had gone. There were splashes and blotches of dark blood on the ground. He saw Berrena being hoisted onto a horse, in front of a guard captain. The captain shouted something and galloped through the gate with Berrena clinging on to him.

The remaining guards dragged the gates together, slammed them close and then dropped the huge barricade beams into their brackets with a crash, while Jarial and a dozen or so people nearby stood and watched. Safe - or trapped? thought Jarial.

He turned, his head bowed, and walked towards some stairs leading up to the walls. As he trudged upwards, he took the shard from his symbol out of his pocket and held it, hoping that by some miracle it would be resurrected. Perhaps if he re-did his marking, it could be re-created. No. He shook his head. He had heard rumours of giftless people that had tried that. It only worked on children. Maybe he should throw his chances in with Berrena, Cairson, Ezera and all their ilk, living in remote dullard villages.

He felt half-tempted to go back to the gate, to try to persuade the guards to let him leave, and try to get to Marden somehow. But it would be folly to do that, if it turned out that this loss was only temporary, or partial, or reversible. It would be wiser and more honourable to stay with his own, in the city. The council would know by now. They would come up with some solution. He had heard from his mother that there was a fortune in collected taxes lying in the council vaults. They could use that to trade. Hueron would survive.

That evening, after a miserable and aimless day spent pacing the city walls and trying to decide what to do, Jarial went to his mother's house.

"Madame Latisse has just this minute come in, Master Sheldman," said the servant.

His mother strode into the hall.

"Ah, Jarry! Thank the Powers! You are safe?"

"As you see."

She walked into the front room and sat down, her head in her hands.

"Mother?"

"What a terrible, terrible day!" she said, looking up at him. "I am exhausted!"

She slumped back on the sofa. Jarial sat next to her.

"We were in council for hours," she continued. "Practically besieged by hordes of panicking idiots. What do they expect us to do? Some sort of miracle?"

"Well, what have you decided to do?"

"Shut the gates, forbid all movement in or out of the city. Sit tight and wait. The gifts will come back."

"And if they don't?"

She looked sharply at him.

"Are you infected with it too? Of course they will. Don't be ridiculous!"

Jarial shook his head.

"I don't think so."

"They will! Or it will turn out to be ... a mistake, or only have involved a few. Believe me, I'll expect we'll find out that there are only a few hundred Hueds affected and the whole thing is simply a trivial incident, magnified out of all proportion by some hysterical idiots."

Jarial took the shards of his symbol out of his pocket and showed them to her. She gasped.

"By the walls, you too?"

"Me too? Mother, where is your symbol?"

Her head dropped. Suddenly her usually serene and confident face looked defeated.

"Gone ... Oh, thank the Founders that your father didn't live to see this. If it's true ... If it's all of us, if it's permanent ... Jarry, this could be the end!"

After a moment she stood up and shook her head.

"No. I'm not going to believe that. We have options. The council is meeting first thing tomorrow. I'll push for a curfew and a lockdown. No one must leave. We will have to think about martial law. There will have to be a ban on looting and hoarding; we will need to impose rationing. And we have money. We can buy supplies from dullards. There are always options."

CHAPTER 13
SEVEN HUNDRED MILES AWAY

Headon Alcastor sat a little apart from the others, staring at the wrecked dome and thinking of the dead and vanished Magi. To his surprise, he realised that he'd begun to shake in reaction to the emotions of the last few hours. Joy and fear were so mixed within him that he did not know what he should feel. He knew that, after his years of torment and imprisonment, he was free; that Felde's son, Riathe, despite his strange, pale and thin appearance, had held, within his tiny pearl symbol, the power to destroy the Magi and their evil. But he also knew that the Hued gifts would have been destroyed as well. What was happening in his city, all those hundreds of miles away?

He turned to watch the grey-clad servants, Felde, his son, and the others, sitting close to one another, embracing, weeping and laughing, jubilant at the realisation that at last they could go home. He thought of Berrena's joy when she would have her son, husband and brother returned to her, and he knew she would forgive Iselle when she saw her with Vallan and their daughter. Then he thought of his own mother and put his head into his hands. At least he knew, from what Felde had heard, that she was probably still alive.

He felt a touch on his shoulder. One of the servants, an old, hunched man, stood beside him.

"Beg pardon, steward, but people are taking the Magi's wine and food without asking you," he said, his face worried. "Should I be stopping them? And now the Magi have gone, what am I to do? I was born here, serving the Magi - 'tis all I've known. I don't know nought about being free"

Headon sighed. He was still seen as the steward, still needed, still in authority.

"Let them have the wine, the food," he said. "The Magi are gone. We should be celebrating."

He took a deep breath, stood up, went over to the low wall round the fountain and stepped up onto it.

"Is everyone here?" he called. "Did you get those from the dungeons and from the farms and the other five apprentices, are they here too?"

There was a murmur of assent.

"Excellent!" he said loudly, and gestured to the pile of glass and brick and metal. "You can see how the dome has collapsed. The Magi's power sustained it and when they were destroyed, it fell. We thought they were indestructible and all-powerful, but they weren't."

He told them how Riathe's pearl had turned their power back on them, killing them. He called Riathe over and asked the boy to stand beside him.

"This is Riathe Sulvenor, the White Hued, who defeated them!"

Everyone cheered. But Riathe shook his head, walked back to his father, sat close to him and put his head into his hands. Headon saw that he was trembling. Riathe had endured more of an ordeal than he had thought. But there was little he could do except ensure that the boy had a chance to rest. He turned back to the crowd.

"The Magi kept us prisoners here," Headon continued. "But that was not the worst that they did. You probably know how poor the Talthen were becoming. It was the spells and actions of the Magi that were draining the land of life. It was their deception that blinded the Hued to the damage their gifts were doing. We need to tell everyone the wrong that the Magi did. How they were the cause of so much evil. That all their blessings were really curses in disguise."

Headon gestured to the others.

"My friends and I are going to travel back over the mountains and go home. As we go we will tell people the truth about the Magi. You can come with us or stay here. You are free to choose. But we need to decide what to do about this land, the buildings, the Magi's possessions - how to share them. I may no longer be your steward, but please listen to me. Let's think what would be best for the people that stay and then meet here at midday tomorrow. Until then, we can feast and celebrate."

A bonfire had been lit in the centre of the gardens and many of the servants sat round it drinking wine in the glowing firelight, under the stars just starting to appear in the deep blue sky. A few servants had found violins, flutes, drums and other musical instruments in the rooms used by the purple Mage. In the warm evening they played jigs and tunes and half-forgotten songs. Some started dancing, while others lay watching them and humming to the tunes, their eyes half-closed with sleep.

Headon went over to where the Hued sat on a slope of the lawn overlooking the bonfire. Nessa lay curled up in Iselle's arms. Headon gently stroked the little girl's hair.

"I think your daughter needs to sleep," he said to Iselle and Vallan. "Riathe needs to rest. And we all need to talk. We'll go to the guest house. I'll get Loira too."

"Loira?" Felde asked.

"Loira Faure. One of the other servants. She is my friend. I cannot tell you how much she helped me."

Once Nessa had been left to sleep in a bedroom and, on Headon's insistence, Riathe had gone to rest too, the others gathered in the sitting room.

Felde looked around. "I remember this room," he said.

Vallan nodded. "So much has happened since then. I never thought I'd be back here, with you."

"This will be the best place for us tonight," Headon said. "We can discuss our plans here. We are free now, but maybe we shouldn't simply ride home without thinking of the others."

They talked late into the night. Vallan, Iselle and Felde wanted to travel back to Langron as soon as possible, but Headon disagreed.

"It's not that simple," he said, shaking his head. "What do you think will happen when the Talthen realise that the Hued have lost their powers? We can't just run back to Langron, to safety. We should consider going to Hueron first."

"Yes, but what will we do there?" Iselle said. "What use will we be?"

Headon shrugged. "Good point. I have no idea."

"Felde, what about the dullards - Talthen - that you met at the Saroche ford?" Vallan asked. "What was it you said about them?"

"Them? That they seemed desperate. They were angry and they hated the Hued."

"It won't be long before they're thinking about attacking the city."

"Aye. Riathe said the Magi were talking about civil war when the gifts failed. If 'tis war, Talthen against Hueds, whose side would we be on?"

Early next morning, when Headon came into the sitting room carrying a tray of bread, pastries, apples and bowls of porridge, Riathe was already there. There were grey-blue shadows under his eyes.

"I couldn't sleep any longer," he said, pacing around the room.

"You need to eat," Headon said. "I got one of the cooks to make us breakfast. I'll wake the others. We still have a lot to discuss and plan."

After the others had woken up, as they ate, Headon said, "I've been thinking. It will take at least a month to get to Hueron. The Talthen may start attacking it before we can get there."

"But we can't possibly get there any earlier," said Iselle,

holding Nessa tightly in her arms. "Are you suggesting that we walk up to the city gates through a horde of Talthen?"

"No. I don't know what to suggest!"

"We really should go to Langron first, to see my mother and sister, and take Nessa there," Vallan said. "How can we leave them in suspense, not knowing what has happened to us?"

"But travelling will be dangerous now," said Felde, "with only us and Nessa. And what can just five of us do, anyhap?"

"I'll come with you, as far as Peveque at least," said Loira, "and if my parents are no longer alive, there will be nothing to keep me there. I know I'm not a warrior, but surely the more of us that travel together, the better. Perhaps some of the other servants will come with us."

"If they all came, that would be over a hundred people," said Iselle.

"That would be excellent," Headon said. "However, most of them will want to stay. Not many have homes or families to return to."

"But we may be able to persuade them," Riathe interjected. Up to now he had listened quietly, but now he stood up. "'Tis true there's only a few of us. But we've got the pearl. Vallan, stand up," he said, staring into Vallan's blue eyes. Slowly, Vallan stood.

"Stand on one leg," Riathe said.

Looking embarrassed, Vallan obeyed. Headon stared in astonishment at Vallan, and then back at the boy's pale, intense face.

"You see," Riathe said. "I've got some of the Magi's powers. People will obey me. Vallan, you can stop now."

"Riathe, that ain't right!" Felde exclaimed. "You can't make Vallan obey you like that!"

"But I had to try it, to see if I could! And I can use that power to get people to come with us."

Headon looked sternly at Riathe. "Maybe, but don't order Vallan or Iselle or me or your father around. You don't understand what it's been like here, being controlled and commanded by those wizards."

"I was trying to help," muttered Riathe.

"You said 'some of their powers'," said Felde, "and you healed Headon's leg. What else can you do?"

"I don't know! Some things, I think. Some of what the Magi could do. I've got to learn how to use this," and he opened his hand and gestured at the pearl, then walked off, flung himself onto one of the sofas at the side of the room, laid there and frowned at the tiny sphere.

"Mayhap Riathe's right and we should tell everyone to come with us," said Felde, after a long pause.

"Hmmm. Possibly," replied Headon. "But I don't think that would be wise. This land is too good to leave empty. If everyone goes the harvest will be wasted. We could take some people but leave enough here to run the farms. If we can get half of them to come with us and leave fifty or so, get them to set up a council to decide how to share the land ..." his voice tailed off, and he stopped, deep in thought.

"What is it?" said Loira.

"Wait," he said. "I'm thinking. War is inevitable, we cannot stop it. We can't support one side or the other, but we can't ignore it. We have to intervene somehow. Restore peace, get each side to listen to what the Magi did and share the harvest between them. If we had some soldiers, an army, we could. I wonder if it is possible ..."

Riathe stood up. He had a visionary look on his pale face and the mercurial shimmering on his skin glistened in the morning sunshine. He stared down at his grey tunic, then lifted his left hand. The pearl resting on his palm glowed faintly, casting a wan light onto his intent expression.

"Aye," he whispered. "'Tis possible."

"What's possible?" asked Headon.

"I think ..." said Riathe, looking around at their puzzled faces. "Aye, I think I can do it. With this. I'm sure I can. We could start such an army. An army in grey uniforms, an army of Hueds and Talthen, a Grey Army. Fighting for peace."

CHAPTER 14
THE GREY ARMY

A few minutes before midday, after hours spent discussing, objecting, arguing and plotting, Headon looked round at the others. "Agreed at last?" he asked. They nodded.

"Excellent," he said, and stood up. "Let's go and try it then."

Outside, it was another warm day, the sun dazzlingly bright, and a small crowd sat on the lawns, waiting for them. Headon counted almost one hundred and fifty men and women.

"More than I expected!" he said in surprise. "There must have been lots of slaves with families hidden away in homes on the outskirts of the land. Still, it's good. It will make what we planned easier."

Despite his words, he did not feel optimistic. He felt that nothing would make their audacious plan easy. But he had to try. He walked forward to face the crowd, stepped up onto the low wall, and raised his left hand in greeting. 'It all depends on this,' he thought, looking upwards for a moment. 'May the Powers help me to find words to persuade them.' He took a deep breath as the grey-clad people in front of him fell silent.

"The Magi are dead," he said, in a voice as loud and clear as he could manage. "The curse they put on the Talthen lands - draining the life, bringing famine and disease – is broken. A good harvest will be coming, either this year or the next."

He heard murmurs of satisfaction, and glanced around to see smiles brightening the faces of those listening.

"The Hued have lost their powers and will need to trade

their wealth with the Talthen for food and goods," he continued. "But we fear that the Talthen and Hued, instead of sharing their riches and food, will attack each other and the land will be devastated in bloody war. No one will gain from that. So we are going to fight for peace! We are going home, to Felde's home, Langron, and then on to Hueron. We will raise an army as we go, of Hued and Talthen, in grey uniforms - the Grey Army. The City Guard are small in numbers and will be in disarray with the loss of their gifts. We plan to invade the Coloured City."

There was a gasp from the crowd. "What?" someone shouted. "Invade? Are you mad?"

"Not mad. No. But - yes, we plan to invade Hueron, stop civil war, and set up a council of Talthen and Hueds, sharing power and goods and food equally."

He paused, and gestured around at the others standing by him. "I, Headon Alcastor; Felde Sulvenor, who is a Talthen; his son Riathe, the half-Hued, half-Talthen who destroyed the Magi; we will lead. Vallan Sapphireborne, a Hued, will be the army captain, Iselle Topazborne will be his second in command, and Loira Faure, a Talthen, will be in charge of the non-fighters and children who come with us. We need leaders, fighters, warriors – and those who love their homes and want to protect them from war."

As Headon looked around, he could see a few excited faces, but many looked dubious, fearful or disinterested.

"This is a huge risk. It may cost us our lives. But it will be worth it to see Talthen and Hued sharing the prosperity that is coming and living in equality and peace. We will start preparing tomorrow and leave a day or so later. Think about this, talk to us, and decide by next morning if you will join us."

He stepped down, feeling as if the words had drained all his energy. He rubbed his temples and turned away for a moment, before turning back to hear the voices of the crowd discussing and exclaiming, and to face their worried questions and dissensions.

The next morning, many of the older Talthen servants said they wanted to stay. But Headon was relieved to see that over a hundred volunteers for the army, including the other five apprentices and many able-bodied men, had opted to join the Grey Army and go with them. He took aside those who wanted to stay.

"You will need some help to run the farms," he said. "We'll try to persuade people to travel south and settle here. There's ample space."

"Aye," said the oldest of the servants. "That'd be good, but who'll decide who gets what?"

"You'll have to appoint a council to allocate land fairly. You could become a country in your own right, trading with the north, if we open up a road over the mountain pass."

The old man grinned. "Fancy me becoming a councillor and running a country, at my time of life!"

"It's agreed then," said Headon. "You'll welcome people travelling over the mountains to settle. I'll come back one day, I hope, see how it's going. In the meantime, will you help us equip the army? We'll need horses, weapons, food, water bottles, the grey uniforms and funds."

"Funds!" the old man exclaimed. "That reminds me, Steward, come with me."

He led Headon to the wing that had belonged to the purple wizard. They went in through a side door, along a corridor, then up some narrow stairs. The old man took a bunch of keys from his pocket.

"I was the purple one's treasure keeper. He kept his jewels and finest pieces locked up in a storeroom. I hope no one else has thought of them, but I don't think many know about them."

Unlocking a door, he took Headon inside. It was a dressing room, with velvet and satin and silk robes handing from hooks and a long ornately-framed mirror on the wall.

"'Tis one of the servants' entrances to his rooms," explained the treasure keeper. "He didn't like us using the main stairs and entrance. Anyhap, let me show you this," he said, and he led Headon into the bedroom and then to another door in the corner, which he unlocked. The room beyond was full of mirrors and glass, with a chandelier hanging above their heads and bright sunlight pouring through the windows. The glittering, flashing light on the shining surfaces confused Headon, but then he made out a dozen tall, glass-shelved, glass-sided silver cabinets. Between each pair of cabinets stood slender-legged tables holding enamelled vases, delicate bronze figurines, and caskets of ivory and ebony. The walls were mirrored, reflecting the sunlight and the treasures in the cabinets: necklaces, tiaras, golden goblets, ropes of pearls, gems beyond number. On a red velvet stand sat nine scintillating diamonds, each as big as a hen's egg. The sunlight glittering off them sent flecks of green, yellow, sapphire and red light dancing over the other treasures.

The man opened up one of the ebony caskets. It was full of the gold and silver coins used by the Hued.

"See," said the treasure keeper. "Funds! He used this to buy gems, those he didn't steal. He could make money out of nought. I've seen him standing here, with coins pouring from his hand into this box, coming out of nowhere. Wonderful gifts he had!"

"You almost sound like you miss him," Headon said.

"Eh? Nay, he was bad, through and through, although he treated me fairly well. But power like that! 'Tis a pity 'tis gone," he sighed. "Anyhap, why don't you take the money and some of the smaller bits of jewellery and some of the gems? Armies need funds, like you said."

"Thanks. Yes, we'll take some of it. But you need to keep this locked up and secret. You may need funds yourself. It can be your country's treasury."

When Headon rejoined the others, Felde and Vallan, with the help of the grooms and kitchen servants, were loading up horses with provisions. People brought bags of food, bundles of arrows and spears, packs of blankets and cloaks. Loira and others had fetched all the grey tunics and trousers from the stores and bound them into heavy bales ready to be carried by packhorses.

"How many horses do we have?" asked Headon.

"Plenty," replied Felde. "Each Mage had his own stable with two or three dozen horses, and some of them are thoroughbreds. There are lots of saddles and bridles too, and there are horses on the farms as well. Everyone will be mounted, even if some of the children will have to ride double. And we've got about thirty pack-horses, and some carts and wagons for the smaller children, like Nessa, to ride in if they want."

"We've got enough weapons, too," Vallan exclaimed. "There are more swords and daggers than I expected. We found a whole armoury in the red wizard's wing, so we've got spears, bows, arrows, even shields and helmets. Bugles and trumpets too."

Headon smiled. "Excellent! Miracles keep happening, don't they? It looks like our plan is succeeding. Where's Riathe?"

"He's in the stables, helping get horses ready," replied Felde. "We should be ready to leave early next morning or the next day. We need banners and flags - grey or white, for the pearl - to march under and Iselle's getting those, with Loira's help."

The banners waved in a gentle breeze as the army prepared to leave two days later, a cavalcade of a hundred and thirty horses, followed by dozens of laden pack-horses. To Headon it looked impressive, but he knew they'd need ten times as many men to invade Hueron.

"We'll travel to the border and camp overnight before attempting the desert," he said.

"What about water?" Felde said.

"I can solve that," Riathe answered, then held his hand out, with intense concentration on his face. The pearl glowed and floated above his palm and suddenly a stream of water poured from his hand. Headon and the others gasped and laughed in wonder.

"At least something is going to be easy," Headon said.

But by twilight, when they had already travelled many miles from the Magi's house, they still rode by a stream that ran through grassy meadows.

"Where's the border?" Vallan wondered. "We should be in the desert by now."

"I don't understand it," said Felde.

"Maybe we misunderstood," said Headon. "We thought the Magi created an oasis in the desert. An island of green. But perhaps they created the desert. Or perhaps it was an illusion? A spell. Perhaps this meadow is what the land is really like. When they died, the power making the land appear desert died and it was restored. They must have made it as a defence against visitors."

"So we've ridden over the border without knowing it!"

"Yes. We really are free. And I thought the land might turn back to desert, but it's the opposite: the desert has turned green. A good omen, I hope."

They camped by the stream that night, then journeyed on, falling into a routine of travelling twenty miles or so each day before setting up camp and training. Iselle taught archery and Vallan organised fencing sessions. Headon could see that some of Vallan's old skill had come back, but he no longer had his gifted insight and Felde could beat him easily. Remembering the times Felde had fought and lost to Vallan before, and all that had happened since, he could hardly believe it. To be riding back with his old friends, along the same path towards the mountain's pass ... He glanced at Riathe, riding beside his father. The boy's face looked intent on the road ahead, frowning slightly. It occurred to Headon that he had not seen Riathe smile since the day of the Magi's death.

CHAPTER 15
PEVEQUE

At Tagrinne they camped for one night, but were unable to persuade anyone to join them, to Headon's disappointment. Four days later they reached Peveque and camped outside the town. Headon, Felde, Riathe and Loira rode into Peveque, heading for the square. At first Loira exclaimed whenever she recognised landmarks and houses, then grew quieter as they got closer. She watched the passing townsfolk and shook her head.

"I don't know anyone," she said. "'Tis all strange after so long away. It doesn't feel like my home."

In the square they paused and dismounted. Loira stood, her hand to her mouth, gazing around. Headon put his hand gently on her shoulder.

"Wait here. I'll find the town chief and ask him to get your parents," he said.

"Thank you," she whispered. "'Tis far more painful than I thought it would be, returning after all this time."

"Felde, Riathe; can you talk to the locals? Tell them about the Magi, and the Grey Army," Headon instructed, and they nodded.

One of the villagers directed Headon to the town chief's house. It was the same two-storey building, even more dilapidated than he remembered, but the chief was a different man, a jovial, red-haired, barrel-chested fellow. When Headon told him about Loira, he stared in astonishment.

"I remember!" he exclaimed. "I was barely a youth then, seventeen I was. I helped in the search. To think, after all this time ..."

When they returned to the square, a group of curious villagers had gathered, talking to Loira and the other two. Loira leapt up and ran to Headon and the chief.

"Loira! Loira Faure!" the chief boomed, enveloping her in a hearty embrace. "'Tis amazing, wonderful news! Welcome home. Your mother and brothers will be delighted! We must take you to her immediately."

"And my father?"

"Alas, he is gone. He died only two years after they lost you. But your mother is still alive, and she lives in a cottage nearby, next to one of your brother's farms. Come, let me take you to her!"

He tucked Loira's hand through his arm, patted it, and escorted her down a side street. She turned to wave goodbye to them.

The town chief returned alone, an hour or so later, telling them, with tears shining in his eyes, of Loira's reunion with her family. "I've left her with them. Well, tell me - how did you find her and what happened to her? Who are you? And what is going on?"

He was quiet for a long time after the story had been told. "'Tis a lot to take in," he commented. "The Magi took her? And they were secretly cursing us? But why? And they appeared so noble. Well, what fools we've been, if your story is true."

"We'd like to meet up with the villagers, the elders and farmers, next morning," Headon said. "And tell them all this. Can you arrange that?"

He nodded.

"And can you sell us any horses, any food? I know things have been hard here for you."

"Aye, but 'tis been easier, since Lord Mavretan's gone," the chief said, with satisfaction in his voice. "For years afterwards we was all of a tremble, expecting the City Guard to come. But they didn't. Mayhap they thought Mavretan was as much of a cursed bastard as we did. We threw his body out onto the fields for the crows to peck at and we ploughed his bones into the ground – only time he gave aught to the town. Served him well, the murdering swine. Zarcus may have been a Hued, but he was fair, and didn't deserve to be knifed by that brute. We don't see or hear aught of the current owner, thank the Powers. So I reckon we'll be able to sell you something. I'll take you round the farmers and see."

Headon was expecting, from what Felde had told them of the drenching rain and ruined harvests of a month ago, that they would be unsuccessful. But he was surprised. The first farmer they spoke to agreed to sell them a horse, and few sacks of wheat left from last year, as he was expecting a fair crop.

"'Twas flattened and spoilt by rain a few weeks ago," he said, "But the weather turned and we've had such sun that it's recovered. 'Twas covered in blight and mould too, but that's gone. 'Tis very odd, but all the others have found the same, and the same with the livestock too. Down the lane there, that farmer lost fifteen sheep to some strange illness and he thought the rest were dying too, but now they're on their feet, eating grass like you wouldn't believe. Well, 'tis been an odd year and no mistake."

In the town centre the next day, under a glorious sunny sky, the farmers, locals and town chief waited for them. Loira was there, and leaning on her arm was a gaunt, faded lady, bent with age but wearing a look of radiant joy. Although lined with sorrow, her face and Loira's were so similar that she needed no introduction. She thanked them for the restoration of her daughter, shaking their hands again and again.

Headon explained to the gathered crowd about the Magi, the curses on the land, and how the Hueds' powers had gone. As he spoke of that loss, many of those listening cheered. When he continued, telling them of the Grey Army's intention to rescue the Hueds from possible war, invade Hueron and set up a shared council, one man shouted, "Why should we help Hueds like that Mavretan, curse him?" and another said, "If you were talking of revenge, then it would be different. But we'd be better off staying here, and not bothering about them, load of greedy blood-suckers!" When Headon asked them to join the army, few looked interested and many turned away.

Riathe strode forward.

"Listen!" he shouted. "I'm Riathe Sulvenor. I'm a half-breed: half Hued, half Talthen; but I'm also a wizard, the Grey Wizard!"

Someone in the crowd yelled, "You don't look much like a wizard! Where's your staff?" and there was a ripple of sneering laughter.

A flush of anger appeared on Riathe's face. He closed his eyes and raised his hand, releasing the pearl to hover above him. It flared and shone bright and Headon felt suddenly afraid. What might Riathe do? But the light faded. All fell silent as he pointed across the town square to two apple trees on the other side. They had black spotted, shrivelled leaves and the few apples they carried were small, green and misshapen. The boy raised his arm again and the white orb above him spun and flashed with scarlet, orange and emerald lights. As they watched the apples grew, swelling, ripening - turning from sour green to rich yellow and red. The townsfolk gasped. One young lad ran across and picked one, biting into it, grinning with relish. "'Tis good!" he commented.

The lights faded. Taking the pearl back into his hand, Riathe turned to the crowd.

"You can stay here and you'll never know what you might have done or seen. Or you can follow us to Hueron. 'Twill be a long and hard journey to battle and danger and uncertain reward. But 'twill be more exciting than staying here. We'll make it easier for you to leave your families. We'll do what we can to make sure they have food 'til you return. You saw what happened to the apples. I'll do that for your crops. Then you can decide if you'll come with us."

Headon seized Riathe's arm and whispered, "What are you promising? Don't say you can do that if you can't. Are you sure?"

Riathe whispered back, "I think so. How many farms are there?"

"There must be three or four dozen – 'tis a big town! What happens if you fail?"

"I can do it," Riathe insisted. He turned away and shut his eyes, holding his hands open in front of him, revealing the spinning, glowing silver light of the pearl. The crowd watched then stirred restlessly, as he stood, silent and motionless.

Headon intervened, "Choose if you will come with us, to battle, to Hueron; or if you will stay here. We need fighters, warriors, leaders; able men and women. Go and see what is happening to your orchards and crops, then decide! If you will join us, return here with horse, weapons and provisions tomorrow morning – wearing white or grey if you can. Tomorrow! The Grey Army!"

The crowd muttered and whispered amongst themselves as they dispersed. Headon and Felde took little notice. They watched Riathe in apprehension. The lad's pale skin looked whiter than ever and he swayed where he stood, as if in a trance, the flickering lights from the pearl reflecting on his hands and closed eyes. Suddenly he staggered sideways. Felde rushed to him and caught him. Headon glanced around. Most of the townsfolk had left, but the town chief was still there, watching with an appraising look in his eye.

"If yon wizard can do what he says, I'll be impressed. He looks too weak and young to do aught, despite those fancy flashing lights. And if he does, it may cost us some of our best men. But mayhap 'tis better that some of the hotheads go off with you than kick their heels in idleness and cause trouble here."

Felde carried Riathe back to the camp. He remained unconscious for almost an hour. Headon paced the tent, waiting for him to recover, half fearful for him, and half furious at the risk he had taken. Felde watched Headon warily.

"Don't be too hard on him," Felde said. "He's but a lad."

"I know. But to do that!"

Round the camp fire in the evening, while Vallan and Iselle were occupied with training and teaching, Headon could not resist haranguing Riathe. "How could you?" he exclaimed. "That was stupid, arrogant ... We work together, otherwise it's chaos!"

Riathe shrugged. "I had to do something. I didn't have time to debate it with you and get your permission!"

Headon threw his hands up. "I don't believe it! Powers above, Riathe!"

"We've got to do something to persuade people to join us!" Riathe said loudly. "You said yourself that we'll need an army of hundreds! So I helped! Why is that a problem?"

"You can't go off and act on your own ideas - we have to work together, not each do whatever we feel like!"

"Well, you won't let me do what I think is best. Why can't I simply tell them to come with us? I could pick out the best and order them to join us!"

"No!" exploded Headon. "We are fighting for peace, freedom – how can we fight for freedom if people are enlisted forcibly like that! No – volunteers, or no one!"

"Headon's right," insisted Felde, leaning forward and putting his hand on his son's arm. "I don't want to force people to join us. We've got to persuade them. Riathe, you've got to listen to him."

"All right," muttered Riathe, "and that's what I did. 'Twas a good idea. Show them something impressive. Feed them too. What else could I've done? Otherwise no one would come with us."

"And what if you'd failed?" Headon said. "Or they'd all seen you faint? You should have stuck to making those apples grow. It was far too ambitious to try to do the whole town. It was a stupid risk."

"It took too much effort, Riathe," Felde said. "You looked almost dead with exhaustion."

"Well, I wasn't dead. 'Twas harder than I thought, but I know it worked. You'll see, tomorrow there'll be dozens who will be clamouring to follow the Grey Wizard."

"Hmm, well, we'll see if you're proved right," Headon said. He paused, frowned and shook his head. "But there are some things I still don't understand, Riathe. The Magi could use their powers effortlessly, so why is it so hard for you? And they said that creating food using gifts was stealing it from others. Is there some farmer or village somewhere who have lost their harvest because of what you did?"

"Nay," said Riathe. "That's partly why 'tis harder. The Magi did take food from others. When they made an apple they took the life from an apple elsewhere. Like from like. They didn't have to do it like that - they were lazy and callous. But I can make an apple using the life from the pine cones and beechnuts in the empty forests miles away. That's what I did. I took power from the woods up in the mountains. But 'twas hard learning how to do it, and harder doing it. I've spent hours practising in the evenings, when I can't sleep. And I don't have all the Magi's powers. Most of that is gone. The pearl took some, when they were destroyed, but only part. 'Tis feeble compared to the original strength of their stones."

Riathe's prediction proved correct. As they rode through the town in the morning, with all the army following, they saw the town chief in the square. He was accompanied by three dozen stout men and a few capable-looking women, some wearing grey shirts or jackets.

"Well, whatever you did, it worked. It seems that everyone's crops and fruit have grown overnight. Even the grass in the fallow fields looks longer. Thank you! These men and women want to go with you. Some of them are good fighters, most of them have got weapons, and they've got provisions too, as you asked."

Headon nodded his thanks.

"I think we'll have companies of fifty soldiers, each under a captain. Like in the City Guard," Vallan said. "We don't have enough horses now, so some will have to be foot soldiers, but that's not a serious problem. Once we get more people we won't be able to travel more than twenty miles a day anyway."

"You're the expert," said Headon. "I'll leave it up to you."

"Right," said Vallan. He glanced round at the forty-odd new recruits. "That makes well over a hundred and fifty. Not very many, though, considering what we are attempting. I think we are lunatics, thinking we can do this."

"It's a good lunacy, though," said Headon. "Better than I had ever hoped. Well, let's find out names and decide who goes in what company. Riathe, can I ask you to do something?" he continued, taking Riathe aside. "I don't want them joining for revenge. For excitement, money, glory, power; out of boredom or despair – fine! But not for revenge. Can you tell? The Magi could."

"Aye, I can tell."

"Do it discreetly!"

"I ain't a fool, Headon!" Riathe retorted. "But instead of leaving them behind, I'll command them not to hurt or injure Hueds."

Headon hesitated. "Riathe ..."

"I will, Headon! 'Twill be better than turning them away, trust me!"

In the middle of the bustle and chaos, Loira came into the square and, running up to Headon, flung her arms around him.

"Oh, I'm glad you haven't left! Headon, I've got something to tell you. I'm not coming with you to Hueron."

"Not coming? Loira, why?" he replied.

"I'm sorry," she said, stepping back. "I'll miss you, but I

can't leave my family again. We can't come with you. My mother's too old for battle, I can't leave her again, and my brothers have wives and children. They're struggling here as we have hardly any land. So I've persuaded them to let me take them to the Magi's land."

"Back to the Magi's land? Loira, I would have thought you'd never want to return there."

She shrugged. "I thought not too, but 'tis a good land now and my brothers could farm there. They could get enough land to make a living and help the existing farmers at harvest. You said they'd need help and you'd send people over the mountains."

"Yes, I did, but not you. I don't want to part with you." He reached out and took her hand.

"Headon, my friend, we were a comfort to each other in a terrible place. But that was all we were, and you know it. Now's a good time to say goodbye, both going to new lives." She held his hand to her cheek then kissed it. "I'll never forget you."

"Nor I you," he said, quietly.

"And I think that we'll be too busy for it to hurt much. Come and visit me in the south if you can, when 'tis all over."

"I'll do my best. Loira, I will want to see you again, remember that."

"I will. Headon, there's another woman who you can trust to look after the children and others riding in the carts at the back. She's called Kera Ransen."

"I know her," he replied. "I'll talk to her."

"Vallan, Iselle, goodbye," she said, kissing them before saying farewell to Felde and Riathe, then kneeling down to hug Nessa. "I will miss you all. Especially you, Nessa. You're the nearest thing to a child of my own that I've had."

She turned to Headon. "Well, goodbye, my friend."

Headon took her hands in his, kissed them, and held her in a close embrace before releasing her. For a long moment, he watched her as she walked away without looking back.

CHAPTER 16
TRAVELLING NORTH

As the Grey Army rode past the gatehouse of Peveque House, Felde saw Riathe glancing curiously at the house. Several of the beech trees lining the avenue had been felled and hacked into logs, and the lawns had turned into hayfields filled with ragweed and rampant brambles. Ivy had scrambled up the grey stone on one side, covering many of the windows and wrapping green branches around the chimneys. The tidy gravelled courtyard had vanished under grass and feathery spikes of willowherb.

Headon, riding at the front, put his hand up to signal that they should stop. Felde turned and saw that Iselle, riding next to Vallan with Nessa sitting in front of her, had stopped already and was staring at the house. Tears ran down her cheeks.

"Iselle?" Headon said to her, gently. "Shall we turn aside to visit? What do you think?"

"No," she said, wiping away the tears. "I can't bear to go there now Zarcus is no longer looking after the estate. He wouldn't have let it get into this state."

"Who does it belong to now?"

"I suppose legally it belongs to me, but Mavretan's cousin will have inherited it. It's obvious he doesn't care for it."

"Maybe so. But the gatehouse is empty," said Headon. "I want to know what the Hueds are doing, whether they've stayed or left, now that the gifts are gone. I'll go – Vallan, you come with me. Wait for us."

They dismounted. Iselle pointed to the house in the far distance. "Nessa, see that house? I lived there once. Isn't it big?"

"Yes, very big. Is that Grandmother's house?"

"No. We've still got a long way to go to get there. "

"Oh. I want to be there. I want to surprise Grandmother, like you said I would!"

They sat by the gatehouse, waiting, while Nessa collected leaves and flowers to make patterns on the grass. The army dismounted. Some idled on the side of the road, some went into the nearby woods to hunt rabbits and deer. It was over two hours later when Headon and Vallan returned, with nine other Hueds carrying packs, and leading a couple of horses heavily laden with bags and sacks.

"There were only six servants and three guards left," Headon said. "They didn't know what to do. They were terrified after they lost their gifts. So I suggested they came with us. Vallan, can you split them up between the companies, at least two in each?"

"Of course," Vallan said, and went to speak to the newcomers.

"Also we've taken all the weapons we could find, not that there were many, and we've - well, stolen, I suppose - some of the money, valuables, jewellery, cooking pots, anything that might be useful. Felde, Riathe, get the quartermasters to help you organise this stuff. It's on the horses."

Felde nodded. Headon turned to Iselle.

"I hope you'll forgive us for raiding your home like this," he said.

She shrugged.

"This means the house is empty and unguarded," he continued, putting his hand gently on her arm. "You know what that means, don't you? But there's nothing we can do about it."

"It'll be looted, won't it? Maybe even destroyed. The villagers, the Talthen, they'll take it."

"Undoubtedly."

"I can still live. I've survived worse, and I never thought I'd even see it again."

But as the army rode off a while later, Felde, busy at the back of the column helping the quartermasters load cooking pots and the freshly-caught rabbits onto one of the packhorses, saw that Iselle lingered, holding Nessa tightly and gazing up the drive towards the decaying building.

They camped a few miles north of Peveque House. That night, Headon gathered the other leaders together for a council of war.

"We have to think, to plan this through," he said.

"Do we? I thought that it's obvious what we're going to do," Vallan said. "Travel to Langron, then to Hueron, and take over the city."

Felde could not help laughing at this. It sounded so simple. But Headon shook his head.

"To do that, we will need at least five hundred more volunteers," he said. "There's nearly a thousand men in the City Guard and I would imagine the City Council will enlist more. They will probably have to impose martial law and they will be aware that the Talthen may attack."

"So we will need more than five hundred, surely?" said Felde. "We've got to break through the city walls too."

"Yes, but we have the Grey Wizard. I hope that Riathe will be able to tilt the balance in our favour."

"How?" asked Riathe. "Because I don't know! The Magi spoke of giving protection to people but I've got no memory, no knowledge of how they would do that. I may be able to break down the city gates, but that's all. I'm struggling to learn how to use this power. 'Tis harder than I would have thought possible. It took me hours to be able to control it so that I could do a simple thing like make an apple."

"But you can do some things easily. You healed my leg in moments," Headon said.

"Aye, that was easy. Healing is simple. The body remembers how it was and all I do is prompt it to restore itself. But you're asking me to feed and protect a whole army! Or do you want me to kill the City Guard? All of them?"

"No! I don't want that! Somehow, we have to take over the city without too much fighting."

"We can't decide how to do that 'til we know how many recruits we'll get and what's happening at Hueron," said Felde. "We should think about getting as many to join us as possible first. Mayhap once we get to Langron, that's when we need to plan."

"True. But we need more." Headon turned to Riathe. "Can you do something to get more volunteers? Do you think that you could increase the crops in villages, as in Peveque? Would that work?"

"I could," said Riathe, "although it will be hard. I'll try. They need the food. But that might not be enough."

He thought for a few moments, frowning in concentration.

"Headon, if you were to talk to the villagers while I watched the crowd, I could tell who was interested or against us. Then if I spoke to those who were hesitant, I could persuade them. 'Tain't a direct command, 'tain't forcing them, just nudging them. Strengthening their desire to fight, weakening their doubts or indecision. 'Tis only doing by my influence what you might take hours to do by speeches."

The evening stars shone in a cloudless sky before they had agreed on their route. Instead of travelling through the less inhabited hills north of Peveque they would to go east to the lowland villages and towns near the Venne River before moving north to cross the Saroche River and on to Langron. The next day they came to a village in the late afternoon, and camped in a field by the roadside.

"Time to try Riathe's plan," Headon said. He took Felde, his son and the Hueds, with a few of the company captains, to ride into the village. He asked someone to find the chief, and then stood on a low wall by the square and started to speak of the deceit, evil and death of the Magi, and of the Grey Army. By the time the chief arrived there was a crowd of intrigued people listening.

Felde stood close to Riathe, watching his son closely and remembering how Riathe had fainted in Peveque, as the boy revealed the pearl and spoke of its power. They both watched the crowd as Headon asked for volunteers to meet them the next day. Felde thought hopefully that many looked interested, but there were also several who turned away, or spat on the ground at the mention of joining with Hueds. Then Riathe said loudly that he would bless their crops in return for their support, raised his arms high, and the pearl shone with a dazzling whiteness over the village.

Despite a drizzling rain there was a crowd in the square the next morning. While Vallan and the quartermasters arranged to buy horses and provisions, using the gold and jewels from the Magi's treasure store, Felde, Headon and the others spoke to the crowd, asking them to join the army.

"Some are undecided. I'll speak to them, persuade them," Riathe whispered to Felde.

An hour later they had recruited eighteen to the army and the quartermasters had bought bread, cheese, flour, butter, a few swords, daggers and spears, and several horses. At the next village they enrolled another twenty-three the same way. By the time they reached the wide expanse of the Venne valley they had nearly three hundred, most of whom were mounted, with over four dozen packhorses laden with food and weapons.

"Excellent! It's going well," said Headon to Felde. "I am beginning to believe that we might be able to do this."

Felde nodded. He too was beginning to believe that this mad plan was feasible. With the Powers' help, maybe they could take the city. But first, Langron. To see Berrena, to see her joy, to reunite her with her son and her brother. That was far more important.

They set up camp under trees north of the village, while a fine, persistent rain drenched the ground and the leaves above them. Felde stretched a rope between two trees and hung his cloak over it to make a shelter for him and Riathe. All around him others were doing the same or draping pieces of cloth and canvas from branches. Under his cloak he slept fitfully until nearly midnight when something woke him. Sitting up and pulling the cloak aside, he saw Riathe pacing to and fro, his hair soaked by the rain. He held his clenched hand to his forehead and frowned in concentration as flickering lights glimmered between his fingers.

"Riathe!" Felde hissed. "Why ain't you asleep? What are you doing?"

Riathe started and turned around, the lights quenched.

"Trying to learn how to use this," he whispered, gesturing with his hand. "But 'tis so difficult! Creating food and increasing crops is getting easier. I'm can pull life from distant forests into the fields and gardens with less effort."

"Good," Felde said. "That's good, surely?"

"Aye. But there's so much more power in it. I can't control it. I can't see how to protect us. How can I possibly make an army invulnerable?"

"We'll have to risk it and fight anyway. Can you do aught about the rain?"

"The rain? Oh. I hadn't thought of that. 'Tis easy. I can shelter us from the rain, even the whole camp." He waved his arm broadly, sweeping the air with the stone alight and glowing. The rain dwindled and stopped.

"How did you do that? How can stopping rain be so easy for you?" Felde asked.

"I didn't stop it, all I've done is move it all downwind a mile or so. I wish I'd thought to do it earlier."

"Mayhap you could do that in battle? Move arrows away from us?"

"Perhaps I could. 'Tis worth a try."

In the gloom Felde thought Riathe looked thinner and paler, his pearly skin almost luminescent.

"Riathe, you should sleep. Don't tire yourself out. You

need to rest."

Riathe nodded and rolled his cloak around himself, lying down next to Felde and gazing upwards. Felde watched his son but Riathe lay there awake so long that eventually Felde gave in and let sleep overcome him. When he woke in the morning Riathe was already up, packing and saddling the horses.

As the army turned northwards towards the Venne River, Headon took Felde and the others aside.

"I think we should send the other five apprentices back to their home towns," he said.

"Why? We need them!" Vallan said.

"They are all from south and west of Hueron. We're going in the other direction. What I'm thinking is that we send them with twenty men each."

"Twenty each?" said Felde.

"That's a hundred fighting men!" Vallan exclaimed. "Are you mad, Headon?"

"No! Listen. We'll get them to tell people about the Magi, to recruit as many as they can, and to meet us at Langron in thirty days' time. We lose a hundred, but we may gain five hundred back. Riathe tells me all the apprentices are keen to help. We can trust them. They know what they owe him."

Two hours later Felde gazed after the apprentices as they rode west, leading their small groups of grey-uniformed men, each with a banner of white and grey flying in the air above them. He could not help his feelings of apprehension as he turned back and looked at the army. It seemed so tiny.

"It's a big gamble," said Vallan. "We may never see them again."

"We'll get more," said Felde, determinedly. "Riathe and Headon are getting good at this recruitment." But he knew he was trying to convince himself as much as the others.

"Thanks," said Headon. "Right, on again. Northwards."

"North and east," Felde said. "We should keep away from Hueron."

"You're right. I don't want any news reaching the city. We've not kept our intentions secret, but I'm trusting that it will be a while before any rumours reach them."

CHAPTER 17
CONSCRIPTION

Screams came from the street below. Jarial paused in his pacing along the city wall. He turned to the other conscripted soldier beside him.

"What was that?" he asked.

They bent over the inner parapet and stared down. Two men in the dark-blue uniforms of conscripts, and another in the black of the City Guard, were pulling a woman out of a house. She screamed again and struggled wildly as they lashed her hands together and hauled her up the street.

"I don't know," the other said. "Perhaps another one found hoarding food? Or spreading despondency? You know," he added in a whisper. "Saying that it's permanent."

Jarial watched the woman being dragged away. "Poor woman," he said.

Suddenly there came a shout behind them.

"Oy! You two! Why aren't you on guard?"

Levin Bluestone, with a detachment of City Guard, strode along the wall towards them.

"Get back to your posts!" he yelled.

Obediently they straightened up and stood by the outer parapet, facing over the southern plains. The midday sun glared full in their faces. Jarial felt the sweat prickling on his back and forehead. His shield was heavy, the leather greaves and dark-blue jacket hot and cumbersome, and his legs ached from the four hours he'd been on duty. Being a conscript was harder work than he'd ever known. But he'd had no choice. Every fit adult under fifty, except those employed on council, hospital or prison duties, had to join the army of soldiers the council had created to help the guards protect Hueron. Jarial shifted his weight from foot to foot to try to ease the aches in his muscles.

"Stand still! Stand still, you scum-faced excuse for a soldier!" snapped Levin. He came up to Jarial and slashed his stick across the back of his neck. Jarial dug his nails into his palms to stop himself wincing.

Levin pulled him around.

"You! Jarial Sheldman! I might have guessed," he sneered, his face so close that his spittle flicked onto Jarial's cheek. "Shirking duty, lolling about ... No doubt plotting to run off like your traitorous girlfriend, that bitch Ezera Mertrice."

Jarial lunged at him. Levin dodged aside.

"You want to be careful, Sheldman. Insubordination? Mutiny?" He paused. "Hmm. Some punishment would be appropriate. Get on your knees!"

Jarial hesitated.

"On your knees, you bastard!"

Levin beckoned the other guards forward. Jarial looked at their cold faces and drawn swords, and slowly knelt.

"That's better. I need to teach you some obedience."

The stick slashed across Jarial's face and blood trickled down into his mouth. With a smile on his face, Levin smashed his fist into the side of Jarial's head then kicked him viciously, knocking Jarial sideways. He curled up on the stones as Levin kicked him again and again.

"Right," Levin said at last, panting. "It's too hot for this sort of exercise. That will have to do as a warning! And when you finish sentry duty, report to the archery grounds. One hundred arrows, before you leave tonight!"

As Levin and the others marched away, Jarial's companion helped him back up to his feet.

"You all right?" he whispered.

"Bruised, bleeding, aching, but I'll survive, I guess."

"Nothing broken?"

"Not for want of trying ..."

"Yes. Bastard, isn't he, that captain? I saw him beat someone into a pulp last week, just 'cos they answered him back."

Jarial straightened up slowly and wiped the blood off his face.

"A beating and a hundred arrows too!" the other added, and spat onto the pavement. "Curse him. Sadistic, vindictive git."

Jarial nodded. "I don't mind the archery practise though," he said. "Easier than sentry duty."

"I hear you're getting good."

"Yeah, thanks." Jarial smiled slightly. The only compensation in all this was the discovery that he was as good an archer as any, now that all the City Guards had lost their advantage. One hundred arrows extra practise was no hardship. And it reminded him of Ezera. She had taught him the basics. He missed her so much, sometimes and some nights, that he couldn't tell if the aches in his muscles and bones were from missing her or from the sentry duty and the marching and the standing and the work.

He stared at the southern plain. The hot sun reflected off the wide lake where the Saroche River had been dammed a hundred years ago, and shone on the empty roads and wide, vacant park-lands. For the first time in his life he could see no boats or sails on the river and lake; no horsemen, walkers or hunting parties on the meadows; no wagons of exported goods on the roads out to the dullard towns.

"What are we watching for anyway?" he asked.

"I don't know."

"Neither do I. This is a waste of time."

Jarial wondered, yet again, if he should leave and find Ezera, or loyally stay and try to protect the city. He stared down past the overhang of the walls to the ground below. Leaving would be hard now that the gates were shut and guarded. The council said anyone caught trying to abandon the city would be imprisoned. He'd have to try at night; he'd need a ladder or a rope. It would be difficult. And dangerous.

By the time the last arrow had thudded into the target, Jarial's arms and fingers were numb and the skin on his hand raw and stinging from where the bowstring had scraped his arm. Vambraces were in short supply, along with everything else. All he'd been given for his lunchtime rations was a small piece of stale bread and even staler cheese.

Jarial walked across the city towards his house, but paused as he crossed the central square in front of the council buildings. His house was empty. Last night he'd lain awake on an unshared bed with his fist jammed into his stomach to suppress the hunger pangs, until the aches and loneliness drove him downstairs into his study to compose yet more yearning, miserable songs on his guitar. He wasn't going to make any money with those depressing and self-absorbed wailings, he thought, even if anyone in the city still went to clubs and concerts.

On impulse he turned and headed towards his mother's house. Inside, he kissed his mother's cheek in greeting, as she sat at her desk, scribbling notes and reading papers with a worried look on her face. She nodded distractedly at him.

"I need some rope," he said. "Is there any?"

"What for? You're not going to - " She looked up in alarm. "Are you?"

"No, of course not. It's just," he thought rapidly. "It's just to tie up some bundles of armour and spears in the armoury, to be sent to Gathen."

"I think there's some in the storerooms," she said. "Here - take the keys."

Jarial went into the kitchen at the back. The cook hummed tunelessly as he stirred a large saucepan.

"Food!" exclaimed Jarial. "Powers above, Thirne, I'm famished! What is it?"

"Only soup. Onions, scraps of bacon rind, some potatoes, and a few bits of barley. Thin as dishwater," said

Thirne, pouring him a bowlful.

"Any bread?"

"You're joking! Haven't seen fresh, decent bread for days."

Jarial stirred the watery broth. A few pale specks of barley floated in the greyish stock. Three weeks ago he would have tipped it down the drain, but now he lifted up the bowl and gulped it rapidly, wincing as the scalding liquid burnt his mouth.

"Got some of these, at least," Thirne said, handing him a wrinkled and spotted apple. "Had to fight twenty others in the market to get them, but there's a dozen in the basket. Just don't eat them all at once."

"May your gift return, Thirne," Jarial said. "You've saved my life!"

There wasn't any rope in the first storeroom, but in the second he found a coil hanging on a nail. As he took it down he saw, in the cobwebbed gloom, a pile of sacks and crates in the corner, and he heard the scuttling of rats. They'd nibbled at some of the sacking and a tiny scattering of grains had trickled out onto the earthen floor. Jarial bent down and examined them, then carefully opened the other sacks and crates.

A few minutes later he stalked into his mother's study and slammed the door. He threw the keys onto her desk.

"Did you think I'd not notice?" he hissed furiously.

"Notice what?"

"The food! Sacks and sacks! Grains, carrots, hams, sausages, cheeses, wine! It's a crime to hoard, or had you forgotten?"

His mother put down her pen and leaned back.

"Jarry, don't worry! It's confiscated food and it's perfectly all right. The other councillors know and they are all doing the same thing. We can't risk returning it to the market, it would cause a riot. Consider it a perk of the job, darling."

"Perk? Surely it's stealing!"

"Sit down and don't be so strait-laced. By the Powers, Jarial, how do you think we're going to survive this if we don't have food?"

"Like all the others. We all starve together! We are Hued! We should be too proud to steal from each other!"

She shook her head.

"You're being stupidly idealistic. As bad as your father was. All starving together? That would be folly in the extreme. You forget, dearest, that I am a leader. A city councillor!"

"What difference does that make?"

"I need to be ... The city needs its councillors to be able to make decisions, to lead, to guide the city through this difficult time. How can we do that if we're half-starving?"

"You should be leading by example!"

"Don't be so melodramatic. I have to be practical. And you need to eat too, Jarry. There'll be food here, if you need it."

Jarial snorted.

"You may as well take advantage of it. It won't last forever, even with me being careful with it. And it won't do you or anyone else any good if you go hungry."

He folded his arms and stared at her.

"You talk about decisions, guidance. The council is doing nothing to help! Curfews, conscription, martial law - what good are they?"

She stood up.

"They are helping keep the city safe, calm, secure! Remember we had riots and looting last week? But not anymore!"

"No - because hundreds were sent to prison!"

"They were looters and rioters! And we are doing things. Why, only today we decided on a course of action that will bring the gifts back."

"Really? What?"

"We are sending a delegation to the Magi."

"Seriously?"

"Yes! As Lord Sapphireborne said, all those years ago when he sent out the four on that ill-fated mission, the Magi are almost certainly the key to it all. He knew that the gifts came from them ..." She looked doubtful for a moment. "Anyway, a dozen City Guards set out this afternoon. All we have to do is keep the city locked down, to survive ... And we will! We can buy food from dullards. We have plenty of money from taxes from the dullards, remember!"

"Folly!" Jarial snapped. "What good will the Magi do, even if you can find them? Utter folly!"

Jarial stormed out. But as he went into the hall he smelt the savoury onions and bacon in Thirne's broth. His stomach insisted. He turned from the front door and went back into the kitchen. Just one more bowl, that's all, he thought. Just this once.

CHAPTER 18
SWORDS FOR MARDEN

Durston paused from his work splitting logs and stared up at the benevolent sky in wonder, as the morning sun suddenly broke through clouds and shone onto the village. After months of rain, floods, storms and dreary, heavy clouds overhead, they had been blessed by a strange shift in the weather. Almost overnight, it seemed. Today, after over two weeks of warmth and sunshine, most of the villagers were setting out to help with the harvest.

"Still seems like a miracle, eh?" said one, as he passed Durston.

"Aye, it does," Durston replied.

"Never thought we'd be cutting corn this early," said another, walking past with a sickle over her shoulder and a young girl holding her hand. Three children ran past, shouting and laughing. Durston watched them scamper to join their families in the procession, then pause, fall silent and step aside. Two Hueds rode down the lane. The villagers drew back sullenly to let them pass.

The leader, an older man with golden-yellow skin and a thoughtful face, stopped.

"Durston Halthe?" he said.

Durston nodded and reached down to pick up his axe.

"No need for that," the Hued said. "I'm Cairson Watergiver. From Marden."

"Oh, are you? The Hued renegade."

"Yes. The Hued renegade." He dismounted. "We've come to collect the rest of the weapons that Ezera Mertrice ordered. This is Tiron Brasque. Are they ready?"

"Aye. They've been ready for ten days. At a cost of ..." He hesitated. "Fifty."

"Fifty!"

Durston shrugged. "Prices are rising. I have other customers who'll take them if you don't."

"Do you? By the seven Founders!" Cairson turned to his companion. "Do you hear that, Tiron? It is what I feared. Two hundred more coming from the city, and now this. But we have little choice. Fifty it is."

"Where's the City Guard woman then? Ezera Mertrice?" Durston asked.

"She got injured," Tiron said. "In a training session."

Durston turned and stared at him. "What! Her? A City Guard soldier?"

Tiron started to speak but Cairson gestured for him to stop.

"It was an accident," Cairson said harshly. "That was all."

"An accident! What happened? How injured is she?" Durston wanted to fire questions at them, but Cairson's hostile look quelled him.

"She has a broken leg, that is all. But my niece's welfare is none of your business. Now, may we proceed?"

Durston walked up the oak-lined avenue that led to the walls of Marden estate. As he approached the gatehouse a long-limbed, grey-haired Hued stepped out, followed by two others.

"Yes? What do you want?" he called.

Durston almost laughed. The men had no weapons, were alone, a quarter of a mile from the house, and the gates stood wide open. An army wanting to invade and loot this place wouldn't have any trouble, despite the twelve-foot high walls. But he stopped and gestured to the bundle slung across his back.

"Taking a sword to someone here. Some woman called Ezera Mertrice. She ordered it. She owes me for it and she didn't come to collect," he said, trying to sound like a bucolic and harmless peasant.

"Oh. All right. She's up at the manor, if you ask someone there they'll tell you where she is. I doubt she's up and about. She's got a broken leg and she has to rest it. Anyway, go on up to the manor."

Durston nodded and strode on up the avenue, shaking his head at the folly of guards allowing him to walk in openly carrying a sword. Several swords, in fact. As he neared the manor house he saw dozens of Hueds bustling about the courtyard in front of the house, talking and arguing, running to and fro carrying logs or sacks or baskets, or walking purposefully to the gardens or stables. People went up and down a flight of broad stone steps to the wide-open doors of the house. Someone pushed a wheelbarrow full of apples past the side of the house, and a woman came round the corner dangling a dead chicken by its feet. She stared curiously at Durston.

He hesitated. He glimpsed a yellow-skinned Hued man inside the house. Durston quickly walked off the gravel path and into a wooded area to the side of the house. He didn't want Cairson to see him. Beyond the wood was an orchard with a young girl watching two pigs eating windfalls. She turned and saw him.

"You made me jump! Who are you? You're a dullard, aren't you? With that odd skin. You're a weird colour."

"Talthen, not dullard," said Durston. "Aye, I am. And you be a Hued. Your purple skin's just as weird as mine."

She giggled. "Yes, I'm Hued, but I'm not as weird as you! And I've got a mark and a symbol, even if I can't use them. When we got here last year Cairson said we can't use our gifts anymore. And he says we have to be nice to dullards like you. Stupid bossy man! He said I have to watch the pigs!"

She poked one of the pigs with a long twig.

"I'm looking for Ezera," Durston said.

"Ezzie? The guard lady? She's inside."

"Where?"

"In her room. Up in the attics. She's right over the front door. She told me she wanted the best view of the avenue. So she could watch for, I dunno, enemies or something. I dunno what she's expecting to come up there. Dragons or wizards perhaps."

Boldness would be the best strategy, he decided. He strode into the house, through the hall and up the stairs. As he ran up the steps he glanced around at the wealth: the mahogany banisters, the tapestries softening the stone walls, the polished sideboards holding painted china, the stained and leaded glass in the windows; the symbols of Hued greed and richness everywhere. He would have liked to smash the windows and yank down the tapestries, but he hurried up a second flight until he reached the top floor.

A corridor stretched to the left and right. Someone, a Hued man, came out of a door. Durston stepped back, but the man turned aside and walked to the end of the corridor without glancing in Durston's direction.

There was a door directly opposite the top of the stairs. It stood ajar. Durston held his breath as he tiptoed towards it. There were sounds coming from the room. A metallic clink and rattle, like a spoon falling onto bare floorboards, then another, and another. Suddenly he heard a voice.

"Missed the lot! Curses! Curse this leg!"

It was Ezera's voice. Durston opened the door and went in. She lay on a bed facing the window, with a pile of pillows supporting a bandaged leg. As he entered, she threw an arrow at a bullseye target hanging on the wall.

"Yes? What do you want now? Can't you leave me alone for a day without forcing your foul medicines down my throat every five minutes?" she snapped without turning her head, and threw another arrow. It hit the plaster and clattered to the floor. "Blast! Missed again!"

She picked up another arrow and swivelled round to glare at him with a mutinous, sulky look. Then she opened her eyes wide.

"Durston?"

"Aye. As you see. Don't throw that arrow at me. I'm not bringing you medicine."

She dropped the arrow and struggled up into a sitting position, hauling a pillow from under her leg and shoving it behind her back.

"How did you get here?"

"Walked."

"What, past the guardhouse and everyone else - you just walked straight in?"

"Aye."

"By the walls! I'll have to talk to Cairson. This is ridiculous. What's to stop anyone, any Talthen or robber or murderer wanting revenge just walking in here and killing the lot of us?" She clenched her fist and thumped the side of the bed, then turned back to glare at him.

"You've got a cursed nerve, coming here at all, let alone to my room. What do you want?"

"To give you these."

He unrolled the bundle and let the swords clatter onto the floor.

"Six. That's all. But I have a feeling you might need them," he said.

Ezera stared at them, then reached down to pick one up.

"Why didn't you give them to Cairson?"

"I wanted to give them to you."

She held the sword up to sight along the edge towards the light from the window, ran her hand along the flat of the blade then balanced it on her palm.

"Folded steel. From the Ceodrinne smithy?"

"Aye."

"I didn't know that dullards had the skills to make swords like these. These must have cost. How did you afford them? Or are you expecting payment?"

"I charged Watergiver double for the last order of training swords."

Ezera laughed and swirled the sword around her head.

Durston stepped back.

"Good for you! These are good weapons. We will need them ..."

She stopped and stared at him.

"Shut the door," she said. "Do you know, then?"

"There are rumours. Tales of panic in Hueron, of Hueds trying to buy food, of barred gates, of people climbing the walls to leave the city. Something has happened. But no one is clear what."

"Oh. Can I trust you?"

Durston pointed to the swords.

"You can see. I'm not your enemy."

"Yes - but who is? All the other dullards - Talthen?"

"Mayhap. But not me."

He took a step closer and knelt down beside her.

"Ezera, what happened? How did you get injured? I've seen you fight!"

She looked at his face for a long time.

"Very well," she said eventually. "I'll tell you. You must promise, by the Powers above and Virtues below, not to tell anyone."

"I promise."

"Get that chair, and sit there, by this cursed bed! They say I have to spend half my time resting, in order for it to heal. I'm not sure I can stand this much longer. I need to be up, doing, preparing, training! This is worse than prison!"

Durston pulled the chair closer. "What happened, Ezera?"

"We were training. Then - in an instant, without any warning - my gift! It died, Durston! I lost it."

"What!"

"It just - stopped. Then Tiron hit me. I couldn't defend myself in time. It wasn't his fault," she said, as Durston stood up and clenched his fists. "I'd said that we could use sharps, and he should go as fast and as hard as he could."

"Sharps! You ..." he paused.

"Yes, a fool. I know. My leg - his sword hit my leg and

broke it."

She reached out her hand, Durston took it and gripped it tightly.

"Breaking my leg was bad enough. But losing my gift! That's far worse. But even that's not the worst. It's catastrophe. It's everyone. We've all lost our gifts, our powers! Every Hued!"

Durston released her hand, and stared at her. Every Hued? Surely that was impossible. He strode to and fro as he tried to understand this.

Ezera seized a crutch leaning against the bed and smashed it onto the footboard.

"Curses!" she exclaimed. "I can't bear this - being stuck here!"

Durston went to the window, stared down at the various Hueds scurrying to and fro outside the house, and muttered, "Every Hued? All the Guards. Levin ... Levin Bluestone. He'll have lost his too." He paused. "If I find him, he'll be easy to kill ..."

"Do you see what this means, Durston? All the implications? Cairson is tearing out what little hair he has over this."

"He said something about two hundred coming from the city."

"Refugees, yes. Frightened, bewildered. Nearly three hundred, in fact, last week, trudging up the avenue in long lines of families, with half their possessions in bundles on their backs. Cairson's been hard put to find beds for them all."

"The avenue's empty."

"It is now. No one's come for days. Either the city's empty or they're imprisoned. Cairson refuses to send anyone to find out. He says we're better staying here and relying on our so-called good relationship with the local Talthen to keep us safe," she said sarcastically. "But he's wrong and I can't do anything! I have to get out!"

As she wedged the crutch under her arm and hauled her

bandaged leg round, Durston heard her suck in her breath with pain. He knelt beside her and grabbed her shoulders.

"Wait, Ezera. I know the implications too, and they're far worse than you think."

"Worse?"

"Keep this secret. If Tulketh knew I'd warned you, he'd kill me."

"Tulketh? Who is he?"

Rapidly, curtly, Durston told her about Tulketh, the plans, the cached weapons, the recruitments.

"They're waiting for the Magi to help, I think. But if they hear that the Hueds have completely lost all powers, that the City Guard are so weakened ..."

Suddenly he pulled her to him and held her. She was so thin, so wiry, so seemingly fragile in his arms, yet so brave. As he held her, she buried her face into his chest and wrapped her arms around him tightly.

"I don't want you hurt," he said. "I thought you'd be able to take care of yourself, but now ..."

"Me too," she said.

"I don't know what it is about you," he muttered. "Ever since I saw you refuse to flog my cousin, I've not been able to stop thinking about you."

"Yes," she said. "I'm the same, but ..." She hesitated.

"But?"

"No matter," she shrugged. "If the world's falling apart around us ... Durston, can you try to find out more, about the city, and come back to tell me?"

"Aye, I'll try."

"They say I should be able to get around on crutches in a few more days. But it will be weeks before I can walk without crutches. We may not have weeks."

She pulled his face down and kissed him fiercely on the mouth. Then she winced.

"My leg hurts like hell," she said. "Aching all the time, and terrible pains when I try to move it. Durston, I need to feel something other than pain ..."

CHAPTER 19
TULKETH'S BARGAIN

The weapons' cache was in a dry shallow cave, its entrance curtained with trailing strands of ivy and clematis, five miles into the forests north-west of Ceodrinne. Durston led the packhorse along the faint trail between alder trees, fallen trunks and tangled bushes. As he reached the cache he heard voices. Tulketh was already there, along with several rough-looking men and women with swords and daggers ostentatiously hanging from belts around their waists. Horses stood tethered to trees, their heads patiently bowed.

Tulketh squinted up at the sun through the branches and leaves.

"I ain't late," said Durston. "You said midday."

"And you've got what we said?"

"Aye. Thirty sword, two hundred arrow."

"We'll check."

"Fair enough."

He started to undo the bundles. Tulketh nodded to his men and they unrolled the cloths and inspected the weapons.

"Good. Here's your fee." Tulketh tossed a small bag of coins over to Durston.

"I'll check," said Durston.

"Fair enough."

"Correct?" said Tulketh, after a pause.

"Aye. But where do you get all this money from?"

"Nought to do with you," Tulketh said. "Don't ask. What you don't know about, you can't be suspected of blabbing about. You lot, get that stuff sorted."

When all Durston's goods had been hidden under branches and twigs in the dark crevices at the back of the cave, they pulled more creepers and ivy down until the entrance was almost hidden.

"You be sworn to secrecy, remember!" said Tulketh.

"I ain't a talker," said Durston.

"And about that other business. You said fifty or more recruits. Be they ready?"

Durston folded his arms and stared Tulketh in the face. "Mayhap," he said.

"Mayhap? Don't you mess us about, peasant! Be they ready?"

"I need to know what for. To attack the city?"

"You've been told. Prison, then city."

"Then what? What about the Hued estates?"

"We ain't in a hurry for them. The city's the prize we be after."

Durston paused, then drew in a deep breath. "What about Marden?"

Tulketh looked at him suspiciously. "Marden? Those idiots? What's it to you what happens to them Hued renegades?"

"They're on our side. Leave them alone."

"You're joking, I hope. Spare Hueds? Nay ... they'll be taken care of, like all the Hued pigs." Tulketh stepped towards Durston, his face threatening. "You ain't on their side? A two-faced traitor?"

"Nay. But I ain't keen on killing innocents. They're trying to do right. Leave them alone, 'tis all I'm asking."

"Never. We be sworn to kill all Hueds."

"Then I ain't going to recruit for you. I don't want any part in any massacres. 'Tis wrong!"

"Wrong? After what Hueds do to Talthen like you? Weakling!" Tulketh hissed. "What's Marden to you? Got some friends there, you rat?"

Durston said nothing.

"You're a traitor, ain't you?" Tulketh said angrily. He

turned away and strode towards the others. But suddenly he turned back to Durston and smiled.

"Of course, if you've got friends there, mayhap you can help. Give us information, and I'll forget your ... indiscretion. We know something's happened. The city gates have been shut for days. No one going in or out. There's been rumours. Perhaps you can tell us?"

"I ain't heard anything."

"You don't want to lie to me, Durston," Tulketh said in a seemingly friendly manner. "You don't want me as your enemy. Just tell me. Have you got allies, friends at Marden? A Hued girlfriend? Someone in the stables or kitchens who helps you out? Nothing to be ashamed of. Get what you can out of them, we say. If you've heard aught about the city, tell me and I'll think about your request."

Durston hesitated. But he'd promised Ezera.

"Nay. I've heard nought about the city."

"You're lying." Tulketh's friendly face changed. "Are you going to help us?"

Durston shook his head.

"You ain't in a position to draw back. You get those recruits you promised. You don't make conditions or beg favours for those Hued swine. You join us, or ..."

"Or what?"

"I asked around the village. Your predecessor - he burnt to death in his workshop, I heard. You were there that night. You saw it. You were a boy, an apprentice carpenter, barely sixteen. You saw him burn to death."

Durston stepped back as Tulketh grinned evilly.

"You be terrified of fire. You back out now, you two-faced coward, and you'll lie awake every night wondering when I'm going to come, in the dark, with my lantern, with a naked flame ..."

Durston remembered the bile rising in his throat at the roasting meat stench, the writhing, the screams, the helplessness. He threw himself at Tulketh and bore him to the ground. For a few moments they wrestled in the undergrowth and brambles and leafy debris. Durston tried to smash his fists into Tulketh's pale face, but the other man wriggled and shouted, until two of his men pulled Durston back and pinioned his arms to his sides. Tulketh stood up, fastidiously dusted the dirt off his shirt and straightened his jacket.

"Shall I teach him a lesson?" one of the men said.

Tulketh shook his head. "Nay. He's a fighter, I'll give him that. We need men like him. I'll put him in the front line."

He came up to Durston and seized his throat, choking him.

"Listen, you scum. We had a deal. You want to get your father out of that prison hell? We help you, you help us. So you get us those recruits you promised. Then you help us take the prison, the city. Afterwards," he smirked. "We take the estates, the towns, Saroche and Marden too. And if you've kept your word, you've fought with us, then whatever - or whoever - it is that you don't want touched in Marden, I'll let you rescue them. Agreed?"

He released Durston.

"I don't trust you," Durston gasped.

Tulketh laughed. "I wouldn't trust me either. But you ain't got any choice. This army, this war, 'tis going to happen whether you help or not. So you may as well join us. 'Tis your only option. Agreed?"

"And if I don't?"

Tulketh shrugged. "Then you be no use to us. You be as good as dead, you and all your Hued friends."

Durston thought of Ezera and of the pain in her face when she told him that her gift had died. Maybe this would be his only chance to save her from the onslaught to come. And he thought of his father and the others from his village, rotting and dying in the Hued prison. Slowly, reluctantly, he held out his hand. Tulketh grabbed it and squeezed hard until Durston's bones ached. "Done! You wait til you hear from us again. Get your recruits ready, warned, armed, then wait. Next spring, at the latest. Remember, we'll take the prison first. And if you betray us ..." He yanked Durston close and hissed into his ear, "I will, I promise, hunt you down and burn you alive."

CHAPTER 20
THE RAID

Jarial stood in a row with the other conscripts as the late afternoon sun brightened the opposite walls of the guard courtyard, casting long shadows behind the trees and buildings. A horse whinnied and, as if in response, a man's stomach rumbled loudly. Those standing by him sniggered. Levin, standing in front to inspect them, snapped, "Silence!" He unfolded a piece of paper. "Orders from the council!" he announced.

"Some action at last!" whispered another conscript to Jarial.

"As you know, those dullard scum are refusing to sell grain, or any food, to us. Despite the gold we offer. So we're going to take what we need from the bastards. I want a detachment of twenty. Twenty decent fighters, not cowardly rabble like you lot, but I'll have to make do with what I've got."

He strode along the lines of conscripts, swinging his baton. "You, you ... you ..."

When he got to Jarial, he smirked. He poked Jarial with his baton.

"Still got a bit of a belly on you, soldier?" he said. "After three weeks on rations. I'm impressed. You can come too. You obviously need some exercise to get rid of that flabby flesh."

Suddenly he lashed out with his fist and punched Jarial in the stomach. Jarial collapsed and rolled sideways. His head hit the cobbles and a sharp burst of pain jabbed his temples. He choked for breath. Levin turned away and strolled down the line of men. "You too, and you," he said. "Right, I reckon that's twelve and I'll be taking eight of the City Guards too. Powers know we'll need some strength as well as this bunch of weaklings. Jarial, you lazy sod, get up!"

Jarial struggled to his feet, still wheezing. He stood as straight as he could.

"Don't let the bastard get to you," the woman next to him muttered.

"Right," Jarial gasped. He wished that he'd had the courage to use that rope to escape. But his heart had failed him when he had stood on the battlements in the dark of the night, and looked down over a hundred feet to the rocky outcrops below. The thought of wandering, alone, the sixty or seventy miles to Marden terrified him too, he had to admit.

Back in front of them, Levin said, "The rest of you lot can go. Dismissed! Right! Squad! Get two hours sleep in the guardhouse, then get kitted up; swords, daggers and spears, no bows on this trip. Then get to the guardhouse at the western gate and get horses from the stables there. We meet there, three hours before midnight."

"Well, full moon, at least, for whatever it is we're doing," said one conscript, as they sat on horses and waited in the deep twilight at the western guardhouse.

"Hope we get moving soon," said another. "Can't stand all this hanging around."

"Anyone any idea where we're going?"

"Taking grain from dullards," said Jarial. "That's what he said."

"Huh! Well, if the bastards won't sell to us ..."

"It's not going to be that easy," muttered another, his voice trembling slightly. "We're not fighters, not like the City Guard were. Can't say I'm looking forward to this."

Two City Guards opened the courtyard gates. Levin and several other guards, in helmets and steel breastplates, were outside, along with two large empty carts pulled by two horses each. Their drivers held lanterns, and more lanterns dangled from poles fixed to the back of the carts.

"Fall in behind the carts," Levin ordered. "Three guards at the rear. We've got a four or five hour ride to a squalid little peasant place called Reshe. So keep awake and alert."

"Reshe? Never heard of it," whispered someone.

"It's near the Saroche. Downstream. About fifteen or sixteen miles, I think," said another.

Sixteen miles, thought Jarial. Ezera had always grumbled that he'd never been far from the city and had no idea about dullards. Well, now he'd find out. Let this not be a punishment detail as well, he thought. He pushed his feet farther into the stirrups and held onto the reins as they rode out of the courtyard and down the deserted street to the city wall. The sentries pulled open the gates.

"Watch out for us coming back," Levin ordered. "Around dawn, I reckon."

The sentries nodded and closed the gates behind them with a thud that sounded loud in the empty stillness.

Jarial rode behind the two carts. As the horses trotted, the lanterns swung and cast pale pools of light onto a mix of apprehensive, calm and determined faces. They rode along the avenue, through stripes of deep shadows and bright moonlight under the trees, and onto the road leading along the river westwards. A breeze rustled the leaves and splashed the water. Jarial pulled his leather breastplate closer. His head felt exposed, but there weren't enough helmets for the conscripts. He'd been lucky to get a breastplate and greaves. His spear was slung behind him, his sword rattled at his thigh and his unused dagger was in a sheath on his belt. He tightened his belt. Despite Levin's taunts, despite the guilty swallowing of bowls of broth cooked up by Thirne, he was thinner than he had been. An owl flew overhead and hooted at their procession.

"Bad omen, that," a woman whispered.

"Hope it's a bad omen for that sod Levin," another

muttered. "Turning thief as well as bully and all-round sadist."

"We're all turning thieves," replied Jarial.

"Don't have much choice, do we? That or starve like rats in an empty cellar."

We should rather starve than this, thought Jarial.

"Quiet, you scum," hissed Levin. "This isn't a bloody pleasure trip. No talking!"

They came to the bridge where the southern road turned left past Sarochen Lake towards the plains. Levin took the right turn and led them west along the river, past a single-storey inn near a jetty with a few weather-beaten boats tied to it, then through a tiny hamlet consisting of a farmstead and a dozen ramshackle thatched cottages. Nine miles downstream they came to a narrow track heading north between fields of cut corn, with a stream on the far side of the fields. The stubble looked grey in the moonlight. Levin held up his hand and the cavalcade halted.

"Reshe is three miles upstream. About a quarter of a mile before the village there's a mill. Conveniently isolated from the village. They've been harvesting so the mill's been busy. We're to raid it."

After thirty minutes of slow, hushed riding they could see the mill, a large brick and timber building, not far from a stand of trees in the shadow of a hill. Clouds were starting to cover the moon but its light still shone white and cold on the tiled roof, shuttered windows and motionless mill wheel. They couldn't hear any sounds other than the rippling of the mill-race, the steady breeze in the trees, the small chink of stirrup and snaffle bits, and the breathing of the horses.

Levin reined in his horse. The moonlight shone pale and stark on his face as he rapped out orders.

"You five guards stand sentry, drawn swords, one on each side, one to the carts, kill anyone who interferes. You three," he pointed to Jarial, a strong-faced ochre-coloured woman called Barecha, and a young lad called Tiere, "round the back. Smash the door and get in. Me and the other City Guards take the main entrance. The rest follow us."

"And if there's any scum inside?" a guard asked.

"We take care of them. Get the grain sacks, flour, anything you find and load up the carts. We work fast, we work silently. And afterwards ..." He grinned. "We torch the place. That'll teach them."

Jarial felt his heart racing and beads of sweat cooling his forehead as he and the other two slipped around to the back of the mill. Barecha looked determined, but Tiere, a pale green-skinned boy, bit his lip, and was shaking visibly. Jarial pulled his sword from its scabbard, then hesitated. Despite Levin's orders, he knew he couldn't 'take care' of any dullard inside the mill. Ezera would, without hesitation, he knew. He thrust the sword back. Barecha pulled out her sword and tried the door.

"Locked," she whispered. She kicked the door viciously. "Help me out here!" she hissed.

Jarial joined her, and they kicked together until the door splintered. They stepped over the broken timbers. Inside it was too gloomy to see much until Tiere lifted the lantern to cast a dim light on millstones, hoppers, cogwheels, and the huge timber uprights supporting the ceiling. Filled sacks had been piled up in one corner, and rough wooden stairs led upwards in another. Tiere put the lantern on a millstone as they heard the crack and thud of the others kicking down the front door of the mill.

Suddenly three men and a woman, all with daggers in their hands, ran down the stairs, shouting loudly. When they saw Jarial and the other two they charged into them. Before Jarial could move the older man leading them stabbed his dagger into Barecha's chest. Barecha slid down the wall onto the floor, her hand futilely trying to pull the blade out as ochre blood spurted onto the floor. Tiere backed into a corner and desperately waved his sword around. His thin face looked terrified. One of the other men, his face raging with fury, bore down on Jarial, yelling incoherently. Jarial snatched at his sword but he fumbled and dropped it. The man lifted his dagger and slashed wildly. Jarial raised his arm to protect his face and the edge of the dagger ripped through his skin. He felt it cut through his wrist and hand and fingers. He clutched the wound and fell to his knees.

The first dullard shouted, "Run! Run for help! Go!"

The third man and the woman hesitated then sped through the door and out into the dark. Suddenly, Levin and the others charged into the room. As Levin brought his sword thudding down on the older dullard's head, the guard behind him grabbed the shoulders of Jarial's attacker. Jarial saw a knife point erupt from the man's stomach. He lurched back in fear as the man slumped forward, then fell to the ground, blood pooling around him.

"You three, upstairs, see who else is here," Levin yelled, pushing the dullard's corpse aside with his foot. "You, stop snivelling in the corner there, you useless bit of damp rag. Who's got the medicine kit? Get the bandages, give them to that kid there, so he can get that sod's arm bound up! Make yourself useful!"

Blood drenched Jarial's hand and arm. As he knelt, he heard it splashing onto the floor. Tiere, his hands and arms still trembling, crouched beside him, pulled strips of linen from the kit and wrapped them tightly around his arm. Jarial shut his eyes and fought against the urge to lie down and faint.

The guards came down the stairs. The leading one shook his head.

"Just the two, then?" Levin asked. Jarial was too dizzy to answer and Tiere said nothing, but turned his face away and stared with fixed concentration on the bandages that he was winding around Jarial's arm.

"Right, you lot, get these sacks into the cart, you others search the building for more. Get anything you find, get it into the carts as fast as you can. Move!"

Levin stood and watched, shouting orders, as the sacks were carried out. Tiere finished the bandaging. Jarial found that his the faintness was passing. He struggled to his feet, holding his useless left hand to his chest. He knew the cut had gone deep. He couldn't feel or move his fingers and the pain from them jabbed up his arm and shoulder.

"You two idiots, get upstairs," Levin turned to them and snapped. "Search up there, since you're no use here loading sacks. Any food, any stores, come back and tell me."

Tiere and Jarial found bulging sacks of un-milled wheat next to hoppers and chutes in a room over the millstones. Levin rubbed his hands together when he saw them.

"About bloody time. Promotion for me, I reckon. We'll need those sentries to help."

He ran down the stairs, grabbed a lantern and went out. Jarial, standing at the top of the stairs, saw him come back in, his face blanched.

"Bastards," he said. "Sentry's been stabbed ... I don't know who. But we'd best get moving. Come on, move it! Get this stuff loaded fast! Hurry!"

Jarial heard shouts. Through the upstairs window he saw twenty or more people holding sharp-pronged pitchforks, swords and spears, some carrying torches. They charged towards the mill. His heart stopped beating for a moment, then restarted, his pulse speeding up as the fear flooded him. Tiere grabbed his unhurt arm and dragged him through a door into a room just off the landing. They heard running footsteps pour into the mill through the smashed doors.

"We need to hide," Tiere stuttered. The room looked like a mill-worker's bedroom, sparsely furnished but with a chest and a bed covered in a coarse woollen blanket. They crouched in the gloom behind the bed, as they listened to the yells and clashes and thuds. They held their breath and tried not to move, but several men ran in, shone lanterns through the darkness and within minutes they were seized, their weapons yanked away, and they were shoved down the stairs.

There were bodies scattered around the mill room. Some were conscripts and guards, but Jarial couldn't see Levin among the slain. A woman knelt by the older dullard, cradling his head in her arms. When she saw Jarial she lifted her head. "Ain't you satisfied with taxing and starving us? You have to come like robbers in the night and murder us too?" she wailed. Jarial wanted to cry out, "It wasn't me! I'm not a murderer!" but his voice failed him as he watched her crouch, weeping, over the bruised, empty face of the dead man. He hung his head and stared at the smudges of blood on the scuffed dirt floor.

"Kill them," someone said. "Kill the brutes."

"Nay, not yet," said another, a stocky, sure-voiced man, as he bent down and rolled over the body of one of the guards. "Seems to me there's something more going on here. We need to ask them a few questions."

"City guards!" gasped a woman, staring wide-eyed at the black uniform. "We've killed City Guards ..."

"Powers help us ..." whispered another. "You know what they do in revenge ..."

"Aye," said the sure-voiced man. "But mayhap we'll be fine. We need to find out why they were here. How many of ours dead?"

"Three, Malk," said another woman. "The miller, his son and Alron. Two of us were injured, but not badly."

"A couple of them escaped," said a man. "Rode off south."

"Three of us killed? That's all!" exclaimed Malk, straightening up. "Yet there were over a dozen of them, and at least six guards! Since when have just a score of us been able to kill City Guards so easily?"

"Easily?"

"Aye! The sentry out there, stabbed in the back by you when you ran for help. You ain't supposed to be able to ambush guards! And one guard can take on half-a-dozen Talthen and barely break a sweat. So how did we manage to kill six City Guards, not to mention all those others?"

"'Tis strange ..."

"And they were stealing food," continued Malk.

"Mayhap all those rumours are true. Search them. Find their symbols."

He turned to the two Hueds. "You bloody coloured swine. Why were you here?"

Jarial shook his head and stared at Tiere. Say nothing, he mouthed. Tiere looked at the ground. Malk grabbed Jarial's left hand and wrenched the bandage off. Jarial stifled a groan as Malk pulled his fingers back. The blood started flowing again. Jarial forced himself to look at his hand. A long, deep gash was open along his wrist and the edge of his hand. Most of his little finger was missing. Stupidly, he looked around the dirt floor for it. His third finger was half cut through. He couldn't move it. I won't be able to play my song about Ezera on the guitar anymore, he thought numbly, then shut his eyes as black fog crept around his vision. I won't faint, he insisted to himself.

Malk stared at his palm.

"Your mark. A flame," he said. "So you be a firemaker."

"I can't find any symbols," said a woman. "But I found this. In a pocket."

She held out two pieces of pale orange glass. It was a sword-shaped symbol, broken in half.

"Ah ..." breathed out Malk greedily. "Ah ... So 'tis true."

He turned on Jarial, yanked his right arm behind his back, took out a knife and held it to his neck.

"Show me a flame, firemaker," he hissed. "Or I cut your throat."

Jarial shut his eyes. The point of the knife stabbed into his skin. He lifted his hand, tried to concentrate and summon a tiny flicker of fire, even a fragment of warmth, onto his palm. But he knew it wouldn't work. The knife pressed harder. He felt liquid trickling down his neck.

"Come on, you gifted red bastard. I want to see your powers in action."

Jarial dropped his hand. He couldn't do it.

"See!" said Malk gleefully, releasing Jarial. "'Tis true! Those cursed greedy Hueds have lost their gifts!"

The others gasped.

"Powers above!"

"This means ... Great Powers and Virtues!"

"Tulketh needs to know this. And Ulban," said Malk triumphantly. "You, and you, get saddled up in the morning. You knew where to find them. Mayhap we don't need to wait until next spring."

He turned back to Jarial and Tiere.

"Look at the boy," he sneered. "Green as a frog. He looks like he's going to throw up."

"Aye, but what shall we do with them?" someone asked.

"I know. I'll deal with them," Malk said, lifting his knife. "Kneel. Beg for your lives."

Jarial looked around. There were too many of them. But he wasn't going to kneel. Tiere was already on his knees, sobbing and shaking. Jarial went for his dagger. It was pointless, of course. Before he could even lunge at Malk he'd been grabbed and forced to the ground. Malk stepped forward, yanked at his hair to pull his head back, and placed the edge of the knife on his exposed throat.

A tall, silver-haired woman with an air of authority strode into the room. The others moved aside to let her through.

"What's going on?" she asked. "Have I missed the fun?"

"Aye, you have, chief," said Malk. "Hueds robbing the mill. We've killed most of them, two scarpered. They killed the miller, his son and Alron."

"Hued bastards," she said dispassionately.

"We caught these two."

"And what are you doing with them?"

"Getting rid of them."

"I ain't sure about that. We ain't killers like them. We don't murder in cold blood. Even bastards like them."

"Chief? You sure?" said Malk. "What then? Let them go free?"

"Aye, but take their weapons. And any money they've got. Search them."

"And we'll have their armour, greaves, everything," Malk smirked as he and the others ripped off their belts, scabbards and jackets, and rifled through their pockets.

The chief nodded. "Leave them enough clothes for decency. Very good. Well, we've got their swords, their horses, two carts, daggers. Not such a bad haul from the swine. How did we manage it?"

"They've lost their gifts."

"What? By my mother's grave ... Interesting. Very interesting. How come them two ain't killed or run off with the rest? Didn't they fight?"

"They were hiding. Skulking and trembling in a corner upstairs."

The woman laughed. "Yellow-bellied powerless Hued! Look at them! Malk, they ain't worth the effort of digging their graves. A frightened boy and a paunchy, flabby weakling! If they were City Guard, I'd say aye, kill them, but they ain't. Let the scum run back to their city and hide there with the rest of them! They can take a message from us."

She seized Jarial's hair, bent down, and hissed, "Tell them, tell those scared rats that we are coming for their city. They'd better choose between running or being killed."

She straightened up, dusted her hands down, and nodded at Malk and the others. Jarial and Tiere were pulled to their feet and shoved through the doorway.

"You heard," Malk hissed. "You heard the chief. Get out! Run!"

CHAPTER 21
RUNNING BACK

Fragmenting clouds shuffled over the moon. The breeze grew stronger and tugged at the wisps of hay in their makeshift beds in the corner of a harvested field. Tiere was asleep, muttering and shivering in his dreams, but Jarial could not sleep. The night seemed the longest he'd ever known, longer even than the night after Ezera had left.

The cold pierced his wounded hand like a blade. He tore strips from his shirt and wrapped them around his hand, then sat, clutching his knees to his chest for warmth, and watched until the darkness imperceptibly became greyness. Then he stirred himself and shook Tiere. The boy's skin and hands felt clammy. He twitched, grumbled and rolled over back into sleep. Jarial shook him harder. Again and again, as they had stumbled southwards down the lane, he'd been tempted to abandon Tiere and run for the city, but he'd looked at the boy's terrified, tearful face and he couldn't do it.

"Come on! We need to move. We have to get to the city."

He dragged Tiere upright with his one good hand.

"Come on, walk, curse you. Walk!"

He bullied and cajoled and insisted and they struggled along the lane. The dawn light grew brighter and the sun rose. They reached the main road and trudged on, resting every mile or so. They came to a bend, and then, less than half a mile away, Jarial saw the ramshackle cottages of the hamlet by the river.

A woman came out of one, carrying two large baskets. She started to walk towards them. As she approached, Tiere stopped and seemed to buckle. "I can't ..." he muttered as he collapsed. The woman paused, looked back over her shoulder towards the hamlet, then stared at them. She walked slowly towards them. Her eyes were wary. She stopped a few yards away. Jarial knelt in the dust and stones of the road, trying to pull Tiere up one-handed. He looked up at the woman.

"You must help us," he said.

She didn't move. He realised that he had sounded brusque, even imperious.

"Please?" he added reluctantly.

"What happened to you?"

"Er - we were attacked."

"Robbers? Here, this close to the city?"

She came close and crouched near them.

"Powers above, you're hurt," she gasped, reaching towards the gory strips of cloth around his arm.

"Yes. And my friend - I think he's just exhausted."

"Wait," she said. Rapidly she walked, with her baskets, back to the cottage. A few minutes later she returned with a jug and a plain horn beaker.

"Here. Water," she said, handing them to Jarial. He drank, then poured some for Tiere. She looked at him with her eyebrows raised. With a start, he realised he was acting like a powerful, ruling Hued.

"Thank you," he said. "You are kind."

"Show me your arm."

Slowly, wincing as the dried blood pulled at the skin, he unwound the bandages.

"That looks bad," she said. "You'd better come with me."

"I can't pay you. We've no money."

She stood up and looked steadily at him with quiet dignity.

"I ain't after money. You may be greedy Hued swine, but

I'm not. I'm Talthen, and I'll help you, though Powers know you lot don't deserve it."

Jarial hung his head. "I know," he said quietly.

"Can he walk?"

"I'll try him. Come on. Lean on me." Jarial, though hampered by his injured arm, managed to drag Tiere to his feet and stagger, supporting him, along the road.

When they reached her cottage, she took them along the side to the back. There was a small fenced vegetable patch with beans and sweet peas climbing a row of tall sticks, alongside a few apple trees under which chickens scratched in the dirt.

"Sit on that bench and rest. I'll get you some food. Don't try anything. I'll scream and I'll be heard, believe me."

She returned with a platter of apples, slices of bread and a bowl of milk. Jarial was so hungry that he found it hard to diligently hand half the bread to Tiere and let him drink most of the milk. The bread was coarse and unbuttered but satisfying, the apples sweet and juicy. He hadn't tasted anything so good for weeks.

"Thank you again," Jarial said. "Are you sure you can spare this?"

She shrugged.

"A month ago I'd have said nay. But things be better. The harvest's surprised everyone. There be food enough and to spare."

Jarial thought of the starving thousands in the city. They had got things so wrong! He put his head in his hands in shame. Tiere leant back against the rough plaster of the cottage wall as the brightening sun lifted over the distant trees and shone on them.

"Your arm!" she exclaimed. "I've got summat that may help."

She went in and came back with an earthenware jar. When she lifted the lid Jarial smelt honey, chamomile, the pungent spiciness of yarrow and other herbs that he couldn't identify.

"What is it?"

"Salve, with arnica. Good for bruises and cuts. 'Tis good, 'tis healing. But 'twill sting."

Gently, with thin, pale fingers, she smoothed the ointment onto his injury. He winced. She was right. But it was a clean, bracing sting that faded. Jarial wound the bandages carefully back around his arm.

"That feels better." He glanced at Tiere. "It looks like my friend is recovering too."

Tiere opened his eyes. Traces of fear still remained on his face but he nodded slowly at the woman. "Thank you," he mouthed.

"I think you've saved our lives," Jarial said. "Believe me, we are truly grateful. I didn't expect such kindness from dullards."

"Talthen! Don't call us by that name!"

Jarial stared at the ground and the hopeful, scrawny chicken darting at the breadcrumbs at his feet. Ezera had been right. He had no idea.

"Talthen," he said.

"Where be you going?"

"To Hueron."

"The city?" She gave him a sharp look. "Why? 'Tis closed."

Jarial wasn't sure why. But there was nowhere else. He'd never manage to walk to Marden.

"He needs to get back to his family," he said, nodding at Tiere. "They'll be worried."

"Will you be able to get in?"

"I hope so. But we're so tired and it's another three or four miles, I think."

He leaned back too. The sun was full on his face, warming and strengthening him.

"Can we rest here for a bit longer?" he asked.

"I ain't sure. I've got to get to market."

Jarial stood up.

"Of course. We should go. Come on, Tiere. I give you

my heartfelt thanks. I'm Jarial Sheldman. What's your name?"

"Liffy Triese."

He held out his hand. She took it in cool, slender fingers.

"Well - you might as well wait a while," she said. "A few minutes won't matter, and 'twill help you. And some time in the sun - 'twill be good for me too."

She sat on the bench beside him, closed her eyes and held her face to the sunlight. Her hair was a deep red, tied back into a long plait. At the centre of her forehead the hairline dipped in a tiny triangle pointing down to her nose. She had straight, dark eyebrows and her skin was the colour of cream. To Jarial it looked oddly pale against the rich red of her hair. A few strands were silver, yet she was young; barely a year or so older than Ezera, Jarial guessed. Her cheeks were thin, and her dress a faded patched green. She turned her head and caught him looking curiously at her, and smiled. Her steadfast eyes were green, flecked with brown.

For a while all three sat in silence. Then Liffy stood up.

"You'd better go. You can keep the salve. I can easily make more. When you get home, bathe your arm in salt water, every day, night and morning, until it heals."

"I should pay you for it. But I've got nothing."

"I told you. It don't matter."

Jarial and Tiere went along the side of the house. When they reached the front Jarial looked back, but she had gone.

CHAPTER 22
REFUGEES

The Grey Army continued through small villages and larger towns, recruiting as they went and camping overnight in thick forests. A month after leaving Peveque they reached the main crossing point of the Saroche River. Headon rode on ahead over the bridge. He slowed his horse. They were travelling as fast as they could, but even so they were only doing twelve to fifteen miles a day, as far as he could work out. There were too many foot soldiers, so they couldn't move as fast as he'd like. The bigger the army grew, the slower it travelled. There was one hundred and fifty more miles to go to reach Langron, then almost the same from there to Hueron. It would be the middle of October, or even later, before they could hope to reach the city. It might be too late.

He watched the army cross. It was an impressive sight, nearly four hundred by now, mostly in grey, or with grey or white strips of cloth tied around their arms, with rippling banners and sunlight gleaming on spears, swords and arrow-tips. But even so, they didn't yet have enough people to take the city.

They had heard rumours of Talthen plans to besiege the city. If they couldn't get there first, Headon realised, they could be facing two armies. But they couldn't travel faster and they had no choice but to take the longer route to avoid the city.

He gazed westwards, towards Hueron. It was hidden behind miles of high moors covered in purple heather and orange bracken and trees turning pale yellow. There was a group of travellers on horses approaching them on the road. They paused to stare at the grey-clad cavalcade. Headon saw they were Hueds and turned his horse towards them, raising his hand to show his mark.

"Are you from the city?" he called. "Is there any news?"

The leader, a tall and stately woman with pale golden colouring, rode towards him. She lifted her hand and Headon saw the mark of a pale flower on her palm.

"We are from Hueron," she said. "Aren't you? How can you not know the news? Surely everyone knows that the Hued have lost their powers and the city is doomed. But who are you and all these? What is happening?"

Felde, Riathe and Vallan rode up to join Headon.

"Vallan, get the captains to move everyone off the road and tell them all to wait, then come back," Headon said. "We need to talk to these people."

The travellers wore cloaks with large hoods pulled over their faces as if to hide their colouring. Five of them were young men and there were three other women, one much older than the others. She rode forward next to the tall woman and looked nervously at the grey-clad soldiers.

"Sefane," she said to the tall woman, quietly, but not so quietly that Headon didn't hear her. "What are you doing, talking to these - these strangers? Can't you see that they are dullards?"

"I am Hued," Headon said. "So is he, as you can see." He gestured towards Vallan, who was riding back towards them. "You have nothing to fear from us. But you must tell us what is happening in Hueron and where you are going. You may not be safe travelling in such a small group."

"Not safe! No, but safer than sitting like rats in a trap in the city, doing nothing, while the dullards could attack at any moment," Sefane exclaimed. "The City Council have sealed the gates in their folly, but, like many, we bribed some of the guards to open the gate at night and let us leave. We are trying to get to Marden. I am Sefane Goldstone, and these are my daughters, sons and sons-in-law, and my mother. But you - who are you?"

"Did you know Lord Dernham Sapphireborne?"

She nodded.

"This is his son, Vallan Sapphireborne, and his son-in-law, Felde Sulvenor, and his grandson, Riathe Sulvenor. I am Headon Alcastor. We were sent by Dernham to find help for the Hueds in case the gifts faded or were lost. Now we are on our way back, with an army, this army, to help the city."

"But it was nearly twenty years ago that Lord Sapphireborne sent you," cried the older woman.

"True. We are late, but not too late, we hope," said Headon. "War is brewing and we intend to prevent it. You say you are going to Marden? Cairson Watergiver's estate?"

"Yes. Where else can we go? There are rumours, dreadful rumours that the city will be attacked. We go to Marden in the hope that we might be safe there."

"Headon, you know that Berrena was persuading Hueds, especially giftless ones, to go there, to Marden, as well as to Langron, don't you?" Felde said. "To live as Talthen."

"Berrena? You mean Lady Berrena Rochale? You know her?" the tall woman said in astonishment.

"Aye. She's my wife," Felde said defensively.

"Oh. I had heard she was married to a dullard."

"Not a dullard - a Talthen!" Riathe said angrily.

"I stand corrected. The world has changed, has it not?" She bowed to Felde and Riathe. "Forgive me. I am honoured to meet the husband and son of so brave a lady."

"If you are going to Marden," Headon said, "then we may be able to help you. Wait one moment."

He took Felde and the others aside.

"Felde, how many Hueds do you think there are at Marden?" he asked.

"Six or seven score, Berrena said," replied Felde. "Cairson visited her and Sarielle a year ago and told us it was going well. He had a hundred or more with him, and Berrena knows of at least twenty more that have gone there since."

"And now that the gifts have failed, others may have gone there too," said Vallan.

"What about a change of plan? Shall we take a detour and escort these Hueds to Marden? We could recruit there. And see Cairson. He must be told about his niece, about Aven's death."

"You're in command, Headon," said Vallan. "Whatever you think fit."

Headon turned back to the tall woman. "We can give you safe passage to Marden."

"Thank you," she replied, "That would be most welcome."

"Do you know Thera Redstone? One of the city councillors."

"Hmm, yes, I knew her. She has left the city, apparently. Rumour has it that she went to Lady Rochale - Lady Sarielle Rochale, I should say, at Langron Manor."

Headon sighed with relief. His mother would be safe there - as safe as anywhere. He noted the swords, daggers and heavy saddlebags on the travellers' horses.

"Presumably you did not escape empty-handed," he said.

"No, we took some, but we had to leave most of our possessions. We can pay you, but not a huge amount. Shall we say two hundred gold pieces?"

Riathe came closer and, looking at the group, said, "One gold piece for every man in the army, and you and those in your group that can fight join the army too. We need coloureds."

The woman looked stunned for a moment, then laughed.

"I purchase my family's safety at a high price, it seems! But it will be an honour to join you."

CHAPTER 23
AT MARDEN

Early autumn sun shone on Ezera's face, warm and bright. But it did not encourage her. She stood, the hard crutch wedged into her armpit and her hand sweating on the handle, watching Tiron and twenty others clashing wooden swords half-heartedly and grunting theatrically with the effort. She could have screamed with frustration. Morons, careless, sloppy morons, who couldn't even hold a sword at the right end and were barely trying! Didn't they realise how vital it was that they could defend themselves? At least her cousin Gabrice, Cairson's nephew, who had recently joined them from Hueron, was almost competent. He was as stocky and square-shouldered as Cairson, and had the same golden-yellow colouring, but he was also strong, surprisingly fast, and encouragingly cheerful. She hoped that he'd inspire some of the others. She shifted the weight from her aching leg, and tried to ignore the weariness in her arms and other leg.

She could hear people gleefully chatting in the orchard. They were filling up the cider press with the windfalls and she could smell the scent of the apples in the breeze, masking the underlying whiff of dung from the stables. When they'd done with the cider making, it would be their turn to be trained. Maybe they'd be more enthusiastic.

Cairson came up and stood by her, handing her a beaker of water. The thought of cider and the feel of the warm sun had made her thirsty. It was tepid but she swallowed it gratefully.

"Good weather for this, at least," Cairson said, looking up at the mare's tail clouds drifting in the blue sky, high over the roofs and chimneys of Marden House.

"Yes. But look at them. Idiots! Their shield work is appalling, they're using the swords like children would."

"Don't be so impatient. It's only their first week. Leave them to it for a minute and come to the front of the house. Watch the archers. They are improving."

Ezera admitted that he was right. Three women archers especially had made great progress, loosing arrows with a gasp and thrum of the strings and then a thwack as they hit the straw targets. "Oh, well done, oh, great shot," they kept saying to each other.

"Right. I admit it, they are good." Though not as good as Jarial had been. Jarial, Durston - Ezera gritted her teeth at the thought of them both. She'd heard nothing from either of them. Men, typical men, she thought, hobbling onto the front lawn by the archers. She wedged the crutch firmly under her arm, seized a bow, nocked an arrow into the taut bowstring, wobbled slightly on her one good leg, then released it, sending it thudding into the bullseye.

"Powers above!" exclaimed one of the women. "That was impressive!"

Cairson suddenly ran forward and put his hand on Ezera's arm.

"Look!" he said urgently, pointing down the avenue to the distant gate.

There was movement, the faint sound of voices and the clop of horses. She could see glints of sunlight from metal - spears? Swords? It looked like a mob, a horde. She gasped. It was an army. They were armed, there were scores of them, hundreds even. What had happened to the gatehouse keepers?

"Curses! Get your weapons!" she yelled. "One of you, to the back, get Gabrice, Tiron, get everyone. Arm yourselves! Now!" she screamed, as they hesitated. "We're being attacked, you idiots!"

"Founders preserve us!" one of the women exclaimed. She ran up and stood by Ezera, arrow on her bowstring, ready.

"Wait until they are in range," Ezera said, loosening her dagger and nocking another arrow. She realised she was shaking and took in a deep breath.

"No," Cairson muttered. "No. Oh, by the walls, it can't be ... No. Surely not."

"What?"

"Wait ..." He walked down the avenue, then broke into a jog. Ezera stared after him. Then she saw, too. The people in front had coloured skin and hair. One was emerald green, one blue, one fuchsia pink. Behind them came Talthen, but she could see a few other Hueds as well. Running ahead of them was one of the gatehouse keepers. He dashed to Cairson and started to speak, but Cairson put him aside and ran to the green-faced leader.

"Headon? Headon!" he shouted.

Headon? thought Ezera. I've heard that name before ... I know that name.

She turned to the others. "Wait," she ordered. "I don't know who they are. But it seems Cairson might. Anyway, wait. I'll find out."

She limped after Cairson. As she neared the group, the leader rapidly dismounted, ran to Cairson and, to Ezera's astonishment, wrapped his arms around him, then stepped back. Cairson put his hands on the man's shoulders.

"Headon! It is you! Vallan, Iselle ..." he gasped. "But where have you been, what happened to you? How did you get here? Who are all these people?" He gestured towards the hundreds of armed soldiers behind Headon

"Uncle? What the blazes is going on?" yelled Ezera. Cairson turned, his face ecstatic.

"Oh, Ezera!" he exclaimed. "You are not going to believe this!"

"So, let me get this straight," Ezera said to Cairson and Headon, the next morning, as they walked out onto the gravel terrace. "There are - were - six evil wizards."

"Magi," interrupted Headon.

"Magi. They created the Hued gifts, years ago. Then Riathe turns out to be a Mage too."

"No," said Cairson. "They wanted to make him a Mage. But they failed."

"But he's a wizard? And a Hued? With a symbol like a pearl?"

"Yes," said Headon.

"Right. And he used the pearl to break the connection, you said, and that's why we lost our gifts."

Headon nodded.

Ezera turned to him. "He shouldn't have done that!" she said.

"He had no choice!" Headon exclaimed. "It was that or die! You have no idea what he was facing. Remember, they murdered Aven. They were going to destroy Hueron, everyone!"

Ezera frowned. "Even so, without our gifts, we're going to get destroyed anyway."

Cairson took her arm. "What's done is done," he said gently. "And at least now we have some hope."

"Hope?" said Ezera, glancing at the army, camped in dozens of tents and makeshift shelters on the lawns in front of the house. "You call that hope? A few hundred untrained soldiers?"

"Yes," said Headon. "Believe me, four months ago, we had no hope. None of us. None at all."

"Anyway," said Cairson, rubbing his hands together. "We've got a lot to sort out. Ezera, we're going to see about provisions. We may even have to kill one of the pigs."

He and Headon nodded at her, then walked round to the back of the house.

Ezera stayed for a while, leaning on her crutch and staring at the campsite. Smoke rose from fires, a few children ran around playing tag and giggling, and groups of grey-clad people sharpened spears, mended saddles or ladled porridge from cauldrons.

She still felt astonished to discover who the three Hued leaders were. Headon Alcastor, Vallan Sapphireborne and Iselle Topazborne; who had been thought lost for ever, and yet had survived capture, torment, and despair. And with them, the two Talthen, father and son, Felde and Riathe Sulvenor. Felde stood nearby, rubbing his hand along the neck of a sturdy, chestnut-coloured mare who nuzzled into his shoulder and neighed gently. He reminded Ezera of Durston, but much older and taller. He looked both strong and weary. And Riathe - the dangerous, powerful wizard who had destroyed the Gifts! Despite what Headon said, could he be trusted? She could see him wending between the tents. His pale, shimmering skin, his blonde, almost white hair made him easy to see among the crowds. His father paused to watch him with a wary, careworn look.

As the lad came towards them, Felde went to him. "Riathe?" Ezera heard him say. "You look tired. Did you sleep?"

"A little. I'm fine, Father. That woman, Ezera Mertrice is her name, isn't it? I need to talk to her."

Ezera limped over to them.

"Greetings, Felde, Riathe," she said. "Er, do you need anything? Let me know."

"Nay," Riathe said. "We don't need anything. Your leg ... What happened?"

"I broke it. When the gifts failed. It's a long story."

Suddenly he knelt on the grass before her. He opened his left hand and she saw the pearl, that hidden and unknown mystery, as a tiny insignificant sphere in his palm. As he touched her leg, the pearl glowed with a faint light and she felt a strange tingling as her bones reknitted and straightened, and the muscles strengthened. All the pain vanished. She gasped, bent down, stroked and stretched her leg, then looked at Riathe's intent, almost fierce expression.

Words failed her. She seized her crutch, flung it high into the air and twirled round and round, laughing with relief. Riathe stood up and closed his hand around the pearl. Before she could thank him, he strode off, flung himself onto the lawn at a distance and sat, staring at the campsite. Ezera turned to Felde. He shrugged.

"By the Powers! I can't believe it!" Ezera said. "Tell him - tell Riathe thank you. A thousand thanks!"

"Aye, I will." He turned back to his horse.

"Right! At last! I can really fight now, I can really start training those idiots properly." She turned to run around the house, to where she knew Gabrice and Tiron were, yet again, trying to teach the Hueds to use swords. But as she turned the corner, Cairson and Gabrice came towards her from the farmyard at the back. Headon was with them.

"Ah, Ezera. We've managed to get a few people sorting out provisions. But we were looking for you, to ask you something." Cairson said, then paused. He looked at her. "Seven Founders, Ezera! Your leg - it's ..."

"Riathe. The wizard. Healed it!" She explained briefly what he'd done.

"I'm so pleased," Cairson said. "Delighted! We need you fit and able to fight. We also need your advice. Headon has asked that we - all of us here - join their army as they go to Langron and then on to Hueron."

"Oh." She thought for a moment, then looked at Headon, at his scarred face and burnt hand. He had the resolute look of a leader who had battled against desperate odds for years but won through. Then she bent down and felt the restored muscle of her leg. "Yes," she said, straightening up. "Yes! I can think of nothing I'd rather do more."

"But it would mean leaving Marden House, the grounds, the gardens, all that we've planted and done here. Gabrice thinks we should stay here."

"Or at least, leave enough here to protect the house," Gabrice added.

"Powers above, why?" Ezera exclaimed. "It would be a waste of people. Don't you see? It's either stay here, and lose the house and everyone eventually, if this rumoured horde of bandits attack it, or leave and lose the house."

"True. I'm afraid that is our choice," Headon said.

"What does the house matter? The people matter! Our best chance to keep them safe is to join this army."

"That's what I feel," Cairson said, nodding seriously. "It breaks my heart to abandon the house, Gabrice, and I know it breaks yours. But it might survive what is coming. There is always a chance that we can return."

Gabrice nodded. "It's your house, uncle. Can't say I'm pleased, but, if that's what you want, I'll go with you."

Riathe glanced across at them, stood up and came towards them.

"Your house ... I think - I know that I can make it safe," Riathe said. "Let me try something."

Riathe walked towards the house front, then held up the pearl. Silvery mist flowed out from it. Ezera stared in amazement as he lifted his hands up and then apart. The mist coalesced into a wide glass wall, twelve feet high, and as thick as a man's body. Gabrice and Cairson gasped. Headon reached out and tentatively touched it. It was transparent, slippery and sheer.

"By the Powers," he whispered. "Riathe ... how can you do these things?"

"Astounding," Cairson said. "What is it?"

"'Tis made of the virtue of protection," Riathe said. "It can't be broken or climbed, although you could get over it with ladders."

"Can you do the entire house?"

"Aye, given time," he said, frowning. "It will be hard work. But, aye, I can. When we're ready to leave, I'll raise it round the house, and the gardens."

"Thank you," Cairson said, rubbing his hands together. "That is good. Very good."

Gabrice nodded his agreement.

"If you do that," Headon said. "Then we can all leave."

"But there's isn't much point me joining the army," Cairson continued. "I'm over sixty. I've never even waved a sword. How can I fight? And there's others like me. Children too."

"We should all go, uncle," Ezera said. "Of course we should join them!"

"And we need other help," Headon said. "Quartermasters, medical help. People to look after children, the sick and old. And the more of us there are, the better our chances."

"Oh. I see. Right. Agreed then," Cairson said, nodding.

"How many people here, did you say?"

"About eight score."

"Excellent! This will help immensely. And no doubt we'll recruit more on the way to Langron. It's important, vitally important, to have Hued and Talthen combined, working and fighting together, in the same companies. I'll go and tell the others. We need to leave tomorrow morning. Time is not on our side."

Ezera felt she could dance. At last! Help, rescue, hope. A cause she could fight for, leaders she could admire and follow. They may not have much chance, but it was better to try and to die, than to live like terrified caged birds in Marden. She looked down at the lightning-bolt mark on her palm. She may have lost her gift, but she could still fight.

CHAPTER 24
MURDER

Several days after leaving Marden, Felde lay, rolled up in his cloak, trying to sleep on the stony ground, when he woke to the sound of shouts, the clash of swords and the whinnying of horses. Leaping up, he ran through the darkness and trees towards the cries, drawing his sword as he went.

Headon and several others were already there, in a clearing on the edge of the camp. So was Riathe. He held his hand out and a pale light from his pearl illuminated the clearing. Six men lay dead on the ground, one in a grey tunic. Two young boys struggled in the arms of grey-clad men, while two other soldiers had seized a lanky, fierce-looking man, who glared defiantly at Headon and Riathe.

"What's going on?" said Felde.

"They were trying to steal the packhorses," said one of the soldiers. "But the sentries spotted them and sounded the alarm."

"They've stabbed one sentry in the back, but he's the only one we've lost," said another. "We've killed the rest of the swine, except these three. What shall we do with them? Kill them too?"

"I'm not sure. Did any escape?" said Headon.

"The wizard says not," the soldier replied, nodding at Riathe's pale figure.

"Well, we can't let them go, but I hadn't planned on taking prisoners," Headon said.

"Let me talk to them," said Riathe, the ghostly light hovering around him. He came close to the prisoners. "I give you a choice. Swear loyalty to us and join the army, or fight one of us to the death. If you fight and win, you're free to go."

Headon cursed under his breath. Felde stepped forward, but Riathe held up his hand to stop him and looked so fiercely at them both that Felde and Headon drew back. Riathe turned and stared at all three prisoners. The two young boys, looking scared and doubtful, dropped their eyes, muttering that they didn't want to fight. But the lanky man spat at Riathe.

"I'll fight you all if I have to, rather than join you cursed lot of traitors and bastard coloureds!" he snarled.

Riathe turned back to Headon.

"The two younger ones are half-starved farm boys, after money to buy food. They can join us and they'll be as loyal as any. But the other – he killed the sentry. He's a robber and a murderer and worse, and I recognise him from when I was at that bandit Ulban Hirshe's house, with the Magi. I'll fight him."

"Nay," Felde said. "Let me do it!"

Riathe shook his head, his face determined. "Don't worry. I won't lose," he said, releasing the pearl to float above him, and drawing his sword.

"Think so?" snapped the robber. He wrenched himself out of the soldiers grip and grabbed one of the swords lying on the ground. He lunged at Riathe, but the boy whipped his sword up and turned the blow easily.

The pearl floated overhead, casting a dim light in the darkness as they circled each other, attacking cautiously, testing each other's capabilities, or so Felde thought. Then the man darted forward, swiping down and across then back, but Riathe parried and riposted, missing by inches as the man side-stepped. He attacked again, fast and accurate, a rain of blows and cuts, his sword moving in a rapid blur. Felde thought with fear that the man might be too good. Would Riathe be able to beat him? He thought he'd seen the sword hit Riathe's shoulder, but the lad defended himself skilfully. Every attack he blocked, although Felde thought

Riathe missed chances to get through the man's guard. Then he realised that his son was deliberately prolonging the fight, knocking the man's sword aside with taunting ease, nicking his skin instead of taking the opportunity to make a disabling wound.

"Fight, won't you, you gutless coward!" the lanky man growled. "Or are you too scared? Scared Ulban will come after you if you kill me?"

At that Riathe started to press hard on his opponent, hitting his sword aside, slashing across his chest and leaving a bloody line. The robber yelled and brought his weapon down upon Riathe's exposed forearm. Felde had a moment of horrible fear, but the sword rebounded from Riathe's arm and the man flinched. The sword dropped from his hand. Riathe stepped back, allowing the man time to pick up his sword. He charged, but Riathe moved aside and turned to cut another scarlet line across the man's back. The robber assaulted Riathe with a rain of blows, every one parried with ease. Frustration on his face, he struck upwards, hitting Riathe's wrist and knocking his arm away. He slashed back down again, aiming for the boy's exposed front. Riathe dodged back and his sword whirled round and down in a scything arc. The man's sword flew aside. This time Riathe did not step back, but sliced across his opponent's face, drawing blood that streaked his cheeks and neck dark red in the pallid light of the pearl. The robber staggered and turned to reach for his sword, stumbled sideways, then fell. As he lay on his back, Riathe scored another red cut along his chest.

"That's for that girl!" he hissed, breathing hard.

"What girl?" the man gasped, staring up at Riathe's icy expression.

"At Ulban's house. The one the blue Mage gave to you, when he'd done with her," Riathe said. "What happened to her? I order you to tell me!"

"That skinny little slut?" he blurted out. "She starting wailing and struggling so there was no bearing her. I strangled her." He struggled up to his feet. "Give me my sword back, you whey-faced runt. I'll kill you!"

Felde dashed forward to intervene, but Riathe slashed at the robber. He knocked him to the ground again, and cut deep across his front. Blood stained the trodden grass around them. Riathe paused, staring down at the pain-twisted face of the robber, before pressing in his sword point and drawing a line from the man's throat down to his stomach and beyond. As he cut, the pearl steadied above him, glowing with a spectral light. The man screamed and writhed helplessly, unable to escape the relentless edge. At last, Riathe thrust his sword in deep and the robber collapsed into a dead and gory heap.

Felde breathed out as Riathe turned away, bitter satisfaction on his face, to wipe his sword on the grass.

"Get rid of the body, someone," was all he said.

"Search him first," Headon said. "See if he's got any money, weapons, decent boots that we can use. Then bury him somewhere. In a shallow grave. Let the rats and foxes get to him."

Headon turned to Riathe. "Are you hurt? He hit your wrist, didn't he?" he asked.

Felde grabbed Riathe's wrist and examined it. "You ain't hurt, are you?" said Felde. "Headon, remember? He's got the same invulnerability as the Magi had. Riathe, what girl did you mean?"

Riathe gazed down at the fading pearl as it settled into his hand. He looked at Felde with bewilderment, then his expression cleared.

"Oh. That girl. At Ulban's house."

"Ulban?" said Headon.

"Ulban Hirshe. I told you! The bandit, the robber chief. A crony of the Magi, curse them. Remember how they were plotting with him?"

"Aye. Planning to destroy the gifts, to start war between Talthen and Hued," said Felde.

"Oh, of course," said Headon. "And, as it turned out,

they didn't need to do anything. It's happening, despite them."

"But, the girl? Which girl did you mean, Riathe?"

"She was at Ulban's house. So young ... I tried to save her but I couldn't. The blue Mage took her and then passed her on to this man. I couldn't find out what happened to her. At least I know now."

"How did you know what the Mage did?"

"I've got all the blue Mage's memories. He gave her to that – to that foul brute. At least he won't murder any other girls. I'm glad I killed him, the bastard."

"Brute or not, Riathe, 'twas not a fair fight. You should've let me or Vallan fight him.".

"Nay. He deserved to die, and I wanted to be the one to kill him. You should think about what I know about him and the others at Ulban's house. Remember what I told you about them. I'm glad I was able to kill one of them. You taught me to fight, father, and I ain't going to be a just a wizard and nought else."

CHAPTER 25
ATTACK ON THE PRISON

Durston ran through the wrecked prison doors, then came to a sudden halt, gagging at the stench. He was in a stuffy, enclosed yard. Yellow foetid liquid trickled between cobblestones and filthy flagstones to a drain in the centre, unhindered by the heaps of decaying straw. The yard was open to the sky, but no breeze came through to remove the smell of urine, sweat and faeces. Wooden staircases led to two tiers of metal walkways lining the yard. Hued guards advanced cautiously towards the gate, but Durston ignored them. Tulketh's men, behind him, would deal with them. Durston ran up and down the stairs, from walkway to walkway, from locked cell to locked cell, his feet clattering on the metal grids of the walkways, shouting out his father's name. All around him gaunt, astonished, scarred faces stared at him. But none of them was the face he searched for.

Dozens of men from Tulketh's forces poured in: unlocking cells with keys taken from slaughtered Hued guards, smashing axes down onto shackles and chains, drawing bolts back, throwing doors wide open. Bewildered, frightened prisoners crowded around, grabbing Durston and others with trembling hands, gasping, "What be happening? Who be these?", or sobbing, "I'm free ... free?" They clutched at each other, crouching in shaking and shuddering groups on the rotten straw and cabbage leaves that littered the stained flagstones in the yard.

Durston dashed to Tulketh, who, with several others, had shoved and threatened the remaining guards into one of the cells. Tulketh twisted the key in the lock, grinned, threw it aside then turned to Durston.

"Well? Seen enough misery and pain to be loyal to us?" he demanded. "Still want your friends in Marden to be spared?"

Durston ignored him, thrust his fist through the iron bars, and seized a guard by the throat.

"Ren Halthe. From Sare. Where is he, you stinking piece of scum? Tell me!" he snarled.

The guard's pale blue face turned paler. He shook his head. "I don't know .. We don't know names ..." he gasped. Durston clenched his fingers into the guard's collar and twisted, harder and harder, until he began to choke, then Durston released him and shoved him back against the others.

"Swine," he hissed, and spat at him. He turned to Tulketh. "My father ... Ren ... he's in here. Or he was ..."

Tulketh shrugged. "They don't know. They don't keep account of who comes in or leaves in a box - or gets thrown into the quicklime pit. Some - " He stared steadily at Durston, his grey eyes narrowed. " - still alive."

The horror drenched Durston. He looked around. Every prisoner was emaciated, with stained rags covering weeping sores on their wrists and ankles, or blood-encrusted cuts and wounds. A young lad knelt by an old woman, and rocked her in one arm. His other arm was a mangled, suppurating stump.

Tulketh glanced at the boy and nodded significantly. "Aye," he said. "'Tis what you think. But there's more. Dungeons. Care to see?"

Durston drew his hand over his eyes, then shook his head. "Nay!" he said. "I've seen enough. I'm with you, Tulketh. Me, and the townsfolk too, I know. When I tell them ... Anyhap, I'll make your weapons, I'll recruit for you. All that I can. Whatever you need." He looked around. "'Tis clear, my father ain't here. He didn't survive - murdered, or driven to death. The Powers above and the Virtues below curse the City Guard for all time, for this."

"I knew you'd see sense. Now, help us get the remaining guards into the cells. A little of their own treatment, I reckon."

They herded the guards into cells. Tulketh ordered the less weakened prisoners to drag the wooden pallets from the cells; along with the flea-infested oakum mattresses, the worn blankets, the tables from the refectory; all into the yard. His men fetched documents and ledgers from the prison offices in the barracks nearby, and more furniture. Then they raked the dank, foul-smelling straw into a pile under the walkways and piled the documents, furniture and mattresses upon it, in a heap as high as a man.

Durston could not repress a shudder when he realised what Tulketh intended.

"Get the prisoners out," Tulketh ordered. "Ten of you stay, and you too, Durston, of course. I ain't going to let you miss this."

One of Tulketh's men lit a torch and passed it to Tulketh. The flames flickered and wavered, and shone a dark orange on Tulketh's high-cheek-boned face. Red glints reflected in his crafty, prominent eyes. He held the torch out to Durston.

"Your privilege, I reckon," he said.

"Nay. Nay!" said Durston. "'Tis too - nay!"

"Be you sure? Not even for your brother, your father, the girl they sent here?" Tulketh sneered.

"Cut their throats and have done with them," Durston said.

Tulketh shook his head. "Too swift. We Talthen demand visible, painful retribution." He jammed the torch into the straw. Others lit more torches and added their flames. One of the imprisoned guards, a woman, started to scream, a high-pitched, desperate screech. Another started sobbing and begging. Durston stepped back and clenched his fists, breathing deeply, but he did not dare intervene. As the smoke drifted up, a breeze took the flames and they licked the wooden stairs and the beams supporting the walkways. The fire grew and crackled, and the warmth spread as the doors of the cells started to smoulder, then burn. Cries and gasps and fear-filled wails came from the cells.

Tulketh turned on his heel. "Out," he said, jerking his head towards the splintered, wrecked doors.

Most of the prisoners, over a thousand of them, stood with Tulketh, his men and Durston on a rise of ground a few hundred yards from the prison. The screams from inside were drowned by the roar of the fire, as bright flames pierced through the narrow window slits and spiralled upwards from the roof and battlements. Durston looked at the satisfaction on Tulketh's face, then turned away. He told himself that the prison guards murdered his father, that they had done terrible things, that they deserved punishment. But this revenge was more appalling than he could bear. Quietly slipping behind Tulketh, and going unnoticed down the slope, he glanced into the barracks by the side of the dark bulk of the prison, where the weaker prisoners were being fed and tended by some of Tulketh's men. Even if his father was gone, at least those people had been rescued.

He strode back along the road that led north. As he passed the governor's house, he barely glanced at its ruined luxury: its smashed windows, overturned and fractured statues; nor did he look at the body of the guard that he had stabbed, lying with arms flung out in a pool of blood on the closely mown lawn. He didn't want to remember how he had felt killing a Hued. It was hard to believe it was only late afternoon, not dark night. The sun shone, and scents from blooming and unknown flowers still drifted from the garden behind the house.

It was only two days since Tulketh had rapped on his door, whispered of a change of plan, spoke of rumours of lost gifts and of another army preparing to bear down on the city, and told Durston of his and Ulban's decision to attack immediately, starting with the prison. And now

Durston's mind filled with unbearable images of the terror on the faces of the Hueds. Could that happen to Ezera now that she had lost her gift? He had not seen her since that day. After Tulketh's threats, he had not dared to go to Marden to see her. He did not dare admit to her how he had switched sides, although his whole body yearned for her wiry strength, for her passion, for her fierceness.

He tore his mind away, and remembered the boy with the mangled arm, remembered the agonised moans of his cousin as he collapsed under the whip of that cursed, foul Levin Bluestone. He would still go through with this revenge. He'd make a thousand arrows to pierce a thousand Hued hearts to avenge his father and brother. He'd join the army Tulketh was raising, and he'd persuade every fighter in Sare and Ceodrinne to join too.

He'd take the city apart stone by stone until he'd found and murdered Levin Bluestone.

CHAPTER 26
LANGRON

Felde knew he would never forget this homecoming. To ride into town, with Hueds as his equals, and his son, a wizard, beside him. To know that there was an army of over six hundred men camped outside the town under their command. To return to Langron, under an October sky, as a hero at last, despite his misgivings that he had done nothing to warrant this triumph. And all he really wanted was to see Berrena, and bring Riathe home.

He was surprised to see so many Hued faces amongst the townsfolk. Numerous people recognised them and called out questions and welcomes, or tried to stop them to ask for news, but they rode on. Kianne ran up and seized Riathe's arm, kissed his hand and wept out a torrent of noisy gratitude to him for rescuing her son Breck, until Riathe pushed her aside gently, saying, "I know, Kianne, I know. But let us get home!"

A tumultuous cavalcade of children, Kianne, her husband Alef Ciard, and other adults, including a few curious Hueds, followed them by the time they reached Felde's house. Laithan stood leaning on a stick in the front orchard, with a basket in his hand, watching Felde's eldest daughter stand on a bench to reach the apples on the higher branches. He turned, saw them, gasped and dropped the basket. Apples rolled over the grass and daisies. Felde's daughter yelled "Mother – they're back! Father's back! And Riathe too!" and ran into her father's embrace. The whole household, Aleythe with them, tumbled out into a melee of elation and hugs and exclamations, and massive flooding relief that near broke Felde's heart with joy. Felde lifted Berrena and whirled her around in delight, before letting her run to Riathe. Then she turned and saw the other Hueds. Her hand went to her mouth, and she paused, her eyes wide with astonishment. "Vallan?" she whispered, "No. Surely not. It can't be ..." and the tears poured down as she embraced him.

"We've got to go to Sarielle," said Felde, later on, raising his voice above the riot and laughter. "Leave the horses, we'll walk, all of us. The children too, Iselle and Nessa, everyone."

The procession set off, in a chattering cloud of stories and questions and explanations and reconciliations. Berrena and Iselle walked apart from the rest, talking quietly together. Felde saw Berrena reach out and put her arm around Iselle's shoulders and hug her closely. The younger children scampered around Headon and their father, demanding stories of the evil wizards, and Felde's eldest daughter reached up to hold her cousin Nessa's hand as she rode on Vallan's shoulders. But Riathe lingered behind, his eyes on his cousin Breck and on the golden hair of Aleythe as they walked together, hand in hand. Felde turned and saw his strained look and remembered that this homecoming was not all unalloyed joy for his son.

Before they reached the manor, they saw Sarielle walking quickly down the road to them, followed at a slower pace by a slender woman with thick, pure-white hair, and tangerine skin and eyes. When she saw them, Sarielle paused, staggered, then fell to her knees, holding out her arms. Vallan took Nessa from his shoulders and went to lift her and embrace her. The other woman stood still, her hands on her cheeks, immobile with disbelief. Then Headon ran to his mother.

Laithan put his arm around Felde's shoulders.

"'Tis as if you've brought them back from the dead," he said.

"But not Jorvund or Aven," Felde replied.

"Nay, but happiness enough, I think. You did well, Felde," Laithan said, watching the mothers holding their sons and stroking their faces in tearful delight, and Vallan calling Iselle and his daughter to come and meet Sarielle.

They walked on to the manor. Sarielle turned to Berrena and Felde, saying, "Someone from the town came and told us that Hued men, one blue, one green, and a pink Hued woman, were riding through the town with you and Riathe. We hardly dared believe it was true. So we had to come to find out! And as you see, Thera is here too – she came to me with other refugees after the gifts failed. Oh, it was so good to have my friend back! And I am a grandmother again too!"

She turned round to Iselle, walking a few paces behind.

"Avenessa is such a lovely name," Sarielle said.

Iselle looked at her with uncertainty.

"How pretty she is – she looks like you, Iselle," Sarielle continued, with an encouraging smile.

"How can you forgive me," whispered Iselle, "after all that has happened?"

"Thera taught me that grudges are heavy things to carry. I've learnt it is best to look forward," Sarielle said. She drew closer and kissed Iselle, who bent her head then lifted her hand to wipe the tears from her cheeks.

CHAPTER 27
COUNCIL OF WAR

"This really is a council of war, isn't it?" said Sarielle. "Do you remember the first one, all those years ago? Twenty years! How lightly we took it then!"

A council of war? Felde supposed that it was. He glanced round the crowded table in the dining room at Langron Manor. The estate manager from Langron Manor, Albis Karne, had joined the army leaders, Sarielle, Cairson and Thera around the table in the dining room. Headon had also invited one of the scouts, a sparsely framed Talthen with darting eyes.

"Yes. I remember it, only too well," said Headon. "Anyway, firstly – the situation in the city. What do we know?"

"Well, Berrena was in the city when the gifts failed," Sarielle said.

"Bee! You were in the city?" Felde exclaimed, turning to her. "What were you doing there?"

"Trying to get the council to change the laws, trying to find giftless and persuade them to come here," Berrena said. "Did you not know?"

Felde shook his head, and reached for her hand.

"What happened? What was it like?" Headon said.

"Panic," she said. "Pure panic. I was terrified." She glanced at Felde, squeezed his hand gently, then shook her head. "I won't go into it. I came back here, with one of the city guards."

"I was so worried! So fearful!" Sarielle exclaimed. "You can imagine. Anyway, she returned, thank the Powers.

Then, a few days afterwards, others arrived, looking for safety. They were so frightened and lost! Oh, I felt so sorry for them! Carrying their possessions, a few on horseback. Some with barely the clothes they were wearing, poor souls!"

"First it was only one or two families a day, then more and more. Too many to count," Albis said. To Felde he seemed less gloomy than usual. He had the satisfied air of a man whose dismal prophecies have come true and who is humming 'I told you so' in his head.

"We managed to find places for them, finding rooms here and there, even in haylofts or in tents in fields," Berrena said. "There must be nearly a thousand in all by now."

"A thousand?" exclaimed Felde. He glanced at his wife with amazement. "Bee, you must have worked all the hours sent to help them out!"

She smiled back at him, with that loving and clear look that he knew so well. "Aye, 'twasn't the easiest of work," she said, shrugging. "But what else could we do? Mother helped immensely, and Albis too."

"We have to get most of them to join the army," said Vallan. "The more Hueds mixed in with Talthen, the better."

"Anyway, eventually they stopped coming," said Sarielle. "Apparently the council have closed the city gates, the idiots!"

"Yes," said Thera. "At first the council denied what had happened, then insisted it was temporary and our powers would return. They made it a crime - treason - to say that the gifts had failed. That put hundreds into jail. Then when riots started they imposed curfews, shut the gates, and started forcibly conscripting men into the City Guard. I'm glad I left before then."

"It's even worse now," Albis said. "Met the last refugee to arrive, five days ago. He escaped by climbing the walls and then swimming across the river at night. According to him there are still thirty thousand trapped in the city.

Imprisoned by the council. No one can leave without their permission. He was talking about martial law, food rationing and fear everywhere."

"There are no limits to the council's folly!" said Thera. "If there is a worse course to take, they'll take it. They sent City Guards out to buy or commandeer food, and when farmers got suspicious, they sent out raiding parties at night. Of course, these were discovered, fought, and many men killed. Now the whole country is aware that the City Guard is weakened, Hueron defenceless and the gifts are gone."

Headon gestured to the scout. "Tell us what you know," he asked.

"'Tis bad. It couldn't be much worse. Did you hear what happened to the prison? The one outside the city walls, where they locked up them as couldn't pay their taxes?"

The others shook their heads.

"Some Talthen stormed it a week ago. They released all them inside, and locked the guards and the governor up in the cells instead. Then they set it on fire, burning them alive," he said with relish.

Sarielle and the others gasped. Felde clenched his fists. So many from Langron had been sent to that prison, and had never come out!

"The governor deserved that, for sure, by what I've heard," the scout said, with a shrug.

"He was - true, he was violent, greedy, sadistic. But to be burnt to death. Horrible!" exclaimed Thera.

"Aye, my lady," said the scout.

"And what's the situation now?" said Headon.

"Now? They've armed the prisoners, and hundreds of others, and there's hordes around the city. They've rolled farm carts and wagons outside some of the gates to block them. There's a thousand, maybe even fifteen hundred of them - 'tis hard to be sure."

"Fifteen hundred!" Felde exclaimed. How could they, with their ramshackle, tiny army take on that number, and then the City Guard? They would need hundreds of the refugees to join them, and weapons, and horses. 'Twas hopeless, he felt.

"That was three days ago," the scout continued. "Most of them are at the east gate. 'Tis clear, to me anyhap, they're waiting for starvation to weaken those inside. I can't think what else they're waiting for."

"How long will that be?" asked Headon. "Thera, what do you think?"

"There's water from the wells and the streams that go through, so it's only food. The bakers, fruiterers, butchers and so on, those sort of trades, they've usually got three or four weeks stock," replied Thera. "And the council did manage to buy some food in. But it's been over six weeks. They'll be starting to run out by now, even with rationing."

"Hmm. Difficult," said Headon. "I think we have about two weeks at most, before those in the city start to starve in earnest. That doesn't give us much time."

"We need more men," Cairson said. "Can we ask Hueds and the Langron townsfolk to join the army?"

"Yes, of course. We have to wait for the other apprentices to arrive, hopefully with more soldiers too."

"Apprentices?" asked Thera.

"The Magi's apprentices. They took five other Talthen lads, as well as Riathe. We've sent them back to their home towns, and asked them to come here. With recruits, we hope. They should be here any day now - if they are coming."

"Well, what's the plan, Headon?" asked Vallan.

"Prepare. Prepare for war."

CHAPTER 28
PREPARATIONS

That afternoon, Felde saw Laithan sitting on a bench in the town square, and joined him in the warm October sun.

"'Tis hard to believe," Laithan said, waving his stick at the grey-clad soldiers bustling through the square, crowding around the blacksmith, and practising on the field. "Hued and Talthen working together."

"Aye," said Felde, watching the preparations: the spears being thrown at targets, the horses being shod, the shields and daggers being allocated. "I can barely believe it myself."

"So many of them. How many now?"

"Over eight or nine hundred now, I reckon, but there are more joining every day. I've lost count."

Yesterday four of the apprentices had rode into Langron, to Headon's obvious relief and satisfaction. The apprentices had brought seven score recruits with them, and the quartermasters were now getting them kitted out.

In the field by the square, several dozen soldiers in a line aimed and shot at a long row of archery butts. Iselle walked up and down the line, watching and giving advice. Vallan stood with her, but when he saw Felde and Laithan he came across and sat with them.

"Well, Lord Sapphireborne," said Laithan. "Nearly ready, I think?"

Vallan grimaced. "I'm not Lord Sapphireborne. My father was, but I'm not. I don't want to own Langron, either. When this is over, I'll deed the property to the tenants. Langron Manor will be enough for me."

They watched Iselle as she continued to inspect the archers.

"She's picking the fifty best ones – she's going to lead a company into battle," Vallan exclaimed. "I said she should stay with Nessa, but she refused!"

Iselle must have heard, because she glanced at Vallan, finished helping the woman beside her to adjust her bow, then came over.

"Nessa will be safe enough at the manor with her grandmother." She tousled his hair and kissed his forehead. "You are leading a company too, yet you forget, my dear mutton-headed one, that you are nowhere near the fighter that you used to be."

"I'm still a captain from the City Guard. You weren't. Of course I will lead a company."

She raised her eyebrows at this.

"Well, I never had a fighting gift to lose, unlike you, and so I'm as good as ever I was. Remember I brought down two men in the forests before Peveque? Look!"

Iselle lifted her bow, slotted an arrow into place, aimed and loosed. The arrow sang through the air, hitting the centre of a target two hundred yards away.

"See!" she said. "I'm as good as you now, if not better. I'm leading a company into battle, whatever you think. I rather like the idea of fifty men to obey my every command," and she gave him a provocative, flirtatious glance, then laughed at his shocked face.

"If I were ten years younger, I'd be going into battle with you, in your company, Iselle," replied Laithan. "But I fear I'd be a more of a hindrance than a help." Felde remembered, with a shock, how old his uncle was. He still looked wiry and strong, but his seventy years of hardship had marked him with deep wrinkles, gaunt cheeks and white hair.

Riathe, Headon and Berrena came into the square and crossed over to join them.

"Felde, Laithan, can you come with us to Langron

Manor?" asked Headon. "Sarielle is waiting for us."

When they met Sarielle at the gatehouse, Headon said, "The manor is more defensible than the town. So we want all those too old or young to fight to move there. Felde, we could do with you and Laithan to help persuade townsfolk to retreat to the manor."

"I'm happy to help with that," said Laithan. "Of course."

"But they'll be still be vulnerable," said Berrena. "It's not that defensible, really, is it, Headon?"

"I suggest that we leave four companies of soldiers for protection," Headon replied.

"That won't be enough, will it, though?"

Headon shook his head. "Hmm, you're probably right. But we can't afford to leave more soldiers behind. We'll need them to take the city."

"I can protect the manor," Riathe said. "With a wall, like Marden."

"A wall?" exclaimed Sarielle. "By the Powers, how can you do that?"

"He can, Sarielle," said Headon. "I don't know how, but Riathe put a wall around Marden. Unclimbable, unbreakable."

"Goodness! Well, that would be wonderful!"

"But you will still have to patrol it," Riathe said. "The only way in will be front and back gatehouses, I'll leave them open. They'll be easier to defend, even with only two hundred soldiers."

"Thank you!" said Sarielle. "I will feel a bit safer, but it is still terrible. To have Vallan and you and Felde back and then to see you ride off to battle and not know if I'll see you again! Try to send news back, as often and as much as you can."

She turned to Berrena.

"That reminds me. Berrena, I hope you aren't intending to go with them!"

"Mother! Ain't that my decision?" exclaimed Berrena.

"I think Felde and I should have some say in it. And you should stay here to be with the townsfolk at the manor. They need their town chief to lead them."

"Well, I'm going with Felde and Riathe. Do you think I can bear to watch them ride away?"

"Berrena, just what do you think you're going to be able to do in a full-scale battle?" retorted Sarielle. "You know very well you can't use a sword!"

"I don't care! I've got to do something! I failed to get Hued status, I failed to persuade the council to do aught, I failed in our plan to warn the Talthen about the Magi!"

"Aye, but Bee, that doesn't matter now," interjected Felde. "The Magi are gone."

"I know, but I want to do something! I can help. I could, I don't know, organise supply lines or something. Be a scout, a messenger, anything!"

"I forbid it! As your mother, I order you to stay here, where it's safe. I can't risk losing you, Vallan, Felde, my grandsons, all in the same battle. Please, Berrena, please!"

"Bee," said Felde, taking her in his arms. "I want you to stay with me. But I can't fight if I'm worried about you. 'Twill be dangerous enough as it is. If you're there ... Look, Bee; stay here and join us the next day. One day apart, 'tis all."

He put her hand on her Binding.

"You being there ain't going to keep me from harm, you know that."

Berrena nodded. "All right. I'll wait one day. Then I'll ride after you. But 'tis hard. And unfair!"

It had not seemed possible to Felde, but over the next few days Langron grew even more crowded and bustling, clamorous with the noise of over twelve hundred soldiers preparing for battle. It appeared to be chaos, but Headon, Vallan and Riathe had set up a large table under an awning and were directing the preparations from there, along with two Talthen captains, their heads close as they conferred over a map. Hued and Talthen working together, Hueron no longer invincible, the Hued powers gone! Felde's mind struggled with the enormity of the changes, as he walked over to join them. To think that Langron, such an obscure town, was the centre of such an unexpected and massive shift in the world!

A sturdy, well-favoured Talthen rode into the square, saw the conspicuous ash-blonde hair of the wizard and called out to him. Riathe and the others turned.

"At last!" Headon said. "The missing apprentice! Halke, is that your name?"

"Aye. Halke Beorse. From Thulron, just north of Reshe."

"Good. We were wondering what had happened to you. The other apprentices returned four days ago."

"I hope I ain't too late," replied Halke. "I went the long way round, east and north, but I've brought over two hundred with me. All armed and ready."

"That makes nearly fifteen hundred fighting men," exclaimed Headon in jubilation. "Excellent! We are nearly ready!"

They talked together for a while, Halke telling them which villages he'd been through and how he'd persuaded Talthen to join, and Headon explaining their plans in response. Riathe listened, then suddenly looked around at something. Felde turned too, to see what his son was staring at. A scrawny, fair-haired man, wearing a pale grey jacket, strolled through the town square, looking with keen interest at the bustling people and purposeful activities. Riathe strode across to him, seized his jacket and pushed him against a wall.

"You!" he hissed. "Who's your captain?"

The man looked terrified.

"Riathe!" exclaimed Felde. "What are you doing?"

"This man," said Riathe. "I know all the Talthen in the army, and everyone in Langron. But not him. He's a spy. From the army outside Hueron."

"A spy! Are you sure? He could have come with Halke."

"Halke!" Riathe called. "Is this one of yours?"

Halke looked at the man and shook his head.

"You see. I'm sure. Headon, come here. See this man?" Riathe gripped the man's jacket tighter and stared into his eyes, as Headon strode up. "Are you a spy?"

"A spy!" Headon exclaimed.

"Aye, but how did you know?" the man replied, his voice trembling.

"Never mind! So what shall we do with you?"

The man gulped in fear at the expression on Riathe's face.

"We'll use him, Riathe," said Headon. "This could be to our advantage."

Riathe looked at Headon for a moment, then nodded.

"Right," he said, turning back to the man. "Listen to me. We won't hurt you and you can go back. But first, tell me the truth. How many of you are there, who leads you, what are you going to do with the city? And would you negotiate a surrender? Speak, curse you!"

"There's over two thousand of us in the Liberation Army and more joining every day."

"Liberation Army?" Headon said, and laughed. "Who are you liberating?"

"The Talthen! From you cursed coloured devils!"

Headon shrugged. "We are not devils," he said. "So who's joining you?"

"People from the villages, and all them from the prison when it burnt down. You may laugh, but they've been liberated. You wouldn't laugh so loud if you'd seen inside that hell-hole!"

"Well - perhaps not. Anyway, your leaders? And your plans?"

"Tulketh Jobe and his friends. He's sent me. We're going to take the city. All the goods, money, houses, horses, jewels. Take the women. Kill the adult Hueds. Take the children as slaves."

"Liberation indeed! And would Tulketh negotiate?"

"Nay. Not for ought you'd offer. They want revenge on the Hued and they're fierce and not easily scared."

"Unlike you!" sneered Riathe.

"Is that the truth?" asked Headon.

"Aye, he's speaking truth."

"Good. Well, more than we thought, numbers wise," remarked Headon. "But the rest is as I expected."

"Listen!" ordered Riathe. "Go back. Tell them there's barely a thousand of us and we're planning to attack in a month. Now go! Run!"

"Clever!" said Headon, as they watched the man scurry down the road. "Lull them into a false complacency. That was a good idea, Riathe. It was fortunate that you spotted him."

CHAPTER 29
BEFORE THE BATTLE

Ezera dodged from tree to tree, then, as she neared the edge of the patch of woodland, dropped to her hands and knees. She scrambled forward, her hands scraping on pebbles and tough grass among the fallen leaves. The scent of damp earth and bracken dust filled her nostrils, and with it a faint smell of woodsmoke. Buzzards circled in the clear sky overhead, calling pee-yow in faint mews high above her.

Then Ezera heard the chink of metal, voices, neighing, the occasional shout. She flattened herself on the ground and squirmed forward as slowly and quietly as she could, through the undergrowth and rustling bracken. Glistening black berries hung from the arching stems of a bramble. Ezera carefully reached her arm up, picked a few and ate them, grinning at their sweet juiciness. During the march from Marden and while in Langron, the Grey Army had had provisions, thanks to the Grey Wizard's powers and the gold that the leaders could give to Talthen farmers, but there was never quite enough of the plain bread, apples and rabbit stew that Ezera had been living on for the last few weeks.

Don't get distracted, she muttered, and wriggled to the edge of the escarpment, then peered through the foliage. The ground dropped away in a hummocky rocky slope, facing south and festooned with feathery clematis, arching rose stems with bright red rose-hips, and dark-berried elderberry bushes. At the bottom, the green meadows of the Hueron plain spread wide. In the distance, she could see glimpses of the river between the willows that lined it and beyond that, the walls of the city. Jarial was probably somewhere in there, she thought, and wondered if she'd see him again. No doubt he'd be a lot thinner, and a lot less proud of being Hued.

She could just make out the many coloured flags hanging limply in the windless afternoon. The east gate was visible and seemed to be, as far as she could see, not blocked. But, on the plain between her and the gates, an army swarmed.

Ezera loosened her dagger, just in case. Among the smouldering camp fires, horses patiently standing, and the patches of dull white and beige canvas upon the meadows, she saw stands of weapons: dozens of spears and swords, bows and arrows, pikes and clubs. Keeping low, all her senses alert for any sound of movement behind her or below her, she tried to count the tents and people. A few sentries stood in groups, but they seemed to be idly talking or gazing at the city, and some leant half-asleep on their spears.

Those sentries should be shot, she thought. They weren't watching at all and weren't going to be a problem. But the army would be. It was bigger than they thought, and well-armed.

She turned and wriggled back towards the cover of the trees. As she went, a bramble scratched her arm with a vicious thorn. She yelped and then cursed, realising she might have been heard by the sentries. Heart racing, she jumped up and ran, dashing from tree to tree, zigzagging from side to side, then speeding as fast as she could. After a mile, she had to slow down. Going behind a tree, she stopped and peered round. No one. She breathed out. What an idiot!

When the army leader, Headon Alcastor, had asked the captains to provide five soldiers to scout ahead, she hadn't bothered to ask her company, but had immediately volunteered herself. "I know the terrain," she'd said, thinking about this oak wood and escarpment, and the clear view that it gave. She had been proud and delighted when, back at Marden, Headon and Cairson had suggested that she became a captain, but if she'd been so stupid as to have been heard by those sentries, then followed and given away the Grey Army's size and position, it didn't bear thinking about. Demotion would be the least of it.

An hour later she reached the camp and went straight to Headon's tent. The other leaders were there, along with the other four scouts, looking at a map spread on the table.

"Ah, Ezera," Headon said. "Your report?"

"I would estimate well over two thousand in the army, maybe almost three. Not many horses, but a lot of weapons. I mean, a lot! And, as we hoped, the east gate is not barricaded, unlike the others. I'm assuming that's the one they plan to use to invade."

"That agrees with what the other scouts said. Thank you."

"Their sentries are hopeless: idling around, not watching at all! We've got a good chance of getting close, using the woods as cover, without being seen or heard, especially if we use these woods here." She pointed to the map, to where a thick plantation of firs blanketed the side of a low hill.

"Ah. I see. Excellent."

"But, even so, 'tis going to be harder than we thought," said Felde. "Much harder."

"Yes. But they don't have many horses. And surprise will help."

"True," said Vallan. "So, silence, no fires overnight, no talking when we move in the morning. Muffled hooves, that sort of thing. I'll get the word out to the captains."

"Thanks. And we have a wizard. Riathe, we are relying on you to do something to tip the odds in our favour."

"I know!" Riathe said. "I've thought and thought, but I can't make people invulnerable. And I can't kill or disable hundred of attacking soldiers at once. All I can think of is to deflect arrows from us. And when attackers are close to me and I can look into their eyes I can stop them. But I want to fight, not hang back and protect others. So I'm going to ride into battle with you, nothing more."

There was a long silence, then Headon shrugged.

"Well, as you wish. The whole thing is a mad and risky venture anyway. But I'd rather die trying to rescue my people in Hueron than imprisoned by Magi hundreds of miles away. So - we move at first light tomorrow and attack as soon as possible."

In the dim early light of the next morning, shreds of mist from the river clung to the grass and trees of the plain below. The air was still, the quietness broken only by the whispering chinks of bridles and stirrups, and the occasional snort of a horse. The Liberation Army's tents were hidden by low lying mist, and the city walls were a pale barrier barely visible to Ezera and the other captains and leaders, as they waited in the resinous dampness of the pine forest.

Headon, his face alert and intelligent, sat on his horse in front of her and the other six captains with their companies. Last night, when Headon told the captains the overall plan, he had explained that because the companies on the left would reach the city wall and be seen by the defenders first, he would lead them. They had put most of the Hued there. "Then maybe the City Guard will believe we are coming to rescue them and won't fire on us," he had said.

Leaning forward and looking left, Ezera could see the pale face and white hair of Riathe, with his companies in grey, and beyond him, the tall figure of Felde, and the mass of soldiers behind him, just visible between the trees.

The light grew. Through the drifting mist, she could make out Vallan and Iselle's six companies of archers, almost half a mile to the west, and hidden from the besiegers by a narrow belt of trees. They were creeping slowly and silently to within bowshot range, on the north side.

Still the camp outside the city stayed quiet, the sentries silent.

Ezera's horse pawed the ground, shaking his mane and

shying sideways. Ezera steadied him with a calming hand on his neck, "Easy boy, easy. Not long now," she murmured. She knew there were hundreds of armed soldiers, many on horseback, behind her and the other captains, but also that there were nearly three thousand on the plain ahead. Even so, her heart beat quickly with exultation. At last, she breathed, at last, a reason to fight! It was hard not to put her heels to her horse and charge gleefully at their enemies, but she bit her lip and told herself to wait.

CHAPTER 30
FIRST ATTACK

The signal came. Felde heard the distant sound of a trumpet, a long single note, and saw the arrows from Vallan's companies flying through the air, hissing down on the tents and sentries. Headon took out his sword and raised it, and Felde heard the captains and leaders shouting "Charge!" He joined in, his heart racing, his breath fast as he roared "Charge!" with all his strength.

With increasing speed, the Grey Army rode out of the forest and down the slope of the hill, fanning out as they reached the grassy meadows around the city. Cantering with spears dipping forward, helmets and shields shining brass and silver, then galloping across the turf, their horses' breath steaming, harnesses rattling, hooves pounding the ground. Foot soldiers ran behind the cavalry, with swords held high or spears levelled toward the enemy.

Headon had said the main aim was to split the other army in two, and then to make it to the east gate. His orders echoed in Felde's head as his companies rode straight into the centre of the Liberation Army's camp at full speed. From the tents ahead surprised, panicked men seized spears from racks and shouted, some frantically trying to saddle horses, others running away desperately. Only a few were ready and armed. As he galloped onwards, Felde could see, through the shreds of mist still clinging to the ground, glimpses of men lying dead or injured from the arrows on the northern flank. Then they were hidden once more, as the opposing soldiers, men and horses, met the Grey Army companies and leaders in violent collision.

The air rang with the clashing sound of the onslaught as

their charge smashed into the first tents and clusters of sentries and horses. They struck men down, unseated riders and sent their horses into a terrified stampede. Weaving between tents and fires, Felde and his men fought and hacked their way through the camp, heading towards the city walls.

Felde glanced to his right and saw Riathe, his pale skin and white hair easy to spot in the melee around him, his sword striking viciously, his face cold and relentless. He heard yells, and glanced round as a group of armed men ran towards them. Breathing hard, Felde defended himself desperately, as he realised that they were now facing the main body of the besieging army; experienced, fierce men, some on horseback, and all well-armed. The advantage of their surprise charge had gone. The Grey Army were forced into a hard fight, as more and more men appeared in front of them. Felde heard the cries as several of his men behind him were cut down, but he pressed on, hoping the others behind him would follow his lead and that they would be able to battle through.

Surrounded by people trying to kill him, he had never felt so alive. Every sense thrilled with alertness, every muscle tingled with power and every nerve vibrated with energy. The blood pounded in his heart and head. His arm ached with the work, his shield dented under relentless blows. Swords clashed, spears drew blood, stray arrows flew past. One struck Felde in the back of his shoulder. He barely had time to snap the shaft off before parrying a thrust from a pock-marked foot soldier's pike with his shield then bringing his sword down with a crashing blow that knocked his opponent to the ground. He turned to face a rider and unseated him with a fast sweep of his sword, pulled his horse aside to dodge a thrown spear, thrust his sword into another's chest then yanked it free, before turning to find his next enemy.

But all he could see were a few score of his own grey-clad soldiers, a couple of captains and one standard-bearer on horses, circling round an empty space between ripped tents and scattered wood-fires. For a brief moment of calm there were no enemies to fight, but he glimpsed skirmishes between the fluttering canvas of the tents, and could hear yells and clashing metal and jangling harnesses, the whinnying of frightened horses, and the groans and screams of fallen men. There was a smell of blood and wood smoke in the air, and red splashes of gore over his arms and the shoulders of his horse.

"Have we beaten them, sir?" gasped one of the captains.

Felde replied, "I doubt it. How many have we lost? How many wounded?"

The captain looked around.

"About a score dead that I know of, and as many wounded - able to ride or walk but not fight. Where are the other companies? What now, sir?"

Felde saw the city walls to their right and thought he could make out, between the tents and horsemen and mist, the main body of the Grey Army near to the gate.

"We've got separated from the rest. Keep together, wounded in the middle. We need to get to the gate."

Suddenly dozens of men rode from behind the tents, between them and the gate, and attacked. Felde's men had to fight their way through. One Hued man fell, his horse brought down by a bearded giant of a man who then tried to cut Felde down, swinging his sword and wounding Felde in the calf before another grey-clad captain dispatched him with a sweeping cut that sliced through his skull.

Felde yelled, "There's too few of us – we've got to get to the others! Ride! To the gate!"

The captains led as they galloped towards the rest of the army, Felde riding behind to guard the rear, trying to ignore the stinging pain in his leg. They were within a few hundred yards of the east gate when an arrow thudded into the neck of Felde's horse, then another and another. It reared up and staggered, nearly throwing Felde, then fell sideways. They crashed to the muddy, churned-up ground together, Felde's leg wedged under the body of his horse, his sword arm crushed under him. His horse thrashed as blood pumped from the pierced arteries in its neck, then it lay still. Felde felt a brief pang of sorrow for his favourite mare, but his leg screamed with agonizing pain, wedged under the horse's bulk. Hampered by his shield, he could not get his sword arm free.

As he struggled against increasing faintness and darkness to free his leg, he heard, among the shouts and clashes, someone yelling his name. He felt them pushing at the dead weight of his horse, cursing loudly, then yanking at his arms and dragging him free. Felde thought he must have knocked his head as he fell; the woman bending over him looked so familiar, with her chestnut-brown skin, short hair and square face.

"Aven?" he exclaimed.

"No, sir. Ezera Mertrice. Aven was my cousin," she said.

"Aye, of course. Ezera. We met ... at Marden."

"Sir, can you walk?"

Felde struggled to his feet. His shoulder and sword arm seemed usable, if bruised, but his leg gave way as he tried to walk. He reeled sideways as the dull hurt in his leg grew into sharp, insistent pain. Ezera grabbed his arm, and he leaned on her.

"Not sure, give me a moment," he muttered.

"There isn't time – I don't think we get the chance for breathers during battles."

Felde laughed, despite the stabbing pangs from his leg and shoulder. He glanced around. The ground mist was clearing but it was hard for him to make out where they were in the chaos of skirmishing groups, over-turned tents and running men.

"You - Ezera - you're a captain in one of Headon's companies?" he asked.

"Yes, I got separated in the fighting. It's been chaos!" she said, a look of excitement on her face.

Then a trumpet sounded; three high, rising notes ringing

out over the noise of fighting.

"Hear that! They've reached the gate!" Felde exclaimed. "Where are the others?"

Ezera pushed her hair back from her face and stared towards the sound. "They're nearly at the gate," she said, then whirled round. "Hells curses, my horse! Oh, what a fool! I dropped the reins when I saw you trapped, and now it's gone. We have to get to the gate! Try to walk."

But before they could move, three opponents ran at them, swords unsheathed.

"Quick, sir, back-to-back, lean on me," Ezera shouted.

She killed the man attacking her, disarming him with an upwards flick of her sword then stabbing him. Felde's sword arm still felt weak, but he parried his attacker with his shield and swiped out with his sword, hitting the man's arm more by luck than skill, knocking him sideways so that Ezera was able to finish him off. The third was an inexperienced lad, looking both fierce and terrified, his wavering sword leaving his guard wide open.

Felde knocked the boy's weapon aside and, feeling as if he was drowning a kitten, struck his head hard with his sword hilt. The lad crumpled sideways. *I hope he is only knocked out*, thought Felde. But there was no time for pity. Some of the strength had returned to his leg.

"Back," he said to Ezera. "Get to the rest of the army."

"Can you run for it?"

"Nay, I can walk, but I can't run. You could leave me, you know."

She grinned and shook her head. "I don't think so!" she said.

"You're a brave woman. Together then."

Watching for attackers, they moved warily backwards to the gate, side-by-side, as quickly as Felde could manage. The fighting around them diminished. Dead bodies and wounded men lay among fallen tents and scattered weapons. Riderless horses galloped, panic-stricken, among the debris. Felde looked behind. The smooth, white walls of the city rose up in the distance and he could see banners fluttering, and make out faces peering over the battlements and sunlight glinting off weapons. Groups of men clustered around the gate, but he could not make out who they were.

Ezera stumbled and fell backwards over a grey-clad body with a dagger sticking up from its back. As Felde pulled her up to her feet a spear, thrown by a scrawny woman running towards them, pierced his shoulder with a thudding, excruciating blow. He fell back and another dart of pain jabbed through him as the arrowhead in his back drove farther in. Ezera leapt at the scrawny woman and wrestled frantically with her. She fell, and Ezera stood up, wrenching her knife out of the woman's neck.

"Sir! Are you all right?" Ezera panted, kneeling beside Felde.

"Nay! I feel like a pincushion. Help me pull this out," he groaned.

She pulled at the spear and yanked it out of his shoulder. Blood flowed from the wound and pooled onto the crushed grass and mud around him.

"I think that was a mistake," murmured Felde. His head spun and a dizzy sickness filled him. He could feel his strength draining away.

Ezera yelled towards the soldiers by the gate, "Help! Over here! Lord Sulvenor is hurt!"

Lord? When did I become a Lord? thought Felde.

She knelt by him, put her arms under him, and heaved, then shook her head.

"You're too heavy for me to carry," she muttered, breathing hard. "I need help!"

Suddenly, from between the bodies, riderless horses and wrecked tents around them, Felde saw a burly man rushing forward, grimacing and shouting and waving an axe. And, from the walls, he heard a distant, urgent cry of "Ezera! Ezera!"

Ezera lifted her head at the sound. "Jarial?" she said, looking wildly around. She stood up. The burly man ran into her and struck her head violently with the shaft of his axe. She fell to the ground, curled up and groaning. The man stood over Felde, the axe raised high above his head. He was so close that Felde could see the sweat running down his cheek and the fierceness in his narrowed, red eyes. The man snarled, saliva dripping from his mouth, then brought the axe down, fast and hard. Felde, with a huge effort, managed to block the blow with his shield. A spasm shot through his arm as the shield edge jabbed into his wrist. The man raised the axe again. Felde was unable to move. His shield arm hung useless. He could not even lift his sword with his weakened right arm. He looked up helplessly at the sharp, crimson-stained edge of the axe above his head.

CHAPTER 31
IS IT RESCUE?

Jarial leaned against the cold stone of the parapet and gazed down at the confusion. He could see thousands of soldiers and riders, a vast moving mass of chaos. They'd heard, early in the morning, a trumpet, then the sounds of shouts, yells, metal against metal, screams, neighing horses and the raging of a furious battle. After the trembling, whispering silence of the city, the noise was shocking. For the last eighteen days, since the army had surrounded them, all they had heard from outside the walls was laughter and taunts, and the sound of wagons being dragged against the gates and of knives being sharpened.

Tiere, standing next to him, muttered, "What is going on? Can you see?"

"It's impossible to see. Too far," a woman nearby said. "Who are they fighting?"

Jarial squinted against the low autumnal sun.

"If they are fighting someone, maybe - maybe it's hopeful. A rescue?" he said. "Do you think they've got anything to eat?"

"Don't be an idiot!" she exclaimed. "Who's going to rescue us or feed us? No, they're scrapping over who's going to - to take the city." She collapsed to her knees, and hid her head in her hands.

A breeze blew the sour smell of sweat; of hungry, sick people from the crowds on the streets below up to them. By now, all the stores had been emptied. They'd slaughtered and eaten all the horses, cats, dogs, pigeons, even the fishes from the fountains. They'd fought each other to get the rosehips from the gardens, and the acorns from the oak trees in the parks. Thirne's soups had become nothing but hot water, leaves, grass and the sweepings from the grain store. Remembering how he had pushed aside a scrawny lad in order to grab at a fallen, bruised apple, Jarial hung his head. To think he'd once been proud of being Hued. Now he was nothing. They were nothing, nothing but a ragged crowd of starving people with no cause to boast anymore. As if on cue, Jarial's stomach rumbled loudly. Someone sniggered.

"A choice between starving to death or being slaughtered. By the Founders, what a choice!" another soldier muttered.

They stood and watched. Levin and the other captains strode behind them, watching too. Levin grabbed the hair of the crouching woman. "Up!" he hissed, and yanked her upwards. Yet again, Jarial wondered how Levin had managed to worm his way back into command after the disastrous attack on the mill at Reshe. Lies and boot-licking, no doubt.

The battle surged, heaved, moved closer to the walls. They could see hundreds of men and women, mostly in grey uniforms, in the centre of the camp, hacking and fighting towards the east gate.

Suddenly Jarial leaned over the wall, with a sharp intake of breath. He could barely believe his eyes.

"Powers above!" Tiere shouted, pointing below.

"Oh, I don't believe it. It's not possible!" someone else exclaimed. "Look!"

The woman leaned forwards. "Hueds!" she gasped.

Levin and the captains ran forwards and pushed them out of the way. As the fighting drew nearer, they could see that some of the grey-clad soldiers were Hued.

"Rescue?" Tiere said. "Do you think it is, Jarial? Are they really ..."

"Yes. Yes!" exclaimed Jarial. "We need to help them!"

He lifted his bow and notched an arrow.

"Curses!" Levin snapped. "What are you doing, you

pathetic excuse for a soldier?"

"No arrows! Don't waste them!" another captain shouted. "Orders are to save them. Put that bow down!"

Reluctantly, Jarial lowered his bow. The armies were out of range anyway. They all stood, silent, watching, hoping.

The mists slowly dispersed and the sun rose into an incongruously blue sky. The battle moved within bowshot and they saw dozens, hundreds of Hueds, their bright coloured faces and hair obvious among the Talthen.

"What are they doing?" one of the captains muttered.

"They're definitely making for the gate," another said.

"Do we shoot them?"

"Shoot our own people? Don't be an idiot!"

"But they've got dullards with them. Look!"

Suddenly, among the chaotic struggling and skirmishing below, Jarial saw a brown-skinned woman wearing grey. His heart beat faster. It couldn't be ... But it was. Ezera! She was with a tall, broad-shouldered dullard - a Talthen - who limped next to her, leaning on her. Jarial saw her stumble and fall. The Talthen pulled her up but then Jarial saw him get knocked down by a spear. As Ezera knelt by him - to help him, Jarial assumed - a huge man with an axe came up behind her. Jarial yelled her name as loudly as he could. He saw her glance up, but it was too late. The man hit her and she fell. Jarial's heart stopped as he saw the axe raised. Rapidly, he lifted his bow, pulled back the string as fast and far as he could, aimed and loosed. He saw the axe fall and rise again. He aimed and loosed again, and again.

Suddenly he felt Levin's arm around his neck, choking him.

"You snivelling, useless lump!" Levin snarled. "Didn't you hear the order! Don't loose! Just leave the bastards to fight it out. I'll have your neck on the block for this."

As he tightened his hold on Jarial's throat, the other captain strode up and shouted into Levin's face. "You're an idiot! Don't you recognise them?" He gestured over the parapet. "That's my nephew, left a week after the gifts failed.

185

And her, over there, see! She's my friend's daughter!"

Levin released Jarial, who sank to his knees, and then turned on the captain. "Then they're traitors. I remind you - we've got orders!" he said.

"Powers curse the orders," the captain said coldly, and drove his fist hard into Levin's cheek. Levin crumpled. The captain turned to the others. "New orders. By the seven Founders, I order you to shoot anyone you see trying to hurt Hueds. And I want a squad of twenty volunteers to go out through the gate with me, to try to meet their leaders and to find out what the blazes is going on!"

Hardly daring to believe that he now had a chance to find Ezera - if she had survived - Jarial hauled himself to his feet. His throat burned, he couldn't speak, but he could put his hand up to volunteer.

CHAPTER 32
PARLEY

Felde stared upwards at the axe blade, his heart pounding with fear. A soft whirring sound cut the air as an arrow flew above him. It pierced the burly man's cheek. He reeled backwards and dropped the axe as another arrow hit his neck and another sank into his chest. He crashed to the ground. Felde struggled up. Blood still poured from his shoulder. Ezera coughed and choked, but she pulled herself up and crawled over to him.

"That was close," she muttered. "A bit too close."

"Where did those arrows come from?" Felde gasped.

"From the city wall. From the Hueds inside, I think."

Felde tried to stand, but he felt light-headed from pain and from loss of blood. He staggered, then fell onto his hands and knees. The early morning mist appeared to be returning. He could dimly make out people and horsemen surrounding them and hear people shouting. Someone pulled Ezera away, but he could not see who it was. Then two white arms wrapped around his chest in a firm embrace. Their paleness shimmered indistinctly in his fading sight as he felt them lifting him up. Heat and strength flowed into his leg and arm. The bleeding in his shoulder stopped. Someone pulled the arrow from his back, but he felt no pain. Energy poured through him. His body tingled. He took a great gulp of fresh, cool air and he could feel the blood flooding back into his limbs. The dimness in his sight cleared. He stood up, blinking and looking around. Riathe stood in front of him, staring at him intensely, breathing out a sigh of relief.

All was bright and clear. Ahead, the city wall glowed pale

yellow in sun, against a blue sky. Felde and Riathe were surrounded by grey-clad men, many on horseback, with Ezera among them. Although the air stank of sweat and blood, although sounds of fighting could still be heard and the soldiers around him looked begrimed and dusty, soiled in dirt and gore, they appeared exultant.

Felde found the others with the company captains by the standards near the gate.

"It worked!" Vallan exclaimed, shaking Felde's hand excitedly. "They've retreated!"

"There's still some minor skirmishing going on, but those on the north side are scattered," Headon said. "The arrows from your companies, Vallan, Iselle, they did the trick. Excellent."

"Thanks," Iselle said, her face flushed. She put her bow down, and looked ruefully in her empty quiver. "I'll need to get some more arrows from somewhere. I'll go and ask around."

"Riathe fought ferociously," Vallan said. "I think many of them were completely unnerved by him. I don't know how many he killed, but between us all, we did well. Hundreds of them killed or wounded!"

Felde looked around to see the Grey Army spread out under the high city walls. Ezera was there, talking to other captains and some of the men in her company. She turned, caught his eye, winked at him, and Felde was reminded again of Aven and her courage and fierceness, so long ago.

"How many did we lose?" asked Felde.

"A hundred men or so, but we have more wounded. Headon had a nasty cut on his arm and I got a spear in my thigh," Vallan answered. "Riathe healed us. He's going round the seriously wounded soldiers, healing them too."

"It could have been far worse, thank the Powers," Headon said. "And we can rest and regroup now."

Several arrows whirred overhead, making Felde glance up.

"The archers on the walls have helped," Headon said, looking up too. "They're protecting us and giving us time to recover."

"They think we're on their side, then?"

"Probably. They can see Hueds in our ranks. Someone from the City Guards shouted down to ask, and I said we were on their side. I'm not sure they believed me, but at least they're not firing on us. And a small group, barely a score, came out of the gate, spoke with some of the captains, and have enlisted."

"Only a score?"

"Yes. There won't be any more. Riathe has sealed the gate in case they attack us from behind." He smiled wryly. "We can only deal with one army at a time."

"What's our next move?"

"Rest while we can and get the injured sorted out. We think there are over two thousand of that army left, so we are still outnumbered. When they've regrouped, they'll attack, despite the arrows from the walls. They won't give up a prize like Hueron so easily."

"It's not over," said Vallan.

"Good!" Felde said. "Do we charge them again, or wait for them to charge us?"

"I don't know which is best. I don't want to get pinned against the city wall so probably we should attack first," said Headon. They looked over the blood-sodden meadows, scattered with dead men and fallen horses, to where the other army swarmed, half a mile away to the south-east. Despite the bright autumn sun shining in their faces, they could see hordes of men re-arming themselves, preparing to fight. A group of a dozen riders cantered towards them across the battlefield. As they watched, the riders lifted up a spear with a torn square of white cloth attached to it.

"Surrender or parley?" wondered Headon.

"What do we do?" Vallan said. "Let's ignore them. Or attack."

"Hmm. No, we won't ignore them. We can use this to

buy time. Felde, I think it would be best if you went, rather than me or a Hued. I want to organise the men here, talk to the captains, and ascertain our strength. Take a company with you, and find out what they want."

As they came within earshot of the group, the captain by Felde's side shouted "Lord Sulvenor wishes to know if you intend to surrender?" Felde drew himself up in his saddle and tried to look lordly, but suspected that he had failed. The other riders pulled up their horses. In front rode a slightly-built Talthen, with high cheekbones and sandy coloured hair.

"Lord? Well, then I'm Lord Tulketh Jobe," he sneered. "Surrender? Not by the Powers. We are being practical. There's little point in us fighting you, or the other way round. Whoever wins won't have enough men left to take the city."

"What do you want?" Felde asked.

"I'm giving you a chance," Tulketh said, with a thin smile. "You can join with us, and share the city."

Felde tried to think what Headon would say. He looked at the huge Liberation Army massed behind Tulketh, and back at the city.

"'Tis a rich prize ..." he said.

"Aye. Plenty for everyone in there."

"We'll think about it."

"What's there to think about? But we'll give you an hour to come back with your answer, or we'll ..." He gestured at the swords and spears in the army behind him.

Felde wheeled his horse round and cantered back to the Grey Army. When he told the others of the offer, Headon smiled.

"Good!" he said. "An hour's plenty of time and means the sun will not be in our eyes so much. I've told the captains to get everyone ready to attack. Vallan and Iselle are taking the best archers to the north side to shoot from there. We'll try to push them back into the river, if we can. But we've lost the advantage of surprise."

"Aye," said Riathe, "but now we have the advantage of fear. Many of them are terrified of me. Headon, let me take our answer back."

"Fine, but why?"

"I have an idea," Riathe said, with a subtle smile. "Something that will make them even more terrified."

CHAPTER 33
SECOND ATTACK

Durston sat, cleaning the blood from his sword with a rag, while the Liberation Army waited. The sudden, merciless onslaught of the Grey Army had taken him, along with most of the army, by surprise, and they'd been driven back. But he'd killed a couple, and wounded several. A graze on his arm stung, but that was all. As he sharpened the sword he wondered what the other army wanted, and who they were. He'd seen both Hued and Talthen in the ranks. He'd heard rumours that the army came from Marden and from Langron. Mayhap he should have gone back to Marden and to Ezera, joined with her, and ignored Tulketh's threats. But then he would not have been able to look for his father in the prison, and would not have seen the horrors and tortures inflicted there by the Hued.

As he finished honing his blade, Tulketh came up and stood over him.

"Heard you and your friends from Sare and Ceodrinne fought well," Tulketh said, with a foxy smile. "Glad to hear it. I had my doubts about which side you were on."

Durston shrugged, standing up.

"Mayhap I'm only on my side. I want revenge, Tulketh. I want to get into that cursed city and find that piece of filth Levin Bluestone and strangle him with my bare hands until his green face turns black."

"Ain't burning down the prison enough for you, then?"

Durston frowned and clenched his fists. The memory of the prison, the horror, the torture, the screams of that inferno would never leave him. But it wasn't quite enough.

Not yet.

One of the other leaders, a thin-faced man with a deep red scar on his forehead, strode up.

"Tulketh, you fool!" he exclaimed. "We should have attacked and taken the city weeks ago. Now we're like to lose it to those traitorous bastards in grey. You idiot!"

"Idiot?" Tulketh said, grabbing the other's arm and twisting it behind his back, until the thin-faced man grimaced with pain. "Say that again and I'll break your arm. You know full well we were waiting for the Magi, like we'd agreed."

"'Tain't done us any good, has it?" the man gasped. "Where are they, then?"

"Hell knows. Betrayed us, swanking around in their hideout down south, taking their time."

Tulketh released him. He rubbed his arm, glaring at Tulketh. "Wherever they are, they ain't here, helping us, are they? I said we shouldn't have waited. And you said wait. You said that them - that lot - weren't going to be a problem!"

"Aye! You heard the scout too! He said they were barely a thousand and they weren't going to attack for weeks."

"He was an idiot! Or he either lied to you."

"Listen, scum," Tulketh hissed, his face close to the other's face. "Whatever he said, lying or not, there ain't no point in arguing about it. We ain't got the Magi, and we've got another army to fight. So we don't need to waste time and energy scrapping. Ulban put me in charge, didn't he?"

"Aye, more fool him. So, you idiot, got any clever ideas left?"

A horn sounded. Tulketh looked up. "That be the hour up. I know what we're going to do. We listen to what they say, but I ain't interested. 'Twas a ruse just to gain time. We still outnumber them. Kill the lot of them, then take the city."

He turned round and strode up to Durston and grabbed his shirt at his throat. "Durston, you rat, I'm taking you with us to the parley. I still don't trust you, so I want you in the front, with my lot, so I can see what you're up to."

Durston and a couple of scores of other soldiers followed, as Tulketh and the other leaders rode over the flattened, blood-stained grass towards the centre of the meadows. Behind them the Liberation Army stood ready, armed and waiting. But only a single, grey-clad rider approached them. Two or three hundred yards behind him waited rows and rows of soldiers, mostly in grey or white, Hued and Talthen. The bright sun glinted off their spear points, arrow tips and swords.

"Doesn't look like a parley," Tulketh muttered to the other leaders. "Good thing we're ready."

Durston stared with surprise at the rider. He was young, barely eighteen or nineteen, thin and tall, with white hair and pale, strangely shimmering skin. He sat easily on the horse, his reins relaxed. He was clearly unafraid, with a faint mocking expression on his face. Suddenly, Durston recognised him. When he'd seen the Magi, months ago, this lad had been one of their new apprentices. He'd been riding at the back of the procession, looking both reluctant and apprehensive. But there was no time now to wonder at the change in the boy.

Tulketh rode slightly ahead of the others, looking at the rider mockingly.

"Well? What's your answer?" he said. "Why've they sent a whey-faced skinny boy to us? Where's his swanky lordship, Sulvenor?"

"Be quiet!" the boy said, turning to the thin-faced man. "You! I've seen you before. You're one of Ulban Hirshe's gang of robbers, ain't you?"

"So what if I am?" he said, glaring at the boy. "Tell us your bosses' answer before I kill you, you scrawny runtling."

"That boy ..." a woman beside Durston whispered to him. "He's - did you see what he did, earlier? He fought like a demon. He killed dozens. They be saying, back in the camp, that he's one of them Magi. A wizard."

"A wizard? A Magi?" Durston whispered back.

"Aye. We shouldn't be insulting the likes of him! 'Tis dangerous!"

As Durston watched, the boy smiled. "Scrawny runtling, am I? No. I am Lord Riathe Sulvenor, the Grey Wizard. And our answer is no. We'd rather lick the mud off our shoes than deal with scum like you. We fight."

"If that's what you want. Right!" Tulketh said, turned and shouted back. "Draw weapons! Get ready!"

Durston drew his sword, and heard the noise of two thousand people behind him shifting their weight, settling spears in their hands, unsheathing daggers and drawing in deep breaths as they prepared to fight.

"One moment! Wait!" the pale-faced boy said. He held up his left hand then opened it. Durston saw a tiny, pearl-like stone on his palm. The boy looked steadily at the army ahead of him, as the pearl floated up until it hung above him. It expanded into a globe that shone, flashed and spun, coruscating blue and silver and steely grey, increasing in brightness moment by moment. Tulketh and the other leaders watched it, their hands on their sword hilts, surprise and wonder on their faces, as the radiance flung long shadows over the grass behind them. Durston held his breath and gazed in frozen apprehension at the dazzling stone as it floated high above them. There was a long moment of silence.

"What is he doing?" the woman whispered.

"I don't know. But get ready."

Durston looked down at his sword, then lifted it and stared at it in horror. It was dull. It no longer shone in the sunlight. Tiny patches of rust appeared and grew over its surface. The edge blunted with corrosion as he watched the rust grow and spread.

The woman gasped. Durston whirled round. She was holding her dagger handle, but the blade had vanished, and splinters of bronze, splattered with verdigris, lay at her feet.

She shook. "Oh Powers ... Powers help us ..." she cried. A man next to her held a spear shaft in trembling hands as the head fell to the ground like a fragile rust-coloured leaf. He cried out, flung the shaft down, then turned and scurried back to the ranks. The Liberation Army soldiers looked at their weapons in bewilderment as, before their eyes, the metal decayed. Durston saw gaping holes appearing in shields and helmets, spears and maces disintegrating into piles of rust, men shouting, cursing and frantically shaking their knives as if they could somehow restore their sharpness. But ahead of him, the Grey Army stood, calm, waiting, their spears still sharp, their swords still reflecting the sunlight from honed edges.

Tulketh swore, threw his useless sword onto the ground and yanked at his reins. The harness and buckles broke, the stirrups snapped. He slid off his horse as the saddle and reins dropped to the ground, and his horse skittered away.

"You ... You cursed whoreson! How are you doing that?" he yelled at the boy.

The boy said nothing, merely holding his hand higher. The pearl, a white radiance above him, shone more and more until light, as bright as the sun, poured from it. Durston shaded his eyes against its brilliance. With a crash of thunder that echoed and rolled off the surrounding hills and a final burst of glare that lit the armies, trees and city walls in white like a flash of lightning, the pearl flared out, dimmed and fell back into the boy's hand. As the noise faded into silence, the boy spurred his horse and rode at Tulketh, Durston and the terrified Liberation Army.

Behind him, the Grey Army followed.

The other soldiers with Durston yelled, turned and scurried back. He could see chaos and panic spreading through the ranks behind, shouting, shoving; people scattering and fleeing. His heart raced with shock and fear. His foremost thought was survival. Everything else was trivial now. He had no chance to get to the city, to find

Levin, let alone to see Ezera again. There was no choice left. Just fight, and hope. But he had no weapons, no shield, no helmet. Nor had the villagers from Sare and Ceodrinne that he'd persuaded to join the Liberation Army, and now they'd be massacred like helpless chickens when a fox gets into the hen coop. He grabbed the spear shaft, and ran towards Tulketh. At least he'd take revenge on that bastard who'd brought them all into this trap.

As Tulketh swore and cursed the running soldiers, Durston ran towards him, shouting, the spear shaft raised. Tulketh turned, saw him and dodged the blow. His grey eyes raging, he flung himself at Durston, who dropped the shaft. For a frantic moment, they wrestled on the ground, until Durston got hold of his throat, and hung on. He glanced up and glimpsed the pale-faced boy thrusting his sword through the thin-faced man, then riding down the other leaders as they tried to escape.

Tulketh scrabbled with his fingers against Durston's throttling hands, then, as they rolled, he wrenched them away and kicked Durston in the stomach. Tulketh rolled on top of him, hammering a fist into his face. Suddenly, a pale hand reached down, seized Tulketh's hair and dragged him upright. Durston stared up at the pale-faced boy, astride his horse, his face cold. The boy thrust his sword through Tulketh's chest with calm precision, then dropped the limp body onto the ground.

Durston grabbed the spear shaft from the ground and stood up. The boy pulled his horse round and rode up to him. Durston stood his ground, his only weapon, the feeble-looking wooden shaft, ready. Sweat dampened his grip on the shaft. His breath came in great gulps, his heart beat in rapid thumps against his breastbone.

The boy looked steadily at him. Durston remembered what the boy had said. He was a wizard. The Grey wizard.

"You," the wizard said. "I'm not sure whose side you're on, and I don't think you know either. So - I give you a choice. Surrender, run or fight."

"Fight," he gasped. He knew he didn't have any real chance, but maybe he could buy time for the villagers to escape.

He held the shaft ready. The other rode at him, sword raised high. As he swung down, Durston blocked the blow with the shaft. The wood splintered and shattered. Durston ducked and swerved. As the wizard yanked at the reins to turn his horse, then charged at him, Durston dropped, rolled, and stumbled away. The sword caught him across his shoulder and back. He fell to his knees, then onto his side. Blood seeped down his side as the cold ache pierced him. He curled up, trying to shield himself, as hope drained from him. All around him roared the noise of battle. He waited for the wizard to finish him off, or for horses to ride over him, or for some soldier to thrust a spear through him. No blow came.

After a few moments, he struggled to his knees and stared around. The horses of the Grey Army had reached the Liberation Army camp. The Grey Wizard rode in the middle of a melee, his sword high, his ash-blonde hair clearly visible, as he and his forces pushed the army downhill toward the river. More and more grey-clad soldiers, mostly on foot, ran towards Durston; towards the battle.

I'm not going to die cowering like a wounded dog in a ditch, Durston thought fiercely. Crimson blood stained his shirt. His left arm and shoulder slumped uselessly, but he held the remains of the shaft in his right hand, splintered point upwards, as he staggered upright.

CHAPTER 34
FIGHTING

From the front ranks of the army, Ezera watched in astonishment as Riathe's pearl rose, glowed and spun. The power! She could hear and see the effect of fear rising in the horde opposite. Headon had briefed the captains earlier, saying, "Scatter, harry them. Take prisoners. But avoid killing anyone unarmed or surrendering. I don't want a massacre." And now, as shields and armour and spears crumbled to dust, she realised why. Headon had known that they would be disarmed.

In the small group facing Riathe, the sandy-haired leader slid off his horse and screamed at the wizard. Then, behind him, she saw a tall man, with fair hair and thin cheeks, staring at his disintegrating sword. Durston!

She drew in a breath and stared, her eyes wide, her fists clenched on the reins. The scum! The two-faced, backstabbing scum! So that's why he'd not bothered to come back to Marden. She'd trusted him! Hot blood rose into her cheeks and her heart raced as anger filled her. She held back, waiting for the signal, but her eyes remained on Durston.

Lightning dazzled her, a roar of thunder deafened her. Riathe spurred his horse to a canter, and the army followed. Ezera saw Durston turn on the sandy-haired leader, and wrestle him to the ground. She stared, puzzled. Why would he fight his own side? But there was no time to wonder. The army swept on. Riathe had killed the other leaders. She watched as he stabbed the sandy-haired leader, then slashed his sword across Durston's shoulders. Ezera rode, spurring her horse to greater speed, her eyes on Durston. Don't let him be dead yet, she thought. Let me be the one to kill him. With a knife, up close, staring into his treacherous eyes.

She pulled up her horse as she saw Durston stagger to his feet, holding a splintered spear shaft. Not dead then, she thought. Good. She leapt off her horse, ran to him, and smashed her open palm with all her strength into the side of his face. He reeled, put his hand to his cheek, groaned and fell. She kicked him.

"Get up, you lying, slimy bastard! Stand up so I can kill you face to face!"

"Ezera?" He gasped, retched, then managed a faint laugh. "That's no incentive to get up ... I'm glad you're alive though."

"What?"

She knelt beside him, grabbed his hair and yanked him to his knees. There was blood on his shirt. He winced.

"By the Powers, I never thought to see you here," he muttered, and smiled at her.

"I'll make you sorry you have seen me, you treacherous piece of filth. You betrayed me! You ran to them - to that rabble - and told them the gifts had failed!"

She hit him again. He seized her wrist and pulled her close to him.

"Nay! I didn't ... They already knew. Rumours ... I might have picked the wrong side, but I'm no traitor!" he hissed. His breath came in gasps. Spasms of pain distorted his face.

"Why're you with them? Why didn't you come back to Marden?"

"I couldn't! Tulketh suspected ... threatened me ... promised me. And then, the prison ..." His voice tailed off. His face grew paler.

Ezera looked at his back. Blood oozed steadily from the sword cut. She swore, and grabbed her pack, pulling out linen and cotton strips. Hastily, she bandaged the wound, then heaved him upright. She'd get him to safety, get him fixed, find out the truth. Then kill him.

"Get onto the horse, you ... you lying, two-faced peasant!" she spat. He hauled himself onto the horse while she held the reins, looking around. Almost all the soldiers in the other army were scattered or fleeing. Sporadic groups of fighting dotted the meadows in front of the river.

"You owe me for this," she snarled. "Another big exciting battle and I'm missing it! Though it looks more like a rout than a battle. And scrapping with unarmed men is too easy anyway."

Durston reached down, put his hand on the back of her neck, pulled her close, and kissed her hard.

"Go and fight then," he said, faintly. "But come back in one piece ... Powers and Virtues, Ez, you don't know how glad I am you're alive."

She drew in a breath, kissed him back, then slapped him.

"Rat!" she exclaimed furiously. "Liar, swine ..."

She jerked at the reins as Durston swayed forward in the saddle, then collapsed onto the horse's neck. Anger and exasperation and not a little curiosity filled her as she rapidly led the horse back to the Grey Army's camp near the walls, calling Durston every foul name she could think of on the way.

Ezera deposited Durston beside a fire within the camp. She pulled off her jacket and belt, tore a strip of grey cloth from her shirt, then tied it round his arm.

"Right. Don't you dare die while I'm gone. If anyone murders you, it's going to be me," she said. "But first, I'm going to find you a medic!"

To her annoyance, finding a medic with time on their hands took a while, but eventually she persuaded a sombre-faced woman to come back with her. She half-expected Durston, the rat that he was, to have run away, but he was still there, lying on the crushed grass by the fire.

"Do your best for this - this swine," she said to the medic. "I want him up on his feet. So I can stab him personally." The medic stared at her, shrugged, then knelt by Durston. She lifted him upright and pulled up his shirt. While she rubbed salve on the wound and bandaged it, Ezera stood, staring at Durston, her hands on her hips. He looked less pale.

"Well?" she said. "Go on. Justify yourself. Tell me why you joined that army of bandits."

"'Tis a long story. 'Tis hard to explain."

"Hard to lie your way out of it, you mean?"

Durston shrugged. "You ain't going to be won over by pretty words, are you? Whatever I say, you'll think that I'm lying." He tugged at the grey strip around his arm. "Does this mean I'm in the Grey Army now?"

"Keep still, can't you?" the medic snapped. She wound another bandage around him. "There. Done. Rest for an hour or so, drink plenty. You've lost a lot of blood." She packed her case and walked away, saying, "I've got hundreds of others to treat. Don't you get yourself wounded, Ezera, will you?"

"Give me a usable sword, Ez. Let me fight!" Durston said, his eyes fierce. Ezera stared at his narrow, tanned face. His level brown eyebrows had drawn together in a frown, his smooth lips pressed together. She remembered fighting him in the rain in Ceodrinne, months ago, and then being with him in Marden. All the things he'd said. The weapons he'd brought her.

"Nothing would give me more pleasure," she said coldly, kneeling beside him and prodding the bandage on his arm. "But you're in no fit state to fight. Not yet, anyway."

"Ezera? Ezera! Zera!" someone shouted.

She whirled round and up, and saw a Hued running towards them. He had red hair and skin, and held a bow in his hand and a quiver slung over his shoulder. He ran to her, his hand raised in greeting, then slowed, before coming to a stop a short distance away.

"Jarial," Ezera said. "Well. You've lost weight."

He glanced down at the belt around his waist.

"Yes. Like everyone in the city."

With a shock, she noticed his hand. She stared at the long, jagged scar, and at the stump of his little finger.

"Yes. I've lost a bit more weight there, too," he said, glancing at his hand and then rubbing it abstractedly.

"Fighting?"

He nodded. "Sort of."

"So, what are you doing here?" She pointed at the grey armband tied around his dark-blue jacket. "Have you joined us? You've dared to leave the city at last?"

"Zera, yes, I know, I was wrong, but ..."

"And you're an archer now?"

"You taught me, remember! And, when you were out there, this morning, didn't you hear me? I shouted to you."

"That was you? Those arrows?"

"Yes. Zera ..." He reached out his hand.

"Good shooting," she said, stepping back. "I'll give you that. And you're in the Grey Army now?"

He unslung his empty quiver. "We were on the northern flank, but we're not needed there. I came back, with the others, to get more arrows, and to get our orders."

"You! A soldier and an archer! Wonder of wonders!"

"I know. Zera, I need to tell you ..."

"Who's this?" Durston interrupted, hauling himself to his feet.

Ezera rolled her eyes. Powers give her patience!

"Durston, this is Jarial Sheldman. Jarial, this is Durston Halthe," she intoned expressionlessly.

"Durston?" Jarial echoed.

Ezera grabbed her jacket, put it on and buckled on her belt. She pulled her sword from its scabbard, checked it was clean and sheathed it, then did the same with her dagger. Both men stared at her warily. If she wasn't so furious she could almost have laughed out loud.

"I don't know if either of you have noticed," she said. "But we're in the middle of a war at the moment. I'm supposed to be leading a company, and they're having all the fun while we waste time here. So, I'm off."

She rapidly unhitched her horse and sprung into the saddle.

"Be good, boys," she said to them, with an ironic smile. "You're on the same side now. No fighting while I'm gone."

She turned and rode away.

CHAPTER 35
NIGHT FALLS

The Grey Army moved camp to north of the road, out of bowshot range of the city. As the sun dropped behind the misty western hills, Felde wound his way between the tents and campfires, looking for the other leaders. A large tent had been turned into a makeshift hospital, full of medics dressing minor wounds. Riathe, Felde knew, had spent several hours healing those who had been seriously hurt, but Headon had told him not to waste his strength on those who only needed time and bandaging to heal. Felde glanced in. It seemed quieter there now. Rows of men and women lay on camp beds or on blankets on the grass. Most were asleep. Among them, Felde saw, with relief, the young boy that he'd knocked unconscious lying quietly with a white linen cloth wrapped around his head. The lad wore a grey armband. He must have decided to join them.

Another group of men went past, carrying sacks and spades and heading towards the battlefield.

"What's happening?" Felde asked. "I thought the fighting was over."

"Aye, it is, Lord Sulvenor," the woman in front said, bobbing her head at him. "We've been asked to collect any equipment and weaponry, from the bodies. And then, lucky soldiers that we are, some of us have got to dig the graves and bury the bodies."

"Oh. That's a grim job."

"Telling me! But someone's got to do it. And the quartermasters have promised to save us a good supper when we're done."

"Provided we bring them back a couple of hundred

arrows!" said another.

Felde spotted Vallan and Iselle talking to a couple of captains. He went over to them.

"'Tis done," he said to them. "I sent three soldiers as messengers. They should get to Langron and back within a few days. Like you said, I've given them a letter for Laithan to commandeer food, and to get some more arrows and swords made, if they can. Let Headon know, when you see him."

"Good," nodded Vallan. "We've taken hundreds of prisoners, and now we'll have to feed them too."

"It was a mistake taking prisoners!" exclaimed Iselle. "We should have - have been more ruthless. I don't care that they were unarmed. It would have been better to have destroyed the whole nest of cut-throats and bandits!"

"We've had that discussion. It was Headon's decision," shrugged Vallan. He turned back to Felde. "These captains are going to take two companies and go through their camp, looking for food, supplies, weapons, tents. Anything useful that they've left behind."

"Do you need me for aught?" Felde asked.

"No. Headon said you need to rest. We're not sure what will happen tomorrow. You can get some food from those men over there. Rabbit stew."

"Again? Still, better than going hungry."

Felde sank down onto the camp bed and started to undo and pull off his boots. His sword arm ached, his hands were blistered and cramped, every muscle was weary but he felt triumphant. He had not failed the test. And he was glad that tonight he'd not be sleeping on the bare ground outside but would be in a tent, one commandeered, like the bed, from the defeated army.

He heard someone come in and turned to see his wife closing the tent flap behind her.

"Berrena! What are you doing here? I thought you were going to wait a day!" he exclaimed.

"Don't chide me," she said, as she went into his arms.

"Bee, I ain't going to chide you. But you shouldn't have come."

"How could I have stayed away?" she exclaimed. "You know what it means to us - to our family - if you fail! I had to know. Waiting - 'tis so hard! And I've had to do so much waiting!"

He held her tightly, and stroked her hair. "Bee, I know," he murmured. "But, even so, this is still a battlefield. 'Tis not safe."

"I know that. But I've seen Headon and the others. They say the worst is over. Headon thinks there'll be little fighting tomorrow."

"Aye, I suppose so. Most of that army has either surrendered, run away, or been killed. 'Tis only the city ..."

"What about the city?" she asked, moving from his embrace and looking up at him.

"We have to take the city. They may fight back."

She shrugged. "Well, mayhap. I still needed to see you, to see Riathe."

"You've seen Riathe? Bee, do you know what our son has done? 'Tis amazing! We'd never have won without him and his pearl. And he fought well too."

"He ain't the only one," said Berrena. Her face shone with pride as she smiled at him. "Headon said you and your companies took the brunt of it, and that you'd fought like the best of the City Guard. That your courage and skill made a difference. But, Felde, are you hurt?"

"Nay. Well, I was, but Riathe healed me. An arrow and then a spear through me. They tore my jacket. But I'm fine," he insisted, as she put her hand to her mouth in horror.

"Let me see! Take your things off!" she said.

"Bee, I'm filthy, I'm covered in sweat, blood, dirt," he said.

"I don't care," she replied.

He kissed the top of her head as she inspected the ripped jacket. When she removed it, the shirt inside was soaked in red-brown blood. She gasped.

"It ain't so bad," he reassured her, pulling it over his head. "Look, the spear went in there, just above the Binding. But 'tis healed."

Wonderingly, Berrena passed her fingers over the small circular scar.

"Is that it? All there is? But there was so much blood!"

"Aye. I thought I'd not survive, I was so faint, bruised and weak. But our son, 'tis his gift. It brought me back," he said, putting his arms around her, pulling her close to him and kissing her.

"I can barely believe it, even now. Riathe, so much power ..." Berrena said, wonderingly, sitting down on the camp bed. Felde sat beside her.

"Power ... Aye. Bee, I'm fearful for him. He's changed. Sometimes he seems so ruthless."

"What do you mean?"

"The prisoners. We took hundreds of prisoners. Headon said they should have a chance to join us, because most of them will have been lied to, or been desperate. So he and Riathe went to the prisoners. They offered them a choice. Join us, or be - be executed. Most said they'd join. But there were some, maybe twenty, maybe more ..."

"Some? Felde, tell me!"

He put his head in his hands. "They said they'd join. But Riathe said they were lying, they couldn't be trusted. That they'd backstab us, that they were part of Ulban Hirsche's rabble. So ..."

"Felde, tell me. It wasn't Riathe, was it?"

"Nay! Thank the Powers! Headon arranged it. They were taken aside, given a meal, blindfolded and then stabbed. From the back, into the heart. Cleanly. I know we had to do that, but 'twas - it seemed as bad as the City Guard decimating Helsund."

"Terrible. But I can see that it was necessary. But - Riathe?" she said. "He's different, you said."

"Aye. He seems - seems torn. He ain't at peace." Felde

took her hand. "'Tain't nothing we can do."

She sat, silently, for a long time. Felde saw a tear slide down her cheek.

"Powers' help him," she whispered, and leant into him. He put his arm around her.

"Bee, Bee," he said. "I may be imagining it. Don't worry."

She leant closer to him.

"I'm glad you're here," he said, after a while. "But you should go back tomorrow."

Berrena lifted up her face and stared at him. "I won't. I spoke to Headon. He thinks there'll be little resistance from the city tomorrow. And he wants me to ride with you, Riathe and him, at the front."

"What! Why?" Felde exclaimed, leaping up.

"Because I'm known in the city!" she said, standing up as well, her hands on her hips. "Because of what I was trying to do – to save them! He says if I'm there he doesn't think the City Guard will attack us. That we'll be seen as rescuers, not invaders. And he's right. You know he is."

"Mayhap. But I don't like it. You won't be safe."

"Nay, but I'll be with you. And I don't notice you being half so concerned over Iselle riding with the army and fighting with them."

"Vallan can worry about her," he laughed. "All right. You know I never could argue with you, Bee. And you'll stay here tonight, with me, despite all my dirt and grime?"

For answer, she only put her hands to his face and kissed him.

"When this is over, Bee, I want to go back to Langron as soon as we can," he said. "To stay there, go back to breeding and training horses. Be with you and our children, and not leave again."

CHAPTER 36
THE GATES

Jarial knew how strong the black oak gates were. And on the battlements of the towers by the gates, a hundred feet above him, archers and City Guards stared downwards. More lined the parapets of the high walls on either side. The coloured flags of the city behind them snapped and billowed in the wind. Scores of arrow points and steady, nervous gazes watched them. They could shoot us easily, Jarial thought. They look frightened and unsure enough to do it. And, no doubt, several hundred more guards are massed behind the closed gates.

He glanced to his left and saw Headon and the other leaders on horses before the main body of the Grey Army. Besides them rode the strange, white-skinned wizard, Riathe Sulvenor, his skin faintly glimmering in contrast to his long grey cloak. And, to his surprise, Jarial saw Berrena Rochale. She glanced apprehensively at the archers above them, and then turned to look at the tall, weathered Talthen beside her: Felde Sulvenor, her husband. He stared up at the gates and walls, awe on his face. Last night, he had shaken Jarial's hand warmly and said a brief, honest thank-you. "You saved my life," he'd said. Jarial looked at his hand. The first time in his life he had shaken hands as an equal with a dullard - a Talthen. The first touch since the gentle, pale hands of Liffy rubbing soothing ointment into his wounds over six weeks ago. And now he stood, in a mixed company of fifty Talthen and Hued archers, waiting.

The leaders waited too. Just behind Felde he saw Ezera,

bouncing on her toes, her sword drawn. Even at a distance he could see the poised, keen expression on her face. She caught his eye and nodded curtly. That skinny, pale-faced dullard, Durstum or whatever his name was, stood close behind her. Too close. Jarial frowned.

Suddenly a stirring and muttering spread through the archers near him. Jarial looked around. The six leaders rode forward. Someone on the city wall above them shouted. He looked up. Twenty or so of the City Councillors, surrounded by guards, had appeared behind the battlements of the tower to the right of the gate. Jarial wondered where the rest of the council were. His mother was there, her face drawn and anxious, her eyes squinting into the glare of the early morning sun. The president of the council stepped forward to a crenel and lifted her hand in greeting.

"Welcome!" she exclaimed. Her voice sounded clear and loud in the cool autumnal air. "Welcome back; Headon Alcastor, Vallan Sapphireborne, and Iselle Topazborne! We are delighted to see you. I assume you are here to relieve the city?"

Headon spurred his horse forward.

"We are Lord Alcastor, Lord Sapphireborne and Lady Topazborne," he shouted. "And these are Lady Berrena Rochale, Lord Felde Sulvenor and Lord Riathe Sulvenor, the Grey Wizard."

"Lords? Are you expecting me to call dullards 'Lord'? By the walls, never!"

"Talthen!" Headon snapped.

"Talthen, dullards, whatever. Headon, I ask again, before we open the gates to you: what are your intentions?"

"Our intentions? You can see ... We have routed the army besieging you. We are your hope, your rescuers."

Several people on the walls above cheered loudly.

"Silence!" exclaimed the president. "Continue!"

"Rescue, yes, but on conditions," Headon said.

Even from a distance, Jarial could hear and sense the whispers and questions spreading through the Hueds on the walls.

"You dare to talk of conditions!" she hissed, staring down at Headon with a fierce expression on her lime-green face, her hands gripping the waist-high wall in front of her.

Headon gestured to the hundreds of soldiers behind him, and to his left and right.

"Yes, I dare," he said. "Our conditions? In return for rescue, protection, food, safety, we demand absolute surrender of power. All councillors to abdicate. You open the gates, we come in, you give us the keys, the authority. The City Guard answer to us. We take the city."

"What? Never!" the president screeched, above the noise of shouts and exclamations from those on the walls.

Headon turned and spoke to the captains on either side. Jarial heard the orders being passed through the companies: shields up, swords and spears ready, nock arrows. He lifted his bow, pulled back as hard as he could, dropped an arrow into place and looked up. "Nay. Aim for the gates," the man beside him said. "That's what I've been told. In case there's a sortie. No point trying to hit them cowards up there, hiding behind them battlements."

Jarial's heart pounded as he sighted along the arrow to the gates. He pulled the bowstring tighter against his vambrace. His tense arms trembled. I could die today, he realised. But, for Ezera's sake, I won't run. She won't see me running. And, at least, thanks be to the Powers and the Grey Army, I'm facing death with scores of arrows in my quiver, wearing a few bits of armour taken off a dead body, and with a decent breakfast inside me.

"Fire!" the president screamed, and the arrows rained down. One pierced the arm of the man by Jarial, and he cursed as he stumbled backwards. Another hit Jarial's shoulder and he suppressed a cry as it bounced off his make-shift leather and chain-mail collar.

"No! Stop! That's my son!" a woman cried. Jarial looked upwards, and saw his mother, her arms stretched out desperately towards him. He stared back at her, as the president shouted, "Ignore her! Carry on, or I'll have you strung up!"

More arrows came. His mother ran towards the president. The sound of cries and shouts blended with the hiss and clatter of arrows. The president turned and Jarial saw his mother, her face twisted with fury, throw herself forwards. They struggled, shouting violently. His mother screamed then, suddenly, the president toppled backwards through the crenel and plummeted downwards, wailing in fear. She landed a hundred feet below, on the stone of the curtain wall. and rolled down until she lay in a twisted heap on the flattened grass and rocks at the base of the wall.

Jarial's mother leaned over the wall and stared at the body for a moment. She turned away, one hand grasping her own shoulder and yelled to the army leaders, "Stop! For the Powers' sake, stop! We surrender!" then the other councillors seized her and dragged her backwards. She screamed again. And still the arrows came.

The Grey Wizard, Riathe, rode past Headon and towards the gate. "Enough!" he shouted. An arrow struck his leg, skittering away. He ignored it. His face shone palely, though dark shadows lay under his eyes. He looked up and lifted his clenched left hand.

"Stop!" he said, in a loud, commanding voice. The arrows ceased. Silence spread, as Jarial held his breath. He could hear the whispers of fear and curiosity running along the walls above them. Riathe opened his hand. A tiny white sphere rose from it. A woman near Jarial muttered, "So that's it. His pearl, they call it. Looks too small to do aught."

The sphere rose higher, spinning and glowing. The dark gates in front of Riathe shivered. He raised his hand higher. Silently, gently, the gates trembled, then crumbled and fell into a slowly blooming cloud of dust that drifted towards the Grey Army before being blown away by the morning breeze.

CHAPTER 37
HEURON FALLS

Ezera gasped as the gates fell. She heard others gasp, muttering and whispering in awe. Riathe turned and rode back, smiling coolly at Headon and the other leaders.

"I told you the gates would not be a problem," he exclaimed. "Destroying is easy ... Shall I destroy the walls and towers too?"

"No!" Headon snapped.

"Riathe!" Berrena cried. "Why would you want to do that? You'd kill all those people!"

"Mayhap I should," he said, shrugging. "Mayhap they need to know our strength, our power. So they daren't resist us. But 'tis fine, mother. I won't."

"Good!" said Headon. "Well, onward. The final challenge."

The army rode slowly towards the walls. Two companies of City Guards, looking resolute but apprehensive, and most of the councillors stood warily behind the wispy clouds of dust that were all that remained of the gates.

At the gap, Headon lifted his hand and the army paused behind him.

"Well?" he said.

The guard commander stepped forward. With an apprehensive look and a slight bow, he handed his sword to Headon.

"The city is yours, my Lord," he said.

Headon nodded. He looked around at the crowds, the guards, the white-walled buildings; down the wide street, then up at the coloured flags still bravely fluttering high above them. He took in a deep breath. Ezera expected him to look triumphant and exultant, but he looked weary and, for a moment, grief-stricken. Then he lifted his hand to the scar on his face, shook his head briefly and rode on. The army followed.

Ezera glanced from side to side as she walked. The streets were lined with still, unmoving Hueds, watching them with fear, their faces haggard and thin, their eyes tense. Not a whisper or sound came from the crowd as the grey-clad companies marched into the city.

At the central square, a mile from the gate, they stopped. Looking around, she saw that it had barely changed, although Ezera thought that something should have altered, given how the whole world had shifted in the months since she'd left. Then she saw Durston's face and laughed. He gazed, open-mouthed, at the vast fountain with its carved statues, at the ornate urns overflowing with late asters and geraniums, at the porticoes, columns and wrought iron balconies of the council buildings, and the copper filials on the bell towers that glinted in the morning sun. He looked astonished, awed and resentful.

"Impressive, isn't it?" she said.

He reached out and seized her wrist. "Impressive? By the Powers', Ezera, I never imagined ..."

"Of course. I forgot. You've never seen the city."

He gripped her wrist harder and turned to her.

"If I had known ... We paid taxes until we were starved, destitute, and for what? For this?" he said fiercely. "Look around you. I ain't the only one thinking this."

She shook his hand off and shrugged. "I know! Why do you think I left the city? But at least, now, things might change. So, shut up, and listen!"

She gestured to the marble steps leading up to the colonnade before the main building. Headon had dismounted and stood at the top, the other leaders beside him. He spread his arms wide.

"Thank you for - for your welcome, for your acceptance," he shouted. "It is good, though strangely bitter, to return to my city after so many years. And in such unbelievable, astounding circumstances. It is beyond belief. Now I am here, I see that we have much to do. I ask your patience. We will bring food ..."

Someone cheered. Headon smiled, lifted a hand and continued. "It may take a while, but it will come. And things will change. As well as your patience, I ask of you that you talk to us, to the Grey Army soldiers, to Talthen and Hueds, about what has been happening in the last few months. Especially ask about the Magi, the authors of so much evil." He paused.

"He does like giving speeches, doesn't he?" Ezera whispered to Durston, with a grin.

"We, your new leaders have a lot to organise and discuss," Headon continued. "But, again, in the names of the seven founders and by the Powers', I thank you."

A faint smattering of applause and a few cheers echoed around the square as he stepped down, but Ezera heard mutterings and grumbles of discontent too.

Headon beckoned the other leaders over to him. He looked across the square towards Ezera and mouthed, 'You too.'

"Looks like I'm needed," she said. "Better go."

"Needed? Ezera, you ... you're ..." Durston stammered.

"Involved? Important? Is that what you mean?" she said, with raised eyebrows, and she patted his cheek. "Oh yes, my dear fellow, terribly important ... Captain, leader ... Didn't you know?"

"Don't laugh at me! How?"

"Headon knew my cousin Aven, and knows my uncle. And I saved Felde - the tall Talthen - I saved his life. Oh yes, further promotion beckons!"

She tightened her belt, checked her sword and dagger were sheathed and smoothed her jacket.

"Before you go, Ezera," Durston said, taking her arm. "Tell me where I can find that rat, Levin Bluestone. His house, the guardhouse, the barracks?"

"No idea," she said. "Ask around. Find Jarial and ask him!" She looked at his frowning expression. "You haven't forgotten that scum Bluestone in all this excitement, then?"

"Nay. I ain't likely to forget. By hell's curses, I'll search every rat-hole and sewer in this city until I find him," he said, then turned and strode away.

As Ezera ran up the steps to the leaders, she heard Vallan laughing.

"I never thought it would be so easy to take the city!" he said.

"Easy?" exclaimed Headon.

"Well, easier than I thought it would be."

Headon turned to Ezera. "Ah, Ezera," he said. "We'll need your help. You know the current City Guards, their captains, their commanders, don't you?"

She nodded.

"Excellent. So, here we are. Back at last."

"And in charge of the city," said Vallan.

"Us?" Felde said. "The six of us in charge? 'Tis hard to believe. And when did we become lords?"

"Since we started leading an army," said Headon. "It's what some of the soldiers call us. I enjoyed saying that to the president. It was a good moment. It made up for a lot of pain." He rubbed his burnt hand thoughtfully.

"Lady Topazborne? Hmm. I like it." Iselle said, and twirled around triumphantly. "Anyway, what do we do now? Look at all these half-starved people!" She waved a hand towards the crowds of Hueds, standing at a distance, watching them warily.

"I think we got here just in time," Berrena said.

"Yes. Well, plans," said Headon. "I suggest that we send two companies to fetch and to distribute the food from the camp. Others can go with some of the City Guard to search the councillors' houses, in case they are hoarding food. So we can start feeding people soon."

"Shouldn't we get the City Guard to join our army?" Vallan said. "We'll need their help to get beds and stabling and things like that."

"Of course. Ezera, can you talk to the commander about that? Also can you ask the commander to search the prison and release anyone in there for breaking curfew or treason."

Ezera nodded.

"And we should tell our soldiers, especially the Talthen, to be friendly and try to get to know people," said Berrena. "It's vital that everyone knows where we are from, and about the Magi and Riathe."

"There's so much to do!" Headon exclaimed. He turned to Riathe, who stood nearby, looking around with a sombre expression at the council buildings, at the inlaid marble pavements, at the white stone walls glowing in the sunlight.

"We'll need your help, Riathe, you know that," Headon said. "We need to know who we can trust. And even with the stores we've got, we'll need more. We need to feed everyone."

"Feed everyone! Do you expect me to conjure up enough food for ten thousand people?"

"Can you?"

"For Powers' sake! Give me some - some respite!" Riathe snapped. He stalked away to the edge of the steps, stomped down and sat on the bottom step, staring moodily at the crowds. Berrena glanced at Felde and the others, then followed Riathe and sat close by him.

Headon watched them for a moment, then shrugged. He turned back to the other leaders.

"As well as food, and the guards, we'll need to set up a new council," he said. "Which raises an interesting difficulty. Should we include any of the current councillors?"

After a while, Ezera decided the discussion was becoming boringly political. She shook Headon's arm.

"Permission to go to find the City Guard, sir?" she said.

Headon nodded. Ezera ran down the steps and then paused. A little girl, with sky-blue skin, curly hair and large wondering eyes, had toddled up to Riathe. Her father hovered respectively and nervously behind her.

"My daddy says you're a wizard," the child asked, her thumb half in her mouth. "Why are you such a funny white colour? Can you make things? My daddy could. He could make all sorts of pretty paper out of nothing, but now he can't. What can you do?"

Riathe looked seriously at her. "Are you hungry?" he asked.

"Very. Mummy says we don't have any food left. But I want my breakfast!" She looked like she was about to wail.

"Shush! Hold out your hands, close together!" Riathe ordered.

Obediently, she held out two small and grubby hands. A roll of bread, a piece of cheese and two apples appeared in them. She squealed in surprise.

"Take them to your parents," Riathe said.

Suddenly, Ezera heard shouts and yells. Several hundred people ran up the east street towards the square, their faces terrified. A child stumbled and a woman snatched her up and rushed on. As a crowd of panicked Hueds poured into the square, Riathe and Berrena leapt up. Headon and the others ran down the steps and stared. Ezera saw smoke rising from near the east gate and drifting over the distant battlements of the city walls, as cries resounded from dozens of screaming mouths, "Murder! Fire!"

CHAPTER 38
INSIDE THE CITY

Jarial had watched Ezera pass through the gate, striding fast behind the leaders. He thought of calling out to her, but she would not have heard him and, anyway, the Talthen man, Durston, walked beside her. The rest of the Grey Army followed, some on horseback, most walking. They marched through the gates. Jarial hesitated for a moment, but the City Guard captain nodded at him.

"Looks like we're invading our own city," the captain said. "Well, they've won. We may as well join the triumphal procession."

Once inside and partway up the main thoroughfare, Jarial paused, looking around, then hung back surreptitiously. No one noticed. He saw other Hueds in the Grey Army run to embrace people in the crowds lining the street or, glancing around, slip away into side streets. Clearly he wasn't the only one wanting to go home, find his family and friends, return to a normal life. He walked back to the gates.

"I'm still City Guard," he muttered, "not part of the Grey Army. Not a deserter."

As he walked round to the stairs leading up to the left-hand tower, he held his breath. He half-expected the captain to come running after him and call him back, but to his relief, he heard nothing more than the distant sound of a thousand men marching and the exclamations from the Hueds lining the street to watch.

His mother came down the steps, surrounded by other councillors. She saw him, and staggered towards him, weeping and crying. She fell into his arms, then whimpered, "My arm, my arm!" as he held her.

"She's hurt. Dislocated shoulder, in my opinion," one of the councillors said. "Best find a doctor. If you can."

"How? What happened?"

"Dislocated in the scuffle when she, the murderous traitor, pushed the president off the wall!" shouted another. "A just punishment! She should be tried for murder! And treason!"

The first councillor turned towards the furious one.

"We've had that discussion and agreed, as things stand, to let Madame Latisse go!" he snapped. "She saved the lives of Hueds! And I for one think that sour-faced, bossy fool of a president deserved what she got. Ordering City Guard to fire on Hueds!"

As they argued, Jarial felt his mother slump against him. Her face looked pale. Gathering his strength, he lifted her up.

"I'm taking her to my house," he said. "It's closest. Then I'll get a doctor or medic or someone. You know where to find me, and her, when you've decided what to do."

She lay, a dead weight in his arms, as he stumbled to his house. Several times he stopped to lean against a wall, trying to recover some strength before staggering on. Throngs of uncertain people filled the streets. He shouldered his way though, ignoring the questions and talk.

Inside, he laid her on a sofa, dropped his bow and quiver, and rubbed his aching arms. She looked less pale. He fetched a tumbler of water from his kitchen.

"I'm going to get a doctor, someone, to come and bandage your arm," he said, lifting her head and stroking the hair back from her face.

"It hurts, Jarry," she moaned. "Oh, I should never have done that ... never! But, dearest, they might have killed you. How could I let her do that?"

She clutched his hand and cried again. Her head fell back, her eyes rolled upwards, and she collapsed onto the cushions. Frantically Jarial chafed her arms, and sprinkled water on her face. Eventually she opened her eyes.

"Jarial? What happened? Where am I?"

"In my house. You fainted. Your arm ..."

"Oh! Yes!" She tried to push herself upwards. "Jarry! The army ..."

"Rest. Lie back, try to rest."

"But the army. There's an army coming. What are they going to do? Jarry, I'm frightened!"

He stroked her face. "Don't be. They are on our side."

"But they've got dullards with them, the ones who've been outside the walls, taunting us, yelling for our blood. Oh, Jarry, what's happening?"

As rapidly as he could, he explained about the Grey Army, about Headon, about Marden and Langron. She gazed at him in disbelief, then dawning grief.

"We've lost then," she moaned. "Lost the gifts, lost the city, lost everything. I'm not a councillor anymore, am I?"

"Not a councillor? Mother, you're lucky you're not in prison for murder. We're lucky we're not all dead! If it hadn't been for that army, we would be!"

"Don't shout at me, dearest," she whispered. "My shoulder ... It hurts so much."

Her arm and shoulder were both swollen. He touched her arm gently and she winced.

"Right," he said. "I'm going to try to find a medic or someone to fix your shoulder. Stay quiet. There's water there. I don't know how long I'll be."

As he went to pick up his bow and quiver, he heard yells, screams and furious shouts.

"What ... What is that?" his mother cried.

Jarial went to the door. Outside he saw dozens, hundreds of Hued, running as fast as possible from the gate, towards the city centre. He smelt smoke. Several houses near the gate were on fire. And, running up the street, a group of Talthen. His gut twisted with fear at the sight. He could see the steely glint of knives and swords, and see the murderous fierceness on their faces. One ran to a tall, balconied house across the street and kicked at the door again and again, until it crashed and broke. Then he and several others ran inside, yelling and laughing.

His heart hammering against his chest, Jarial dashed back inside, pushed the door shut and slammed the bolts across. Rapidly he closed and bolted the shutters to the windows.

"What's happening?" gasped his mother.

"I don't know!" he shouted, grabbed his bow and quiver and running upstairs.

From the bedroom window he could see more houses on fire, more Talthen running, with knives in their hands, through the streets. He gasped in horror. Three dead Hueds lay in a crumpled heap. Their coloured blood mingled and spread around them. Was it another invasion?

He shouted for help and looked wildly around, up at the city walls and along the street. Where were the Grey Army, the City Guard? All seemed chaos: running, terrified Hueds being chased by ferocious men, flames blazing from windows, smoke rising. Even the sky appeared chaotic. Dark swirling clouds eclipsed the blue morning sky. But Jarial barely registered the strange sky. His hands trembled, but he managed to nock an arrow and sight along the shaft.

Two of the invaders ran into his garden. One seized the bay tree, in its terracotta pot, that stood by his front door. He snapped the bole and then threw it onto the ground with a curse. The pot shattered, dark soil and red shards scattering over the path. The other Talthen hammered and kicked at his door.

Jarial shook with fear, but he had no choice. He loosed. It was impossible to miss at such close range. The man at the door fell. Blood spurted over the doorstep. Jarial yanked another arrow out and aimed. His hands were steadier now. The arrow went through the chest of the other man.

Three more ran up into his garden. It took five arrows, but he managed to stop them. But still more came. One paused, lifted a bow, and shot back. Jarial ducked out of the way just in time. He loosed, killing one, nocked and loosed again, wounding another man.

The sky above grew darker. A wind rose and howled among the towers and chimneys and roofs.

Jarial nocked his last arrow, breathing hard, and aimed. Powers knew what he would do once that arrow had gone. And his mother ... What would these terrifying men do to her?

A crack exploded above him. He dropped his bow as a bolt of dazzling lightning speared down with radiating blue-white fingers and struck the high filial on a roof opposite. For a searing moment the city blazed in overwhelming, intense white light, then darkened.

Thunder roared and roared, on and on, around and above him, in a cacophony that terrified him. He crouched, his hands over his ears, and stared upwards at the black, tormented clouds, as the explosive tumult swirled high above him. More and more lightning struck the city buildings. Then, with a sound as if the clouds were being ripped open, torrential, drowning rain cascaded down onto the city.

CHAPTER 39
HEADON'S MISTAKE

Ezera ran to the crowd, grabbing the arm of a woman. "Murder? Fire?" she snapped. "What's happening? Who's killing people?"

"Dullards!" the woman gasped. "Hundreds of them! They killed my friend, her husband. They've got torches, swords!"

"What? Dullards? Grey Army men? Powers above, no!" she exclaimed.

"No! I don't think so. Not yours ... After your army," the woman said, in a shaking voice. "We were just by the gates, talking to neighbours who'd gone to Marden, when suddenly we heard them. Groups of them, running, pouring in. Swords, spears. They started killing people. Looting, setting fires ... Oh, Founders help us!"

Ezera ran to Headon and the others. Riathe stood up and joined them.

"The other army?" Felde was saying.

"Yes, scum from the Liberation Army," Vallan said. "They must have followed us into the city."

"No ... Oh, no," Headon whispered. "I should have thought of that. I should have left a guard, sealed the gates. They'll be in the streets. Looting, killing ..."

He crouched down, his head in his hands.

"What are we going to do?" Vallan said. "Headon! What do we do?"

"I don't know," he muttered.

Vallan looked around. "We'll need to find them. Stop them."

"Street fighting? They'll be everywhere by now," Headon said, standing up. "And they'll be more."

"Sir, we can still do something," Ezera said. "We've still got over two score companies and the City Guard."

Headon breathed in deeply. "Yes. Thank you. What do you suggest?"

"Leave half here, to protect the rest of the Hued. Take the rest, spread out. Street by street, door by door. Searching the houses."

"That would work," said Vallan. "We have to try."

"You're right. I'm sorry. Yes ... Leave half the companies here, with Berrena, and the City Guard."

"Iselle and I could take some, seven or eight, fan out to the north. Felde with some to the south."

"Yes. Ezera, Riathe, you come with me east. Riathe, can you come and seal the gates? It will be hard street fighting. And the houses on fire. How do we stop the fire spreading?"

"I can handle that," Riathe said. "But tell the companies, anyone not in the Grey Army, any Talthen, who is looting, setting fires, or has blood on their swords, kill them. No mercy. I said we should have destroyed all that army in the first place!"

"Yes, but it's too late now," Headon said. "Anyway, as you say, we can't afford to be merciful now. Well, let's get prepared. As fast as we can."

Ezera dashed back to where her company had been sitting, relaxing and chatting, at the side of the square. "Get ready," she exclaimed. "We're going to be needed. Looks like street fighting after all. The city's being invaded again!"

In less time than Ezera expected, they marched, with drawn swords, towards the east gate, following Headon and Riathe. She glanced around, but only saw the occasional Hued running towards the central square, looking terrified. As they neared the gate they saw bodies on the street, houses with doors smashed in or thrown wide open, and flames flickering inside.

"Dullard bastards!" someone in her company hissed.

Ezera spun round. "Don't you call them that!" she snapped. "Call them Talthen! And this hasn't been done by Talthen. This is those rats and bandits from the Liberation Army, damn them to hell!"

"Where are they?" another soldier said.

"I don't know. Hiding in the lanes, ran away when they saw us coming?"

And if Durston is with them then I will slit his chest open and tear out his lying, stinking heart, she thought, gripping her sword tighter. She could see smoke rising from near the wall and, with a shock, realised it came from houses on Jarial's street. She turned, hesitating. Jarial wouldn't be there, he'd be in the square, no doubt, and she had more important things to do. She could look for him later on, assuming they both survived.

At the gate, Headon strode forward and stared at the open space. The road and plain outside were scattered with bodies, tents, dead horses, and burnt out camp fires, but no one visible moved.

"Why didn't I think to seal the gates earlier?" he muttered, then turned to Riathe. "I assume you can do something?"

"I can, I think," Riathe said. He lifted the pearl and closed his eyes. Slowly, as Ezera watched in awe, the dark oak doors, the heavy iron bars, appeared as faint shadows, then coalesced into solidity. She heard gasps from the companies behind them.

"Good," Headon said wearily. "Well done. Now, at least, they are trapped. We split up, one company per street, and hunt them down."

"What about the fires?" Ezera asked.

"Oh. Yes. Riathe?"

Riathe held his hand higher. Pale flickers of light glimmered around it. He opened it and the pearl hovered above him. It turned and glowed. In the blueness of the sky overhead dark, foaming clouds formed. They twisted and writhed as they grew. White lightning flashed against the blackness, as the sun was quenched by the tormented storm clouds.

"Powers above!" someone gasped as a bolt of dazzling lightning speared from the dark and struck a building nearby. Ezera flinched despite herself, and another soldier screamed, as thunder exploded above them, the lightning striking the city again and again.

Her heart thudded. She lifted her sword, taking in a breath to steady herself.

Headon turned, and shouted about the tumult of the storm. "You know what to do! Go!"

"Stop gawping! We have work to do! Swords ready and follow me. First street on the left!" she yelled, as Riathe stared upwards, lifted his arms and stretched his hands wide apart. Rain poured from the sky.

CHAPTER 40
SECOND BEST

Jarial watched from the window, his heart thudding, as the Talthen in the street, bloody swords dangling from their hands, stared in fear and astonishment at the strange, tormented sky. The deluge drenched them, the street, and the roofs, while the blood on the cobbles mingled with the widening pools of rain water. Two of the men ran to Jarial's door. He picked up his bow, nocked his last arrow with trembling hands, loosed and missed.

Suddenly, through the roar of the rain, he heard shouts, and scores of soldiers ran down the street from the city centre. Those in front had grey jackets or wore grey or white armbands. Jarial saw that some of them - three or four - were Hueds. They held drawn swords, and in the flashes of lightning their determined faces glistened with rain water. The Talthen at his door turned and fled, with the others, followed by the fast-running band of Grey Army soldiers.

A white arc of light struck a chimney opposite, then thunder rolled and echoed and faded away. Jarial saw a few more Grey Army soldiers running down the street. He pulled his dagger out, dashed downstairs and yanked the door open.

In the street he paused. He could hear distant shouts, over the sound of wind and rain, but see no one. He looked up. The swirling clouds had stilled and the wind had dropped. Jarial shivered in the drenching cloudburst, and hesitated.

"Jarry? Jarry?" his mother called.

He went back inside. She had heaved herself upright, and stared at him with wide frightened eyes.

"What's going on?" she cried. "That terrible noise!"

"I don't know," he said. "I think ... I need to find out what's going on. Lie down. You've got to rest!"

She nodded, and lay down, sobbing quietly and trembling.

Jarial locked the door and ran down the deserted street towards the gate. He could hear his heart pounding in his chest and feel sweat prickling his armpits and back. Through the rain and gloom he saw someone running towards him. He recognised her as a woman from another City Guard squad, and grabbed her arm.

"What's happening?" he asked.

"Those bastards ... They got in! Killed people, hundreds, I heard," she panted. "But the wizard, the other army, they've stopped them. Most of them prisoners or killed, thank the Powers! Lord Alcastor asked me to take the news back to the others in the main square."

Jarial released her arm and she dashed away.

So, it's over, he thought. He stood, drenched and breathless, as the rain poured onto his head, his arms and his dagger, and ran down to the cobbles. It was quieter. The only sound was the hiss of water falling onto the fires. Steam and smoke rose from dozens of burning houses. His neighbour's house was ablaze, red flames flickering in every window. He hoped to the Powers that the family had escaped, but there was nothing he could do. He looked at the bodies of the three dead Hueds. One lay, face upwards, arm flung out and a bloody stain on his shirt. Jarial recognised his distorted, pain-filled face. He was the owner of the bar around the corner. Jarial stood, silently, gazing at him, then turned and walked back home.

Even a week later, he could still smell the acrid scent of soot, burnt wood and ash lingering around the eastern streets. He stood on the walls, gazing at the road leading out from the city, as a chilling wind sent grey clouds across the sky, covering the sun. More rain had fallen overnight and the stones of the parapet were wet and cold under his hands. At least food was coming in to the city - at a price, of course. He could see two wagons, piled high with sacks and potatoes, lumbering towards the gate. A Talthen followed them, carrying a basket of eggs, and with several plucked chickens swinging from his belt.

Below, several hundred yards from the walls, a few dozen people dug graves, others lowering shrouded bodies into the finished ones. Jarial shivered. Over a thousand dead in the massacre, mainly Hued.

He turned away, walking rapidly up and down, wrapping his arms around himself and stamping his feet to warm up. Guard duty was becoming both chilly and dull.

He heard quick steps coming up the stairs to the battlements. Turning, he saw Ezera running up them then striding towards him. There was a bandage around her arm, and a red graze healing on her cheek. She paused, and held up her left hand in formal greeting. Jarial stepped forward, his arms held out, then stopped and let his arms fall to his side.

"Ezera!" he said. "I wondered where you were. I haven't seen you since that day ..."

"I've been busy," she said. "I called at your house. Your mother was there. She said you'd be here."

"Yes. She's living with me now that she's lost her council position."

She tilted her head sideways and looked him up and down. "Still in the guards? Archer?"

"Still in the guards. And you? You've been fighting again?" he said, pointing at the bandage.

She laughed.

"Always! But not recently. That's from a week ago. I've got a quieter life now. Captain of Lord Alcastor's personal guards. I'm a rising star, Jarial."

"Oh ..." And I'm fading, he thought. "Well, congratulations from a humble foot soldier." He bowed. "I'm honoured to be visited by such an illustrious personage."

"Don't be an idiot, Jarry! And it's only because Headon - Lord Alcastor - knows Cairson. And he says I remind him of my eldest cousin, Aven Lachaire. They were friends, years ago."

She sat on the low stone benches and stared out over the plain. Jarial looked at her and thought she looked even more confident and energetic than ever, yet somehow more remote.

"Great views," she commented.

"But still dull, boring and cold work."

"Especially after all the fun of last week!"

"Fun! Not sure I'd call it that!" He leant on the wall, close to her, and gazed out.

"So, what are you going to do, if this is too dull?" she asked.

"What can I do, Zera?" He showed her the stump on his hand, where his finger had been. "I can't make fire, I can't play music like I used to, not that that ever bought me a living. I've got a friend who's thinking to set up a trading business, buying firewood from Talthen and selling it here. I could help him. Drive the carts out and back, do the accounts, do the haggling. I know about firewood, if not much else."

"Good idea. Trading - turning business man? And leaving the city?"

"I have left the city before, you know! And now we're safe, secure ... It should be fine."

"Secure!" She snorted. "I'm not so sure! There's still a lot of resentment out there. Rat's nests of thieves, bandits; remains of that damned Liberation Army." She waved her hand towards the pale hills on the distant horizon.

"But we've got the army, the City Guard, the wizard."

"The Grey Wizard?" She turned to him. "I'll tell you something, Jarry. He ... He is not safe! Not stable. There is something about him. As if he can only just control himself."

She stood up and paced too and fro.

"Really?"

"Yes. Really. I wasn't frightened during the battles, even in the street fighting, though that was dangerous enough; but I am scared of him."

She was silent for a moment, then sat back down. She shrugged.

"Anyway, that's enough of that."

Jarial leaned towards her and tentatively touched the graze on her cheek.

"Street fighting. That's how you got this, and your arm?"

"Yes. It was bloody, intense. But exciting! And we beat the scum. You were involved, weren't you?"

He laughed. "Sort of. I was down to my last arrow. I never thought I'd be so glad to see scores of armed soldiers running towards me!"

"Even if they were Talthen? Dullards?" she said, grinning.

"A man can change his mind, can't he?"

Ezera stood up, put her hands on the parapet and leaned over, looking down at the newly-dug graves, then out and around, and finally up at the flags on the tower by the east gate. The coloured ones were faded and ripped. Above them a new grey silk flag, with a white circle in the middle, billowed and cracked in the wind.

"A new era," she said. Turning to Jarial, she ran a finger down his cheek and then over his dark blue jacket. "Uniform suits you, Jarry. And I like the shorter beard."

He put his hands on either side of her face.

"You always looked good in uniform, Zera."

She ran her fingers through his hair, and pulled his head down. They kissed. Her lips were hard and firm on his, and he felt her breasts pressing into his chest as she moved closer.

"We had our differences, but we've also had some good moments, haven't we?" she asked.

"Some extremely good moments."

"Until we disagreed about the Talthen."

Jarial stepped back. An image of that Talthen, with his pale blue eyes and mismatched brown skin, and Ezera kneeling close beside him, came into his head. He grabbed her wrists.

"What is this about, Zera? Why did you come to find me? What about that man, Durstim, or whatever his name is?"

"Durston?" She wrenched her arms from his hands. "What about him?"

"Tell me ... Does he matter to you? Is he still hanging around?"

"Still hanging around? Well, for your information, no! He's gone to Marden, as part of the Grey Army, on protection duty! And then he's going to Ceodrinne, to see his family."

Jarial folded his arms and glared at her.

"I see," he said. He couldn't help himself. It was as if someone else said the words for him. "So your dullard lover has left you, and you're settling for second best?"

Her hand flew up and slapped him hard. He staggered back. Her face reddened with fury.

"You ... You bastard!" she snapped. "I came to find you, to talk, to decide ... But now ... Curse you, Jarial. At least you've made it easy for me!"

She turned on her heel and strode away. Jarial rubbed his cheek and stared after her. So that was how she felt. Well, if she could get entangled with someone else, so could he. And he remembered Liffy Triese, from after that disastrous raid on the mill, and how her dark red hair had tumbled over her pale, serious face as she spread ointment onto his wounded hand.

CHAPTER 41
THE BRIGANDS' HOUSE

Durston and Ezera marched with the other soldiers along the narrow track that lead uphill through sparse forests. Eyes narrowing, Durston seized Ezera's arm.

"Him," he muttered, pointing ahead. "'Tis him, ain't it? That rat, Levin Bluestone?" His breath hung in clouds in the frosty air.

Ezera squinted ahead through the shadowy gloom.

"Yes. I reckon it is."

"Good," Durston growled. "I never could find the brute in the city."

"I expect he was hiding from you." Ezera laughed quietly. "Heard there was a Talthen searching for him, and skulked in a cellar."

"Like the coward he is," Durston said. "So why's he here?"

"Tempted by the extra pay for this little picnic, no doubt." She looked at the scowl on his face. "Cheer up. Otherwise I'm going to think you regret coming back from Ceodrinne."

Durston grunted and stared ahead. The leaders paused at a bend in the track. Felde, Vallan and Iselle stood aside as Riathe stepped closer to the tall hedge of holly that lined the track.

"What're they doing?" someone near them whispered, then gasped as the holly trees swayed and parted to reveal a locked gate. Cold moonlight shone from its spikes and curved, wrought-iron railings. Riathe gestured briefly and the padlock crumbled.

The gate swung wide. As the companies walked through, Durston pulled Ezera to the back of the column.

"I'm going to get to him," he said in a fierce whisper. "'Tis too good a chance to miss."

"I wondered whether you'd abandoned your idea of revenge. You've not said anything in the month since you came back."

"I ain't forgotten. You know what he did. How can I let a murdering scum like him walk the earth?"

Ezera nodded. "True. What do you want me to do?"

"Keep out of it. You've got your job, your position. I don't want to cause you trouble."

"Cause me trouble?" she hissed. "I can handle myself!"

"Don't be a fool, Ezera! I ain't going to risk you being court-martialed. 'Tis my business, not yours."

Ezera glared at him, then shrugged. Perhaps it was his fight. It had been his village, his cousin, his father.

"All right. Have your own way. I expect I'll be busy enough without chasing round after you and Levin as well," she whispered, as they followed the rest through the gap in the hedge.

Shards of white moonlight flecked the trees ahead. Ezera could not see beyond them, but she thought she could smell a faint trace of woodsmoke beneath the scent of leaf mould.

Felde and Vallan quietly reminded the soldiers of their orders.

"Absolute silence, until the first signal," Vallan whispered. "And you all know what to do on the second and third?"

Ezera and the others nodded. "Yes. Get out as fast as we can," someone muttered.

"Good. Four squads from each of the two companies are going in, two more are going to get the horses from the stables, and the archers and the rest are to surround the house."

Iselle came up and nodded briefly to Ezera, Vallan and

Felde. "The archers are ready," she said. "We're waiting for Riathe to lead."

Bending low, creeping forward through trees, they came to a sloping meadow, pale grey in the moonlight. In the centre of the bowl-shaped dell, Ezera saw the brigands' house, the lair of the elusive Ulban Hirshe. It looked like a peaceful, sturdy house, with high gables and tall chimneys, white stone quoins, and ivy clinging to the brick walls between dark mullioned windows. Stone wolves guarded a studded, heavy door. Silence filled the dell as they crept into positions around the house and its outhouses and stables.

Clouds blew across the sky and veiled the moon. In the deeper gloom, Ezera could barely see the pale figure of Riathe standing before the door, staring intently at it, his shoulders tense, his hands clenched by his side. She glanced at Durston beside her. He nodded, his face taut and grim.

Riathe released the pearl. It rose, glowing brightly. The light glinted from sword points, knives and dozens of arrows nocked on bows, pointed towards the house. Shadows deepened to black in the dazzling light, and the roof of the house glistened silver. The light grew and outshone the moon. Riathe paused, staring at the house for a long time. Ezera shuddered at the tormented, vengeful expression on his face. Then he clicked his fingers and the door shivered, cracked then fell into fragments. Ezera, Durston and the other squad members ran forwards into the house, weapons unsheathed.

The hall was empty, apart from two scrawny greyhounds stretched out on the quarry tiles before a dead fire. A wooden stairway led upwards, and several closed doors lined the plain brick walls. The dogs lifted their heads and barked briefly.

"Leave them. You go left, you right, you to the back," Ezera ordered. "The rest, upstairs with me."

At the top of the stairs a sleepy-eyed burly man staggered, shirtless, from a room. He stared at them.

"What the ..." he grunted, then lunged at Ezera. She dodged, and Durston's fist thudded into the man's side. He rolled sideways and tumbled down the stairs. Running left, Ezera slammed open the next door. A young, white-faced lad cowered in a corner, next to a plump grey-haired woman. They shrank back, shaking visibly.

"Out!" Ezera snapped. "Out, hands in the air, no weapons, and you won't be hurt."

By the time she, Durston and her squad reached the last rooms on the corridor, Ezera reckoned they'd dispatched six bandits, and another dozen, including servants and mistresses, had run downstairs and out, hands in the air. They'd be taken prisoner and fairly well treated, as long as they didn't try to fight. She and her group checked a few more rooms: empty. The sounds of combat, cries of surprise and yells of defiance from the other parts of the house had faded.

"Right, done, time to get out," she said. But as they followed her squad to the top of the stairs, Durston pulled her back.

"Levin!" he hissed. She turned, and saw Levin run into one of the rooms on the other side. Durston ran after him, sword drawn. Ezera followed, but Durston reached the door first. He dashed in and slammed the door shut. Ezera heard the sound of bolts. She tried the door. It was firmly closed. She hammered on the panels.

"Durston! Durston, you idiot, let me in!"

Through the door, she could hear Levin exclaiming and shouting. Durston yelled, "You murdered my cousin, you sent my father to that hell-hole of a prison!", then there were no more voices, just the sounds of blows, steel on steel, crashes and two men's angry wordless sounds.

"Durston, you rat, you'd better let me in!" she shouted, slamming her shoulder against the unyielding door again and again.

Suddenly she heard a single trumpet blast. The signal!

"Get out!" she screamed. "Durston, get out!"

The sound of scuffling and fighting still filtered through the locked door. Swearing, she threw herself at the door one last time, then kicked it violently, again and again. It didn't move. She ran downstairs, through the emptied hall, outside and round to the side of the building, ignoring the circling ranks of soldiers, the groups of chained prisoners, the astonished looks on the faces of Felde and Vallan. At the side of the house, she counted the windows and looked up. Yes, she could see glimpses of two men struggling together behind the leaded panes of glass.

The final signal, two long blasts, sounded. She looked back and saw Riathe stepping towards the front of the house and raising his hands. The light from the pearl above him turned from silver to gold, then to lurid orange.

"I'll kill Durston for this," Ezera muttered as she ran to the ivy snaking up the buttresses and bricks. Someone yelled a warning. She didn't glance back but grabbed at the ivy stems, wedging her toes into the indentations in the masonry as she started to clamber upwards.

She gasped as the wall became warm. Heat started to radiate from the bricks and the stone window sills and jambs. Through a window nearby she saw the flutter of a red tongue of flame. Ezera reached up, seized a stem and pulled. It broke. She felt herself slipping and reached out sideways to grab at the mullion of the window. She screamed in pain.

The stone scorched her. She fell, clutching her blistered hand, and thudded onto her back. Above her, the ivy shrivelled, blackened and burst into flames.

"Durston!" she cried, desperately, "Durston!"

Someone grabbed her arms and dragged her away from the building. As the walls shimmered with heat, she struggled against the arms pinioning her, biting her lip with fear and pain, watching the window above. It shone yellow as if all the inside of the room blazed with a roaring fire. The light glowed carmine, until the whole house reddened as if dipped in blood. Smoke rose from the roof and the tiles shook and cracked. A split opened in the roof and flickering flames rose into the sky. Ezera could not stop herself from crying and shaking.

A figure appeared at the window above her, a black silhouette against the orange and yellow flames. It became two figures, struggling and clutching each other and reeling towards the window. They crashed through the glass and fell, among splinters and shards and smoke. There was a cry of agony, suddenly cut off. The figure underneath jerked and then collapsed. The man on top lifted his head and crawled slowly away. It was Durston.

Ezera cried out, wrenched herself free and staggered towards him. Others ran to him, and the other, and pulled them away from the building.

"By the founders, it's Levin," one said. "And his neck's broken."

"No great loss," another muttered.

"What happened?"

"Four of them," Durston paused, coughed and gasped. He groaned and rolled onto his side. Blood trickled from a slash across his back. "We had to fight them ..." he stuttered, in a hoarse voice. "Got trapped ... Heard signal, couldn't break through in time."

Ezera knelt by him and pulled him into her arms, wincing at the pain from the burn on her hand.

"You idiot," she muttered.

She looked up and around at the house as it shook. Beams and bricks groaned as they twisted and buckled. Glass in the windows shattered. A chimney stack fell. Most of the soldiers stared at the blazing house, but many glanced with fear and awe at the expression on the wizard's face in the blood-red light from the pearl.

"Enough, I think," Riathe said, so quietly that Ezera could barely hear him against the roar of the conflagration. He raised his hands and then dropped them. The house became a single fire. Flames and smoke reached up into the dark sky, covering the moon. The meadow filled with the heat and light from the burning. The glare lit the horrified, amazed faces of the watchers in crimson, orange and bright gold. With a great crack, the roof fell, the walls crumbled, and even the stone wolves by the door vanished into the inferno. Riathe stared at the consummation, his expression filled with a terrible satisfaction, until all that was left was a chaos of ash and embers and billowing smoke that brought stinging tears into their eyes.

They bivouacked in a glade in the woods, a mile from the burnt-out shell of the building, but not out of reach of the drifting scent of smoke and ash. As Ezera bandaged the wound on Durston's back, Riathe strode by. She thought of asking him to stop and heal Durston, but something about the intent, fell expression on his face stopped her.

"Gone to interrogate the prisoners," a soldier nearby said. She poked some more wood into the fire, then reclined back on her mat and pulled a blanket over herself.

"Why?" Ezera asked.

"I heard he's trying to find someone called Ulban Hirshe," she replied, as she interlaced her fingers behind her head and stared up at the pale moon. "I don't envy him if the wizard finds him. He looks murderous."

"Ulban Hirshe ..." said Durston. "Aye. I know the name."

The woman closed her eyes. "I'm exhausted. Long night ... And now it's going to be too cold to sleep, even with this pathetic excuse for a fire. Who'd be in the army, eh?"

Ezera turned on her side and moved closer to Durston.

"Quick thinking with that lie," she whispered.

"What lie?"

"About fighting four bandits and being trapped."

"Oh. That."

"How does it feel, to have killed the rat?"

"I didn't," Durston muttered.

"Huh?"

Durston looked away. "'Twas the fire ... If I'd known the

wizard meant to fire the house! Ezera, it ... Anyhap, I lost concentration. Panicked. He stabbed my back. I ran to the window; the door was all flames. He grabbed me, we struggled, we fell, but I was on top. I heard his neck snap as he hit the ground."

Ezera shrugged. "He's still dead, though. It's done."

"Aye. But ... 'Tis no satisfaction in it."

He rolled over and pulled his cloak up over his hunched shoulders.

The night became bitterly cold, their mats and blankets too thin for a late autumn night in lonely forests. By morning Ezera felt chilled to the bone and had only managed a few hours' sleep, before being woken by Durston groaning in his dreams and muttering about fire and Levin, and rubbing fitfully at the wound in his back.

Ezera reluctantly got up, wrapped her blanket over Durston, kissed him, and went to find Felde and the other leaders. They were deep in a discussion with Riathe. She coughed. They turned.

"Er, sir, I gather I and some of my company are supposed to be escorting you to Langron," she said.

Felde looked uncertainly at the others. Iselle shrugged, and Riathe rolled his eyes sky-wards.

"That was the arrangement," Vallan said, spreading his hands wide in exasperation.

Felde flung a saddle onto one of the horses taken from the stables.

"'Tis complicated," he muttered. "But 'twill be just the three of us. Me, Vallan, Iselle."

"What?" Ezera said. "But, sir, the danger ... We've destroyed this nest of scum, but there may be others!"

"Aye," snapped Riathe. "You should have an escort!"

"We'll be fine now that we've got horses," Felde said. "'Tis only four days riding. And there ain't enough other horses for an escort."

"True," said Iselle. "We can ride, and get there faster. An

escort, having to walk, would slow us down. Felde wants to see Berrena, and I want to get back to Nessa."

"Who's Nessa?" Ezera asked.

"Our daughter," Vallan said.

"I should come with you!" Riathe said.

"Headon needs you in the city," Vallan said. "It's your duty to go back."

"For what? For pointless, endless meetings; for reading the councillors' dull, fearful little minds, persuading them to do this, to approve that. A tame wizard, doing Headon's bidding. I'm tired of it! Duty? Curse it!" He flung his hands up and stalked off. Felde stared after him.

An hour later, Felde and the two others rode away. Ezera noticed, with a feeling of relief, that Riathe submitted to being embraced by his father. He stood, intently watching them as they disappeared between the trees. Then he turned away, slowly wiping something from his eyes.

"Sir?" she said.

"I know," he said, wearily. "Back to the city."

CHAPTER 42
NOT A COWARD

On the road to Langron, winter frost crisped the surface of the snow and drew hoarfrost on the twigs and grasses. The branches of the trees stood out in stark filigree against the heavy grey sky. Last night had been clear, but the bright blue of early morning had clouded over as snowflakes started to fall.

Felde shivered as the flakes landed on his bare neck. They had ridden for two days, in chill autumn air, and now it seemed that winter was coming. Despite the cold nights, as they had sat round the fire in the evenings, talking quietly of all that had happened, peace enveloped Felde. The three of them had needed this time alone, to remember and to re-connect, without the distraction of a dozen City Guards escorting them. The quiet and the companionship were a blessing, and they were going home.

Now Iselle and Vallan rode in front, talking about what Nessa may have been doing with her grandmother and whether she'd like Hueron when they took her there. Felde went a few yards behind, pondering over the changes of the last few months and yearning for hot food, a blazing hearth and, most of all, for the warm arms of Berrena, only a day's ride away.

Ahead of them, six men trudged through the thickening snow. They parted to let the three horsemen through. As Felde and the others rode past, suddenly the men drew daggers. Three of them seized the horses' bits while the others pulled Felde and the Hueds off their mounts. Before they could react, Vallan and Felde's swords were thrown aside. A swarthy fellow pinioned Iselle's arm behind her, grabbing a handful of her hair with his other hand. She screamed as he yanked her arm and hair. Felde and Vallan found themselves caught too; strong, ruthless men holding them with knives at their throats. Felde cursed their folly, riding unaware and alone into such a trap. He struggled but could not break free. The bearded man holding him laughed and pushed the tip of his knife into his neck.

"Keep still," he growled.

A dark-haired, lanky man walked up to Vallan, holding a long, narrow dagger. Felde recognised him.

"You're from Helsund, ain't you?" he burst out.

"Aye. Helsund. You know it?" the man said, turning to look at Felde.

"I was born there."

"Then you'll know all about it. Keep out the way and you won't get hurt. We ain't got no quarrel with Talthen. Just them murdering, greedy, thieving Hued swine."

He pressed the dagger point against Vallan's chest. "All those men murdered, my grandfather dead, my parents dying of famine while you feasted in your bloody city," he hissed. "Well, 'tis our turn now."

Felde thought frantically. A coward would say nothing and would escape. But he wasn't a coward. A reckless idea came to him and he burst out, "Stop! Let me do it! Let me kill him!"

The lanky man swung round. "What?"

"I hate him! Let me get my revenge on him," Felde exclaimed. "The Hued murdered my grandfather too, in Helsund. You don't know what this cursed brute did to us - to my wife, to my niece."

With a sudden lunge, he wrenched himself out of his captor's grip and spat at Vallan, who flinched as Iselle cried out in fear.

"What're you doing riding with them, then?" demanded the man.

"'Tis for the money. They hired me as a bodyguard."

"Some bodyguard!" sniggered the burly man holding Vallan.

"Aye, a bodyguard. I had to!" Felde said. "You know what 'tis like. 'Twas either that or starving. Let me kill the bastard, for my wife's sake, for my niece's sake!"

The lanky man looked at Felde, at his height and muscles and air of strength, and at Vallan and Iselle's shocked faces. He laughed.

"All right! Prove it. If you kill him you can join us and help us wipe out the whole damned lot of them. You look like you'd fight well. Give him a knife," he said to one of the others, then stepped behind Felde, grabbing his left arm. He hissed into his ear, "I'm right behind you, watching you. Don't try aught clever or you'll feel this," and the point of his dagger pressed into Felde's side.

The burly man pushed Vallan forward. Felde ran the knife tip along Vallan's throat as his blue eyes gazed squarely back at him. He winked at Vallan and drove the knife deep into the neck of the burly man, who dropped to the ground.

"You filthy bastard traitor!" yelled the lanky man holding his arm. Felde knew the dagger had been thrust into his side, but felt no pain. It can't be too deep, he thought, as he pulled his arm free and rammed his elbow into the lanky man's stomach, who stumbled backwards. Felde shoved the knife hilt-first into Vallan's hands. Vallan ran to Iselle's captor and stabbed him. She yanked herself free, leaving a mass of purple hair in the man's fist. She pulled her own dagger from her belt as the two other ruffians dropped the horses' bridles and came towards them.

Felde whirled and charged into the bearded man who'd been holding him, smashing his fist into the man's face and knocking him to the ground. The lanky man staggered up and rushed at him, pulling another knife from his belt, but Felde threw himself forwards. His weight bore the other downwards and he rained ferocious blows at the man's face.

He heard Vallan shouting and glimpsed him grabbing his

sword then stabbing the bearded man as he lay facedown on the grass. The thickening snow swirled around them, grey and white, as Felde struggled with the lanky man, hitting him again and again. As the man writhed under him, Felde looked around briefly and realised that Vallan had slashed at one of the two ruffians, felling him. He saw the final ruffian backing away, looking at Vallan and his gore-covered sword, at the four bodies on the ground, at Iselle, dishevelled and breathing hard but her knife ready. The man leapt onto one of the horses and fled.

Felde's arms felt numb and he knew his strength was draining away. He battled desperately to keep his grip around the other's throat. Vallan and Iselle ran to him and pulled the lanky man away. The man rolled on the blood-stained ground, clutching his throat and groaning, his face bruised and crushed. Vallan stood over him and thrust his sword down into his heart.

Felde staggered upright, but weakness came over him. He glanced down and saw scarlet blood pouring from a gash in his side. He slumped to his knees, then fell sideways. Vallan tore off his jacket and shirt and held them over his wound. Iselle ran to the horses and pulled towels and bandages from the saddlebags. As they tried to staunch his wound, he saw the flowing blood drench the cloths and bandages, spreading onto the grass and staining the white snow red.

"I'm sorry ... that I spat at you ..." Felde muttered. Breathing came hard. He blinked to clear a growing blackness in his sight.

"It was a good plan, brother," Vallan said. "Headon will be impressed."

"Tell Bee ..." Felde whispered.

"Tell her what? Felde? Felde!"

Vallan's voice grew fainter. Felde no longer had the strength to speak. He could feel Iselle's fingers clutching his, and her tears dropping onto his hand. He could no longer see the white snow, the grey sky, the dark trees. The last words he heard, before the darkness and silence took him, was Vallan calling his name.

CHAPTER 43
GOVERNING

Headon picked up a green chalcedony paperweight from his desk and thoughtfully rubbed its carved facets as he gazed at the heaps of reports and letters on his desk. No matter how many hours he worked, the piles never diminished. Sighing, he placed the paperweight on the highest pile, straightened up the papers neatly, then walked over to the window. It had a view of the main square, where market stalls of colourful vegetables and verdant herbs stood between shops with vibrant displays of cloth and ceramics. Talthens wheeled barrows laden with sides of ham and flitches of bacon. Headon could hear the traders calling out:

"Cheeses: matured, creamy, beautiful cheeses!"

"Dyed and printed cotton, cheapest in town!"

"Cooking pots, the best in the city!"

He could almost smell the yeast and cinnamon from the bread and cakes mingling with the briny smell of the smoked fish. The market started earlier each day, and had more goods on offer, more stalls, more produce. He noticed a Hued woman talking, almost flirting with a Talthen trader, smiling at him and laughing at something he said. Some things at least, Headon thought, had improved in the last few months.

Returning to his desk, he picked up the next letter. A request, a demand almost, from a councillor; that Talthens should not be allowed to live within the city. The author had written 'dullard', not Talthen, and Headon could imagine the scorn and distaste on the writer's face. He frowned. The next task, after the marking ceremony had been declared illegal, would be to take action, somehow, to stop people using the term 'dullard'. He recalled his feelings as he'd waited in front of the Grey Army, when he'd looked down at the masses of enemies on the plain before the city, and he smiled wryly. Leading the assault and invading the city had certainly been easier than governing it.

He heard a quiet knock at the door. "Come in," he called. Riathe entered.

"You wanted to see me?" he said, a scowl on his face.

"Ah, yes. But, first, come and see."

Riathe came in and gazed out of the window with an uninterested expression.

"Well, what of it?" he said.

"Look at the market. So much has changed. We almost appear to be prosperous. And we - you - have helped. I didn't think we'd survive the remainder of the autumn, let alone the winter! Struggling to feed everyone, even with your help. It seemed like the easier times would never come."

"But they did."

"And better than expected. The Magi's curses really have been lifted, the gifts are no longer draining the land. I am almost optimistic. But there is still so much to do! How to reduce the prejudice, the resentment, how to reconcile people - I cannot see the way yet."

Riathe did not reply. He put his hands to his temples and leaned against the glass, staring down. Headon looked at him with concern. Headon had long since reverted to normal dress but Riathe still wore the grey uniform. He looked taller and thinner, his face ashen white, almost gaunt, his eyes deep-shadowed, the opalescence on his skin stronger. He turned away from the window and wandered around the office, picking up a bronze penknife from the desk and examining it before replacing it, moving from the fireplace to the desk and back, as Headon sat at his desk, glancing through a few more documents before putting them aside.

"What did you want to see me for, Headon?" Riathe asked.

"Well, I intend to travel to the old Magi's land next month to find out how things are there," Headon said. "We will open up a trade route with the people there and try to persuade or bribe some Hueds to move there - it's a good land. And I want to see Loira again."

"Loira?"

"I don't know if you remember her. A friend of mine. She helped me at the Magi's house, but she came from Peveque."

"Oh. Right. Do you want me to come with you?"

"Perhaps. But we need to get this legislation about the marking ceremony passed first. I need your help for this."

Riathe frowned. "The usual? Find out who is likely to vote against it, and persuade them otherwise? Yet again?"

"It's the only way!" Headon snapped. "Until we have more Talthen on the council!"

Riathe shrugged. "As you wish, Headon. It is very useful to you, ain't it? Having a tame wizard?"

Headon stared at the sour expression on Riathe's face.

"I thought you wanted to help. That you cared," he said, hesitantly.

"Cared? Not much, no. Why do you care, Headon? You spend hours, hours and hours, at this." He gestured at the piles of letters and documents on the desk.

"Why?" Headon hesitated. "Riathe ... Hundreds of people died in that invasion. It was a massacre, and it was my mistake - my fault - for leaving the gates open. The guilt haunts me. I don't want to be remembered for that. I want to be remembered for building peace, for working for justice, for prosperity. I would do anything for this. To stop the prejudice, the discrimination. To try to make things fair. How can that not matter to you?"

"Matter to me? You will hate me for saying it, but nay, it doesn't!" Riathe exclaimed. "I'll work with you, Headon, for justice, for prosperity. I'll do it because 'tis right, but I don't care about it and don't expect me to!"

He strode back to the window, gazing outward with a dark look on his face. Headon considered remonstrating, but while he thought what to say, there came a sharp knock on the door.

"Come!" Headon called. A captain from the City Guard walked in and saluted.

"Excuse the interruption, sir, but Lord Sulvenor asked to be informed immediately. Sir, they have tracked down and caught Ulban Hirshe and the remaining bandits. He is about to be committed for trial."

Riathe turned round.

"At last! Where were they hiding?" he exclaimed.

"In the forests north-east, seventy miles away from the north road. There were over forty of them. Sixteen were killed but we took the rest, including Ulban, alive."

"How did you find him?"

"One of the rabble we captured last month squealed," the captain said. "Sold his comrades for six months less in prison, the scabby little worm, and told us where Ulban's hideout was."

"How many men did you lose?" asked Headon.

"Fourteen, sir, and several injured."

"Fourteen! They put up a fight then!"

"Yes, sir."

"Well, thank you. You may go."

Headon turned to Riathe.

"More men dead! For the sake of one bandit chief and two dozen robbers! Riathe, is it worth it? Finding Hirshe has become an obsession. Why?"

Riathe shook his head.

"'Tis hard to explain. The hatred I've got for the Magi and for Ulban and for all the evil they were planning - 'tis like a fever burning me up. I'm glad to have him taken at last. I've got to see him destroyed," he explained, adding in a subdued, intense voice, so quiet that Headon barely heard him, "then I can get free of it all."

"Free of it all? Riathe, there is something seriously wrong. You are not well, I can see," said Headon in alarm, looking at Riathe's pallor and the shadows under his eyes.

"Nay. I can't sleep, but that's not the worst. Headon, I'll tell you after Ulban's committal. But you can't help me."

Headon stared at Riathe.

"I will tell you later, Headon!" Riathe exclaimed. "But I need to finish this with Ulban first!"

CHAPTER 44
THE TRIAL

Sunlight poured through the upper windows above the empty balcony as Headon followed Riathe into the council chamber. Only a couple of dozen council members occupied the curved benches, and the two judges sat at a desk facing them, with the council scribes beside them. Soldiers guarded the doors. In the centre of the room a man stood, facing the judges, with two soldiers flanking him. His arms were folded defiantly but beads of sweat glistened on his bald head. Headon looked at him with curiosity before taking his seat next to the council secretary on the front row.

"Is that feeble-looking man really Ulban?" he asked Riathe.

"Aye. Thinner. And not as well dressed as when I last saw him. No fine lace, no linen shirt, no gold chains. But aye, it's him."

The senior judge nodded to them both, then continued reading the formal accusation. "Ulban Hirshe, you are charged with murder, robbery, with plotting robbery, with plotting murder, and with treason. We will now hear the evidence for this accusation."

Riathe paced up and down as the witnesses were interrogated. After the soldiers involved in capturing Ulban, a guard brought in a grey-clad gaunt man, who gazed at Ulban with fear as he was pushed into the witness stand. Riathe leaned forward.

"You," he hissed. "I remember you. You were a servant in his house. You told me what Ulban was. Now, tell the council."

The gaunt man glanced at Ulban then stared at Riathe. "Aye, I recollect you, you were one of the apprentices, weren't you?" he said, slowly. "I've been promised protection, ain't I?"

Riathe nodded.

"Good," the man said. "Well, Ulban, curse him, he's a thief, a leader of thieves. Ambushing travellers, robbing, murdering, enslaving. Banditry, call it what you like."

Ulban leaned forward and shook his fists at the man. "Lies!" he shouted. "Lies, all lies! You back-stabbing traitor! Didn't I pay you enough when you worked for me?"

The servant shrank away from Ulban, his hands lifted in fear, as one of the soldiers hauled the prisoner back. "Scum! Don't speak unless you are instructed to!" he snapped.

"It's not lies," the gaunt man said. "He's a bandit, a robber, a worse than robber!"

"Indeed? A robber?" said one of the judges. "Robbing Hueds? Or dull ... I mean, Talthen?"

"Anyone he could. Course, Talthen ain't generally rich enough to rob. But Ulban, his lot, they'd sometimes attack Hueds, if they could get away with it. As long as there weren't no City Guards around."

"Ah ... I know of people who'd travelled north and been ambushed. But we were never able to track down who'd done it. The bandits wore masks, gloves, or killed their victims." The judge glared at Ulban with contempt and fury. "Get this greasy swine, this Ulban, back to his cell. We will hold a full trial in ten days time and I hope that I will have the sentencing of this scoundrel!"

Headon breathed a sigh of relief. Perhaps now Riathe could put aside his obsession with Ulban. But as the soldiers came forward to take Ulban away and the council rose to leave, Riathe jumped up and strode towards the judges' desk.

"Wait!" he said. "There's more. There's something that Ulban Hirshe knows, something that would hang him ten times over. 'Tis important that you and the council and all the Hued know this. That you know, from him, what he and the Magi were planning."

Headon got up and took Riathe's arm.

"Can't this wait, Riathe? Until the formal trial?"

"Nay! I can't wait. Not another day! The sooner this is known, the better."

"What is known?"

"Ulban won't tell you willingly. But I can make him."

Headon shrugged. "Very well. Are you willing to allow Lord Sulvenor to interrogate the prisoner further?" he asked the judges.

"Yes. Intriguing," one said and the other nodded.

"Good. Riathe, he's yours," Headon said, sitting back down. He noticed Ulban's hand trembled as he wiped sweat from his face.

Riathe turned to the scribes. "Be sure you write down all that he says. And I want his account public, for everyone in the city to know it."

A murmur of interest ran round the benches. Riathe stared at Ulban's defiant face.

"Do you remember me?" he demanded.

"Nay. I've never seen you before in my life," Ulban snarled, glaring at Riathe.

"Do you know what this is?"

The pearl, faintly glowing, rose from Riathe's hand and hovered above Ulban.

"A magic trick? How the hell should I know? Let me go! 'Tis all nonsense. I'm innocent; I'm only an innkeeper. I've done nought wrong," he burst out desperately. Beads of moisture on his brow glistened.

The sunlight in the room faded, as if a cloud had passed over the sun. The pearl grew. A baleful blue-green light shone from it, casting strange shadows on Riathe's face. Headon held his breath in fear, but did not dare move.

"The truth now, Ulban," Riathe said in a cold, quiet voice. "Tell us the truth. As a robber, as a chief among other robbers, how many men did you control? Were you in league with the Magi?"

Ulban was shaking. The council chamber was silent as everyone leaned forward to hear him.

"Aye, aye, damn you. I'm a robber, I've sheltered and helped the Magi, there were three hundred and sixty other thieves under my command. You bloody wizard!" He made as if to lunge at Riathe, but the soldiers pulled him back.

"Where are the men now?"

"Some died at Hueron last year, some you've got in prison, some are in the northern mountains in a hideout two score miles north-west of Helsund, others – I don't know."

Riathe turned to the scribes. "Have you got that?" he asked, and when they had finished writing, he rounded on Ulban again.

"And the Magi? Tell us what you and they were intending to do about the gifts and symbols, what you were going to get the Talthen to do, how Hueron's destruction was planned."

Ulban shook his head and sank to his knees. Sweat poured off him, as he grovelled before the pale figure of the wizard. The pearl glowed brighter. He looked up at it, then at Riathe's implacable face. In a faint, terrified voice that seemed to be forced out of his throat, Ulban told the council about the Magi's scheme to persuade the Talthen to attack the Coloured City, about their plan to offer help to the Hueds and then destroy the symbols, how the Magi had been contriving the massacre of the Hued. The judges and the councillors gasped and stared with shock at each other and at the shaking figure of Ulban. Whispers of amazement and fury echoed around the chamber.

"Then, when most of the Hued were dead and the Talthen weakened by war, I would have robbed and looted at will, taking what I wanted from the city and towns." His voice tailed off.

"Hang him," someone cried. "Powers' above, hang the swine from the tallest gallows that we can build!"

"Mercy ..." Ulban muttered. "I ask your lordships for

mercy."

""Tain't all, though, is it?" Riathe said curtly. "Your men started attacking and robbing Hueds and encouraging Talthen to look for revenge. Your cutthroats were behind the murder of Lord Felde Sulvenor, my father, weren't they?"

"Nay, nay, that wasn't us. After the city fell, I and any of my men that were left fled back to our northern bases to hide."

"You are lying! Tell me the truth, Ulban!" insisted Riathe, as the strange light from the pearl pulsed around him.

"I can't! I don't know who they were!" sobbed Ulban. He jerked upright, his back arched and his right arm pulled behind him, the hand pushed upwards by some invisible force. The soldiers started forward but Riathe whirled around, his face contorted with anger.

"Stop!" he commanded. "Leave him!"

They stepped back. Headon rose to intervene, but Riathe's fierce grey eyes met his with such force that he felt compelled to back away.

The greenish light grew and the stone spun and shone, flickering black threads rippling across it. The silver shimmering on Riathe appeared flecked with darkness and strange reflections. Headon could smell the fear-drenched rank sweat upon Ulban, who started to whimper as his arm moved higher.

"Last chance," said Riathe, his voice inexorable. "Did your men kill my father?"

"Nay! Nay, nay!" Ulban gasped, agony in his face.

Riathe held up his hand. In the sudden silence the sound of his fingers clicking rang loud. At the sound the memories flooded Headon with cold, and his heart paused for an instant. Then he heard an echoing snap in Ulban's arm. The man fell forward, moaning and writhing. His face was ashen, his arm dangling at a sickening angle. One of the councillors cried out in horror. Headon shrank back in overwhelming dread at the terrible expression of satisfaction on Riathe's face.

Slowly Riathe's expression changed and the green light faded. The pearl sank back into his hand. Late afternoon sunlight flooded the room from the high windows. The compulsion keeping Headon from moving broke and he leapt up. He barked to the soldiers, "Get a doctor for that man! Get him treated, then back to jail!" Then there was uproar, people shouting in shocked voices, men rushing to fetch help, others trying to leave the chamber, cramming the doorways in their panic. Riathe turned to Headon, a shocked look on his face, and staggered towards him. Headon ran to him, grabbed his arm and pulled him to the door, then pushed him along the corridors and up the stairs until they reached his office. He shoved Riathe inside, followed him and locked the door behind them.

CHAPTER 45
OBSCURITY

Riathe stumbled forwards a few steps, then collapsed onto the rug and curled up, shaking and muttering. His pale skin looked even paler than usual, almost grey. Headon stretched an arm towards the boy's thin shoulders, then withdrew it and stepped back. He sat at the edge of the room, his back against the wall, and watched Riathe in trepidation.

Eventually the trembling and strange mumbling faded. Slowly, wearily, Riathe got to his knees and knelt, staring at Headon with wide, horror-struck eyes. He shook his head.

"I should not have, I know, Headon," he said. "Foul, vile ... I should not have done it."

"No," Headon said. "No, you shouldn't have."

"But I had to find out who killed my father. And - I failed." He hung his head and rubbed his temples.

"You didn't know that Ulban wasn't responsible. Anyway, we'll find them eventually. We're scouring the northern hills for the rest of them."

Riathe stood up. He looked down reflectively at his left hand and muttered. "You're right. It was a waste of time." He snapped his fingers quietly.

Headon flinched.

"Don't be frightened!" Riathe said. "I ain't going to hurt you!"

"Frightened!" Headon leapt to his feet. "Frightened! Riathe, I saw Aven killed like that. The Mage broke my leg like that. By simply snapping his fingers. Do you have any idea how you doing that made me feel?"

"I didn't know," Riathe said, looking appalled.

"No, you didn't know! But, even so, Riathe, in the name of all the Founders, what is going on? You torture Ulban, you say you're not free. Your hints, your looks, not sleeping ... What is wrong with you?"

The boy said nothing, but he looked at Headon with a distorted, wretched face.

"I'm not so much frightened of you, as frightened for you," Headon said. "What is it that is wrong?"

Riathe held up his left hand. "Mayhap you should be frightened of me. There's so much power in here." He walked over to the window and stared out, then said quietly, "There's a sentry down there. He looks bored. Waiting for his shift to finish, waiting to go home to his dinner, his wife, his children. I would give everything to be like him. Obscure ..."

"Why don't you?"

Whirling round, Riathe snapped. "I can't! It's eating me up, and I can't!"

"What?"

"You don't see it, do you, Headon? I told you! The blue Mage, damn him to all eternity, gave me all his memories, all his desires. I can remember, Headon! I can remember what I - he - did to Iselle, to Vallan, to that girl at Ulban's house, and to all of them!"

Headon shrank back against the wall. "Great Powers, Riathe ..." he muttered.

"And that's not all! When I broke Ulban's arm, oh, Headon, it was - it was bliss. Such enjoyment!"

"No, no, Riathe. Not you ... Not like them. Not the Magi. No, not like them."

"Aye," he said, nodding miserably. "Like them. That's what I am scared of. That I'm turning into a Mage."

He sat down, clutched his knees to his chest and rocked to and fro. There was such utter bleakness on his face that Headon went over and put his arm around the boy's hunched shoulders.

"I'll help you," he said, eventually. "We'll all help."

Riathe shook his head. He reached inside his jacket and took out a folded white cloth. Listlessly he opened it. Inside a lock of golden hair glistened.

"This is Aleythe's," he said.

"Aleythe?"

"Aye. I think you met her, at Langron, briefly. I loved her, centuries ago it seems now. I would have fought dragons for her. That's why I went to the Magi, and asked to be an apprentice. To save her. When she said she loved my cousin, not me, I felt - such grief! I wish I felt that now!"

"Wish you felt grief? Why?"

"Because when I saw her again, afterwards, in Langron, all I felt was contempt for a pretty doll-faced nothing of a girl. And ... and lust. I wanted to force, to take ... Ugh! Foul! Vile!" He lifted his arm and bit down hard on his wrist.

"Fight it, Riathe. You must fight it!"

"I have!" He leapt up. "For months! And months! Always fighting it! And I'm so tired. Just tired. I feel a thousand years old. A thousand years of ... of murders and cruelties and vile, vile desires. All there! Stuck in my head! I'm so tiring of fighting them, and I'm losing. Giving up ..."

"There must be something we can do!" Headon said, standing up.

"The best thing you could do would be kill me, Headon," he said in a deadpan quietness. Going over to the desk, Riathe picked up the penknife. Headon watched in trembling fear as Riathe ran the edge hard along his skin. He held his unmarked arm out to Headon.

"See? Nothing. You know, I think, how impossible it is to kill a Mage."

He turned away and put the knife down, and leaned on the desk. Headon could think of nothing to say or do. In the silence, the sounds of the market filtered through into the room. After a few minutes, Riathe turned back.

"I'm not glad my father's dead. Of course not. But I am glad he died still proud of me. Knowing nought about this. About what I did today. About what I am becoming."

"I see. Yes. I can see that."

"I'm full of these of these foul desires. There's nothing good, no good desires, nothing good that I enjoy anymore. Not even seeing my mother, my cousin, my family. Not riding, not eating, not drinking, nothing. The only thing that is left is this vile, vile desire to hurt people!"

Headon stared at his friend's gaunt, tormented face.

"I wish I could help you," he exclaimed.

"Mayhap you can. I can barely sleep and if I do, I have nightmares." He rubbed his eyes. "Horrible ones. Full of cruelties. Can you give me something to make me sleep better?"

Headon nodded.

"Good." He sighed. "That will help."

"I'll do that. Is there anything else? For the Powers' sake, there must be something!"

Riathe lifted his closed hand to his forehead. "I must find a way," he murmured. "Aye. There might be a way, only ... Headon, before you go south, come with me to Langron."

"To Langron? To see Berrena?"

"Aye."

"Escort, or just us two?"

Riathe laughed bitterly. "Why should we need a City Guard escort when you've got a Mage?"

"Well, I suppose not."

"But ..." Riathe paused. "Aye. Best have someone else. Someone we trust. Ask your captain, Ezera. She'd do. Aye, Headon, just us and her."

CHAPTER 46
LADY ROCHALE

The flashes of gold from celandines and anemones peeping through the spring grass did nothing to lift Ezera's spirits. To call this journey dull was too complimentary, she thought, scowling at the pale green leaves of the trees shaking in the breeze, and up at a buzzard soaring above. No bandits, no attacks, nothing exciting. Ezera remembered her last trip with Headon, and a few other councillors, to negotiate a trade deal for grain with a Talthen town in the south west. That had been much more exiting. She grinned at the recollection of thwarting a inexpert assassination attempt on her boss. But this trip? Dull in the extreme!

Headon had been quiet and preoccupied, talking little and constantly glancing with concern, even trepidation, at Riathe. The Grey Wizard had been sullen and dour, riding a little behind them and occasionally snapping impatiently at Headon when he asked him to rest or to eat. Apart from the tinge of fear caused by his strange behaviour, Ezera felt bored. Simply bored. Durston would have smiled sardonically and remarked that he would have thought she'd had enough excitement last autumn. Now, if he'd come too ... They could have sparred, practised archery, sneaked off together into the depths of the forest in the night. But he was in Ceodrinne.

I miss him, she thought. But I don't miss Jarry at all, do I? No, this ache in my bones, in my gut; it's for Durston now. So that's decided, at least.

They crested a hill. The road sloped downwards for about a mile. The other two let their horses amble onwards, but Ezera could bear it no more. She slammed her heels into her horse's flank, put her head down and galloped down the slope. Of course, Headon looked at her disapprovingly as she swept by, but she shrugged it off, and by the time they arrived in Langron he'd forgotten and was gazing around at the town with interest. Riathe looked around keenly too, his face slightly less grim.

The town seemed almost as busy today as it had been six months ago when the Grey Army had filled it with the noise and activity of hundreds of soldiers preparing for battle. But instead of archery butts and piles of shields and swords, there were market stalls and traders selling everything from fresh lettuce to great bolts of woollen cloth.

In the centre, by the side of the square, stood a tall marble monument. Headon and Riathe dismounted and stood before it silently for a while. The folded steel blade of a sword, high on its face, glinted against the pale stone. Ezera dismounted too, and knelt to read the gilded inscription.

> *Lord Felde Sulvenor*
> *"Brave men be rare as gold"*

"He was brave," she said. "I wish I'd known him better."

Headon nodded. "True. And you only know half, a quarter, of his story. Anyway, Riathe? Shall we carry on? On to Berrena's?"

On the far side of Langron they stopped at a square brick-built house, with an orchard of blossoming apple and pear trees shedding white petals onto the long grass in front. Ezera stared at the simple building, the plain slate roof, the five small windows, the unpainted wooden door.

"That's Lady Rochale's house? But she's the daughter of Lord Sapphireborne! Surely she'd live in Langron Manor, not this - not a place like this?"

Riathe frowned at her. "'Tis my home!" he snapped.

Ezera shrugged. "My mistake," she said. She supposed it was a step up from the thatched wattle and daub cottages of the rest of the town.

"Felde - Lord Sulvenor - lived here too," said Headon. "Remember she married him when he was only a Talthen horse-breeder. I suppose you never had occasion to see their house before."

As they dismounted and tied their horses to the fence rail, Berrena opened the door and ran out.

"Riathe! Oh, I'm so pleased to see you! 'Tis been too long, 'tis been months," she exclaimed, taking him into her arms and holding him close, stroking his hair and face. Then she released him and stepped back. She nodded to Headon, then glanced briefly at Ezera, and lifted her hand.

"Lady Rochale," Ezera said, bowing back and lifting her hand in greeting.

"Welcome to Langron," Berrena said. "Ezera Mertrice, is that right? I'm glad to see you. And Headon, you too, of course."

She turned back to Riathe, put her hands on his shoulders and looked steadily at him. "Riathe, you look so tired! By the Powers, you're not well, are you? What is it?"

Riathe shook his head. "Nothing, mother."

"Something is the matter." She turned round. "Headon, what is wrong with my son? He looks exhausted. What have you been making him do?"

"'Tis nought to do with Headon, mother," Riathe said, taking her hands in his. "Aye, though, you are right. I am tired. So tired! But I'm glad to be home."

He turned away and walked slowly into the house. Berrena beckoned Headon and Ezera in too.

"Come into the kitchen," she said. "I'm sure you're hungry."

In the kitchen, Riathe stood surrounded by a group of boys, girls and youngsters, his siblings, Ezera assumed. The smallest, a lad of nine or ten, pulled at his arms and shouted with excitement. Riathe gently disengaged the boy's hands.

"Not now, Gerik," he said. "Let me sit down first."

"Aye, make space, all of you," Berrena said. "Let our guests sit down too!"

The tallest girl poured water for them from an earthenware pitcher, while another cut slices of bread and put a bowl of apples on the table. Ezera perched on a window seat, crunching one of the apples, swinging her leg and watching the embraces and exclamations of the family. Headon stood, quietly watching Riathe with that same expression of wary concern. Berrena sat down next to Riathe.

"Any news, mother?" he said. "Looks like the town is going well."

"Aye, it is. Now that the taxes have been reduced so much, thanks to you and Headon, 'tis better. We had a good harvest and the shepherds are up to their knees in newborn lambs this spring too. The increased trading with the Hued, that as well, 'tis all helping."

"Good. And are Aleythe and Breck well? I want to see them."

"Very well," she replied. "They were married early in the winter, but you knew that, I know. They live only a few houses down the road. Breck helps with the horses and is out there now, with Aleythe. Gerik, run and fetch them, will you? Shall I tell your grandmother and Kianne that you're here?"

"Nay, not yet. Tell them later on today."

Aleythe and Breck came in, with the young lad Gerik behind them, as Riathe and Headon discussed the changes Headon had implemented in Hueron and exchanged Langron news with Berrena. Ezera looked curiously at the couple. She remembered Breck from six months ago, but had never seen Aleythe, a pretty, fair-haired, pale-skinned slip of a girl. Riathe nodded to Breck, rose and went over to them, taking Aleythe's hands in his.

"Aleythe, you look well," he said.

"Thank you, Riathe," she murmured in an awed, shy

voice.

Riathe reached inside his jacket and took out a folded cloth. He opened it. Ezera leaned forward to see a lock of golden hair.

"Do you remember giving this to me?" Riathe said.

Aleythe looked at it, raised her eyes to him and nodded.

"Do you remember, Aleythe, when I kissed you? All those months ago?"

The girl shot a glance at Breck, who stared at Riathe with wide-eyed surprise. Ezera couldn't blame him. She'd never have put Riathe down as a romantic type. Berrena and Headon looked equally astounded.

"Aye, but I never told Breck," she whispered.

"Breck, you knew I loved Aleythe," Riathe said. "I know you won't begrudge me one kiss, such a long time ago."

Breck nodded. "I did know. And, given what you did for her, for me, I don't begrudge you that. You know that!"

"Give me one kiss now, Aleythe," Riathe said, in a low, serious voice, taking her hand again.

Aleythe stared at him, "Nay, I can't ..." she said.

Breck moved forward as if to protest, stammering, "Raithe ... 'Tain't right!"

Berrena put a hand on his arm, and he sat down, looking suspiciously at Riathe.

"Please, Aleythe," said Riathe. "Breck, you don't mind, do you? You can trust me. All I ask is one kiss."

Breck hesitated, and then nodded. "Aye. We owe you everything, and I do trust you. But Riathe, it won't do any good, you know that."

"I know," replied Riathe.

"All right," said Aleythe and she kissed Riathe on the lips and stepped back, staring at him. He looked at her as if waiting for something. Then he turned away.

"Headon, can you give me that sleeping potion you said you had?" he said, in a drained, flat voice.

Headon nodded, reached into his rucksack and pulled out a small bottle.

"Just a spoonful," he said. "It will help. I can see you need to sleep."

"Thanks." Riathe stood for a while, looking down at the bottle, and at his closed left hand. He went to the door, then turned around.

"Headon, there's something I've meant to ask you for a long time," he said.

"Yes?"

"Your scar. On your face. And the burns, the damage to your hand. You've never asked me to heal them. But I could, you know. Shall I?"

Headon put his hand up to the knife scar that ran from his brow to his chin. He shook his head. "I had thought, once, to ask you," he said. "But - these scars - they are a reminder. They are my story. I can't explain clearly, but they are part of me. But, thank you."

Riathe turned away. "I do need to sleep. Mother, I'll go upstairs to rest for a while."

As he went out, Berrena turned to the children and told the tallest girl to go to the manor to tell Sarielle her grandson was home, and added, "Gerik, you go and help Breck. I need to talk to Headon and Ezera."

"Aye, come on lad," said Breck. "Give me a hand with the horses."

"I was just about to clean out the chicken hutches," said Aleythe. "I'll go and do that. But I hope Riathe is all right. He's odd. Different, and not just from being a wizard. I'm worried about him!"

"We all are," said Headon.

"I mean, I hoped he'd forgotten about me. We hadn't seen him hardly, for months. I know he didn't come to our wedding, but I could see why. And then – well – you saw it. I didn't know what to do, it was so odd the way he asked. I'm frightened of him! What if he asks again? What shall I do?"

Breck put his arm around her. "Don't worry, Ally. I don't think he'll ask again. Come on, we've got work to do. Gerik, you too. Leave these folks to talk politics."

When the kitchen was empty, Berrena turned to Headon.

"What's wrong with Riathe?" she demanded.

"He can't sleep," replied Headon. "But that's not all. You need to talk to him. He is suffering, but I can't help him. It may be that he only needs rest. The sleeping drug may help, but I'm doubtful."

"Headon, is it serious?"

"I think so."

There was a long silence. Berrena turned her face away. When she turned back to Headon Ezera saw tears in her eyes.

"I can't bear it if anything happens to him," she cried. "I've already lost so much! I miss Felde every moment of every day. You know, I knew the moment it happened. As if something huge had been pulled out of me."

For an instant, her hand fluttered to her heart. Then she shook her head.

"He was brave, after all, but I wish he hadn't proved it like that. I almost wish he'd run away."

"Berrena, what can I say?" Headon said. "We know. Losing him was a great loss. We all miss him."

"I couldn't carry on as town chief. Not without Felde. You knew I'd resigned, didn't you?"

"Yes. Riathe told me," nodded Headon.

"And my gifts too. It has taken me months to get used to losing them, and that isn't all. I tried for years to get the city council to reduce the taxes, to stop the forced labour, to trade with Talthen. I failed in all these! But you succeeded. You and Riathe and the Grey Army. I'm glad you did. But my failure – it shames me." She put her head in her hands.

Headon reached out a hand and hesitantly stroked her arm. "I think I understand," he said. There was a long moment of silence. Ezera looked at the sobbing woman and curled her lip. Forget it, move on, she wanted to say, but this was Lady Rochale, who had persuaded so many Hued to leave the city before the gifts were lost! Otherwise, Powers alone knew what would have happened to them all. She slipped off the window seat and perched on the bench next to Headon.

"Lady Rochale, do you know why we succeeded?" she said.

Berrena looked up, surprise on her face.

"We took the city because there were over four hundred Hued in the army, fighting alongside the Talthen," Ezera said earnestly. "Do you know where they were from?"

Berrena gazed at her. "Aye, well, of course, I do," she said. "From Langron and Marden."

"Yes! Because of what you did. If you hadn't persuaded them to leave Hueron, if you hadn't helped make those two safe refuges, we'd have had not only a smaller army, but one that was almost all Talthen. We'd have lost far more men against the other army, and we'd have had to fight the City Guard to take the city."

"Ezera's right," Headon said. "Without that, we may well have failed. Take comfort. You did succeed in something, even if it was not what you planned."

Berrena nodded.

"I want to ask you something," Headon continued. "Will you become a city councillor? An ambassador between Hueron and Langron and other towns?"

"Oh! On the council?" she exclaimed. "How ironic!" She stood up, walked around the room a few times, then turned back to them. "Aye, I will. I don't even need to think about it."

"Excellent. Can you come back with us to Hueron to take your seat? For a few days, at least?"

"Aye, of course. Kianne, Aleythe and Breck can look after the children for a week or so." Her face brightened. "Headon, there is something I'd like to do, and being on the council would help."

"What?"

"Set up more schools. In every large town, and in Hueron. Schools that teach reading, writing, mathematics, but that also teach history – the story of the Magi and the gifts and the Feorgath. To make sure that all the Hued and the Talthen know what has changed, and why."

CHAPTER 47
AN ENDING

As Berrena and Headon started to enthusiastically discuss schools, how to get teachers, how to combine Talthen and Hued children into the same classes and whether to charge or to make them free, Ezera stood up.

"I'm a fighter, not a politician," she said. "I'm not much use with this. I'll go and see to the horses, shall I?"

"Yes, good idea."

"Aye, Ezera. The stables are round the back. Breck and Gerik should be able to show you where things are."

After they had stabled, rubbed down and fed the horses, the other two went to the tack room to clean and polish saddles. Ezera lent on a fence staring absently at a couple of chestnut mares eating the young grass. They appeared to be in foal.

She thought about Durston. Perhaps she should ask Headon for a transfer to Marden. What could she do in peacetime now? Maybe set up a training school there? Consider settling down? How dull that sounded. But she couldn't continue to live in the city and barely see Durston.

Suddenly, arcs of white lightning split the air around her. In the dazzling brightness the horses reared, neighing in terror. Thunderclaps crashed and roared. Ezera put her hands over her ears to block out the deafening clamour. Then, as quickly as it had started, the din and the lightning stopped.

Ezera whipped around, half-expecting to see the farmhouse in ruins. There was only one person who could trigger something like that. She pulled out her sword and ran to the house. If Riathe had done something terrible, if he'd hurt someone ... She wouldn't hesitate, wizard or not.

Inside, the kitchen was empty, but she heard Headon and Berrena running up the stairs, exclaiming. She caught up with them as Berrena flung open a door. Inside, Riathe lay crumpled on the floor, unmoving, his eyes closed. The silvery gleam on his skin had gone. His left arm spread wide across the floor, the palm of his hand open. It lay empty.

Where's the pearl? thought Ezera, looking around wildly, as Berrena dropped to the floor next to Riathe, trembling as she stroked his face and called his name. Headon knelt beside her, and gently shook Riathe's shoulders, then felt his pulse and put his ear to his chest.

Breck and Gerik appeared at the door, looking terrified. The lad ran to Riathe and yanked his arm, crying loudly.

"Hush," Headon said. "Let me lift him onto the bed. He's got a pulse, he's breathing."

Against the dark coverlet on the bed, Riathe looked chalk-white. Berrena put her arms around him, but he did not move. Ezera could barely see the faint movement of his chest as he breathed.

"The sleeping potion!" exclaimed Headon, looking around.

"It's here," Ezera said, pointing to the bottle by the bed. "It's full. I don't think he's drunk any."

Kneeling beside the bed, Headon shook Riathe's shoulder with more force, then looked at Berrena, concern and fear in his face. She clutched Riathe's hand, stroking his thin cheeks, calling his name. As she called to him, Aleythe ran in.

"What's happened?" she cried, clutching at Breck's hand. "Oh! Riathe! What's happened to him?"

"We don't know!" exclaimed Berrena. "Riathe, oh, Riathe - come back!"

"Aleythe, get some water, quickly!" Headon said. "I don't know what he has done, but his pulse is very weak and he is barely breathing. Riathe, Riathe, wake up! Wake up! What have you done? Where's your pearl?"

Eventually, with a long indrawn sigh, Riathe opened his eyes. He slowly lifted his hand and gazed at the round scar on his palm.

"Riathe! Oh, thank the Powers! What happened?" Berrena caressed his face. "Your skin. The pearliness has gone. You look like my son again."

Riathe lifted his head, looking at them with faint exultation.

"I did it," he said, his voice so low they could hardly hear him. "I destroyed the desires, the memories and the stone."

"What? How did you do that?" Headon exclaimed.

"I knew the trick, the knack, from the Blue Mage. I worked out how to reverse it. I used the power of the pearl on myself. It was so hard! But I'm as I was before. The memories, his memories ... Gone, thank the Powers. Then I turned the stone on itself. It's destroyed, but losing it has destroyed me too, I think ..." his voice tailed off.

"The pearl? It's destroyed?" exclaimed Ezera. "Like when I lost my symbol? But how can you do that?"

"I don't understand," Berrena said. "Why would you do that?"

"Ask Headon, he'll explain," Riathe murmured, as his head fell back.

"Riathe, Riathe, don't go! Not you too! Riathe, please. Headon, please, save him. There must be something you can do!"

Aleythe came in with a glass of water and paused, staring at Riathe's stillness. Berrena went to take the water but Headon put his hand on her arm.

"Let Aleythe give it to him," he said.

The girl knelt by Riathe's side and slipped her arm behind his shoulders, raising him so she could put the glass to his lips. A gleam of sun shone through the window onto her. Her hair hung loose, glowing in the light as Riathe took a sip of water.

"Ah," he murmured. "I've got no strength left. Aleythe,

please ...?"

Tears in her eyes, she put the glass aside and leaned down, her golden hair falling around his white face. She touched his lips with hers for a moment. His words were so quiet Ezera could barely hear him. "I feel that my heart is breaking again," he whispered, gazing at the girl. Ezera stared and wondered, but this was all a bit beyond her.

"Riathe, lie down," Headon said. "You have to rest."

As Riathe lay back with his eyes closed, his breathing sounded shallow and laboured. Headon checked his pulse again. "It's a bit stronger," he said quietly. "I think all we can do is wait. Ezera, open the window, let some fresh air in."

Berrena knelt by her son's side, holding his hand in both of hers with her head dropped onto it. Her shoulders shook with quiet sobs. Riathe lay unmoving; his face empty, his eyes closed. Outside a lark sang, warbling high, praising the blueness of the sky and the breeze blowing all clouds away. They all listened as the birdsong soared and lifted. The sun strengthened, filling the room with golden light. Riathe opened his eyes, and he smiled.

EPILOGUE

As the hot summer sun blazed down on the city street, Durston leant down and gave Ezera a slow, lingering kiss.

"I won't come in with you, Ezera," he said

"Why not? Are you worried? Jealous?" she said, with a grin.

"Nay. Not anymore," he said, running a finger along her cheek. "But I'd feel out of place. 'Tis best you go alone."

Ezera shrugged. "Fine. You're right, I guess."

"I'll head back. Finish packing." He raised his eyebrows. "I expect I'll have to repack the mess you've made of your bags."

She laughed. "Well, I can think of better things to do! Anyway, I won't be long. I just want to - you know."

Durston nodded, kissed her again briefly and strode away along the street.

Ezera knocked on the door. It was opened by a slender Talthen woman, with cream-coloured skin and dark red hair.

"Who the blazes are you?" Ezera exclaimed. "Where's Jarial?"

The woman stepped back. Jarial appeared in the hall.

"Who is it, Liffy?" he said. "Oh. Well, Ezera! It's been a long time. Months. Come in. Come right on in."

He held the door wide. Ezera looked curiously at Liffy as she entered then Jarial enveloped her in his arms in a crushing embrace.

"Good to see you! Right - introductions! Ezera, this is Liffy Triese. Liffy, this is Ezera Mertrice. I told you all about her."

Liffy glanced at him, then turned to Ezera, smiling tentatively and nodding. Ezera looked her up and down, lifted her hand in greeting and nodded back, then looked questioningly at Jarial.

"Yes, it is what you think it is," Jarial said, putting an arm around Liffy's waist. "We'll be married this autumn, and you and Durston can come and dance at our wedding."

"Congratulations! No, honestly, I'm really pleased," Ezera said. "I knew you'd find someone else. Tell me, Liffy, does he cook as well as ever?"

Liffy laughed. "Aye! I'm getting plump on his food!"

"Chicken with cream and tarragon? Flat breads with spicy sauces?" Ezera grinned.

"You remember my triumphs, not my failures," Jarial said. "What about the raisin cakes that didn't rise, the burnt rainbow trout?"

Ezera grinned. "Best forgotten, I reckon."

"Anyway, shall we share some wine and talk? Have you come for any particular reason, or did you just smell the roast lamb while you were passing?"

"I've come to say goodbye, Jarry."

He looked seriously at her. "Goodbye?"

"Can we go up to the walls to talk? You don't mind, Liffy, do you?"

They walked along the walls to the south-western gate, to where the Saroche river curved and wound along the plain.

"At least there's a breeze up here," Jarial said, leaning against the parapet. "Cooler. So, Zera, you're leaving. Where to?"

"West." She gestured towards the distant valley and the hills faintly visible on the horizon. "I asked Lord Alcastor for a transfer. Me and Durston, we're going downriver, to a garrison in a port, about a hundred miles away."

"To the sea? Powers above!"

"Yes! There's a small town, called Talband or something,

with a harbour, and not much else except fishermen. The council want to start trading overseas and along the coast."

"More adventures for you, Zera! It suits you. You never wanted a quiet life."

"Unlike you." She sat down on one of the stone benches. "Yes. I can't wait. I've never seen the sea."

"Durston's going too?"

"Yes. He'll be setting up a smithy, an armoury. I'll be training, learning how to sail. Oh - and there's someone else."

"Who?"

She laid a finger on his lips. "Swear by the Founders and the walls that you won't tell anyone?"

He nodded.

"Riathe Sulvenor."

"What! The wizard? But ... But there's been all sorts of rumours. That he'd died, been murdered, been banished. Someone said that he'd lost his powers and killed himself."

"He did lose his powers. To be honest, he did it deliberately. I've no idea how, or why. But now, he needs to vanish. So he's changing his name and joining us at Talband."

"Extraordinary! The whole world is changing. Who would have believed we'd see what we have seen?"

"Don't get philosophical, Jarry. It doesn't suit you."

He laughed. "I can't say I've missed your sharpness, dear Zera. But, seriously, I'm pleased for you. And Durston too."

"You can come and dance at our wedding too, if you want."

"I would want too." He leaned closer, and kissed her cheek. "For past times' sake. And I'll sing too."

"Sing?"

"My new career. The timber trading business is doing well, and Liffy makes and sells ointments, salves, tisanes. I grow the herbs, she chops them up. We're fairly well off now, thank the Powers, and I'm starting to write and play more songs."

279

Ezera glanced at his hand. He held it up and turned it too and fro.

"Yes, even with this. I've learnt to play three-fingered. But - song-writing!"

He hummed a few notes.

Ezera jumped up. "I recognise that! It's called 'The Seasons', isn't it? They were playing it in the bar three nights ago."

"I wrote it. Well, Liffy taught me the words and the tune, and I tweaked it. Changed the rhythm to something a bit more interesting, put a minor bridge into the middle, and started playing it with some of my friends from our old band. And it caught on."

"Amazing."

"Yes! Honestly, Zera, it's just exploded." He flung his arms wide. "The song-writing is brilliant. With all that's happened recently, there's endless inspirations. Wars, hunger, sieges, invasions, evil, wizards ... My latest song - well, you inspired it."

"I did?"

"It's about two rivals in love, meeting on a battlefield." He winked.

Ezera burst out laughing. "Play it for me and Durston one day, Jarry. We'll be coming back now and then to visit."

She glanced upwards.

"It's past midday. Durston will have packed. Time to go. One last one of your huge bear hugs, Jarry?"

As she ran down the steps, the tune Jarial had hummed came into her head, and she strode along the street, singing cheerfully.

> *When spring was in the air,*
> *He saw that she was fair,*
> *He promised then and there,*
> *To be her hero.*

> *Oh, know your own true love, for wealth's a liar,*

THE CITY

Brave men be rare as gold, true hearts as sapphire.

He thought her love was strong,
But a rich man came along,
And when summer was gone,
she'd left her hero.

He went with horse and sword,
Through autumn mist, and swore,
He'd go to die in war,
an unwanted hero.

Brought back in winter frost,
Deep wounds sliced through his chest,
She mourned what she had lost,
a valiant hero.

Oh, know your own true love, for wealth's a liar,
Brave men be rare as gold, true hearts as sapphire.

The End

ABOUT THE AUTHOR

Cathy Hemsley is a radical Christian, software engineer and author. She writes a blog about writing and reading Christian fiction called 'Is Narnia All There Is?', is involved with various charities to help struggling people in her home town of Rugby, and is a trustee of a charity, '1 John 3 Beira' that helps rebuild houses and lives in Beira, Mozambique.

This is her third book: the first is a series of short stories, called 'Parable Lives'; the second is 'The Gifts', the prequel to 'The City'.

https://isnarniaallthereis.wordpress.com/

Printed in Great Britain
by Amazon

75957553R00163